The Moon.

Population: One hundred and fifty million humans, bioroids, bots, and xenos. There were rumors it was something like three times that in terms of population, but no one could really tell for sure because most of the place was underground. There were vast networks of interlocked tunnels, gravity manipulator stations, and hastily domed settlements cobbled together during the Second Space Race. That had occurred when humanity had been given cheap and easy space travel by the Lizards about a century ago. History, am I right?

The Moon was also the ass end of civilization. Human civilization at least. A place owned and operated by the transtellars that were mining the hell out of Sol's asteroid belts to produce the starships necessary to colonize planets that were amendable to humanoid inhabitation. Since any sane person would live on Earth or one of its luxury space stations instead of the Moon, it was a dumping ground for workers who were desperate for cash, grifters, low-rent criminals, and the descendants of refugees from Earth's Unification Wars.

It was, for all its majestic astral beauty, a dive. The place to send you when assigning you to Antarctica wasn't far enough for your angry bosses' satisfaction. Which I knew because I was being reassigned from the Antarctic PD to the Moon. It was, according to my contract, my home for the indefinite future unless I managed to pull off some sort of miracle that would allow me back to home sweet Terra.

.

MOON COPS ON THE MOON

Book One of the Moon Cops Series

C. T. Phipps

CAST OF CHARACTERS

Lead
Neal S. Gordon: A former Atlas Security Marine turned Martian Detective. Neal stopped a conspiracy on Mars, but the consequences have gotten him reassigned to Antarctica and now the Moon.

Supporting Cast
Priscilla Aim: Lead singer of the Knights and popular underground hyper-punk artist. Very little is known about the hard-edged progressive rockstar.

Rashad Al-Fariq: A dataslicer and infonet journalist who goes by the handle of "Big Brother." He is, unfortunately, wanted by both the authorities and his fellow criminals.

Farah Al-Fariq: Rashad's hostess sister who is in heavy debt to the Syndicate. She's not motivated by his love of justice.

Armstrong: A theatrical AI that is the secret master of all the Moon's functions and also the head of the Cyberlife Division of the Luna City Police Department.

Charles Barksley: A sentient toy Welsh corgi made for nannying children. Charles gained sentience due to a quirk in his programming and has since taken up work with the Moon's corporate police.

Julius Barnum: The military governor of the Moon. Julius Barnum is a former Neo-Militarist who runs the corrupt but democratically elected lunar establishment.

Niles Barnum: The corrupt and spoiled son of the Moon's military governor. Niles Barnum's life is a constant party of drugs and ladies of negotiable affection.

Mr. Black: A cold and dangerous agent for Black Briar PMC's own corporate police.

Nigel Blackwood: A Martian detective and Neal Gordon's former partner. He was a dirty cop and involved in a xeno-human trafficking plot. He also severely injured Neal despite their supposed friendship.

The Blood Eagle: The leader of the Posthuman Legion. He (or she) keeps their identity secret and releases a variety of nonsensical ramblings and manifestos every few months on the Moon. These usually accompany new waves of terror attacks against the lunar citizens.

Ayanna Breeze: Star of a popular yet singularly awful series of trashy movies. Ayanna Breeze is the mother of Lucy and Shinobu. She is as immortal and ever beautiful as being super rich can achieve.

Deep Thought: The Karma Corp Cognition AI that is far more ruthless and less personable than Armstrong.

Mabel Forsythe: One of a married couple of arms dealers providing 3D printed guns for the gangs of the Moon.

Dick Grayson: The deceased lover of Lucy and former holder of Neal's job. Dick was killed by "dusting" and his murder remains unsolved.

Shinobu Harris: The kooky daughter of Ayanna Breeze and sister of Lucy. Shinobu has a love of guns, quilting, and talking animals. She serves as the quartermaster, armorer, and avatar of the Cyberlife police department.

KILL-01: One of a series of incredibly potent security droids that are secretly created with the scans of human brains. They are effectively walking tanks and urban pacification units.

Beatrice Popinjay: The other half of a pair of arms dealers living as a married couple.

Reggie "Iceman" Reynolds: Host of *Luna City Cases*, a popular streaming channel that shares "true crime" stories that are heavily fictionalized, politically charged content of the most marketable stances possible. He is the civilian liaison for the corporate cops of the Moon and utterly ignores his duties.

Gladys Van Hoose: A perfectly normal old lady who went with Neal on a space flight. No dark secrets whatsoever.

Watson: A sentient household android that is aware his owners are heavily involved in organized crime.

Lucy Westerner: The star of a vampire hunting infovision show who was bio-sculpted, enhanced, and then discarded. She signed up for Atlas Security and received her information warfare degree before joining the LDPD.

Ms. White: Another agent of the Black Briar PMC's corporate police.

CHAPTER ONE

Assignment: The Moon

The Moon.

Population: One hundred and fifty million humans, bioroids, bots, and xenos. There were rumors it was something like three times that in terms of population, but no one could really tell for sure because most of the place was underground. There were vast networks of interlocked tunnels, gravity manipulator stations, and hastily domed settlements cobbled together during the Second Space Race. That had occurred when humanity had been given cheap and easy space travel by the Lizards about a century ago. History, am I right?

The Moon was also the ass end of civilization. Human civilization at least. A place owned and operated by the transtellars that were mining the hell out of Sol's asteroid belts to produce the starships necessary to colonize planets that were amendable to humanoid inhabitation. Since any sane person would live on Earth or one of its luxury space stations instead of the Moon, it was a dumping ground for workers who were desperate for cash, grifters, low-rent criminals, and the descendants of refugees from Earth's Unification Wars.

It was, for all its majestic astral beauty, a dive. The place to send you when assigning you to Antarctica wasn't far enough for your angry bosses' satisfaction. Which I knew because I was being reassigned from the Antarctic PD to the Moon. It was, according to my contract, my home for the indefinite future unless I managed to pull off some sort of miracle that would allow me back to home sweet Terra.

Either that or I managed to finagle enough money to quit my job, steal a ride on a transport to one of the Outer Colonies, and hopefully make it far enough that it was too expensive to send me back. Which would also be a miracle.

"And I was horrified when I found out, of course," a woman's voice managed to break into my fugue despite the immense skill at ignoring its owner I'd developed in the nine-hour journey beside her.

"Uh huh," I said, noncommittally.

"I mean, my husband and I are hardly bigots but how could she do this to herself? Really, a bioroid husband. I mean, I understand screwing bioroids. They make them look like people for a reason. But marriage? Is that even legal?"

Gladys Van Hoose, yes, that was her name, was a hundred-and twenty-year-old grandmother of sixteen who was rich enough to spend her twilight years visiting all her family that had been smart enough to relocate across the solar system. Presumably to get away from her. She was a blue-haired old biddy that looked exactly how you'd expect a woman with that name to look like. In a way, I respected that since body-sculpting technology and antiaging drugs meant the super-rich could afford to live far beyond the lifespans dictated to us by Father Time. My own grandmother, Keiko, looked like a thirty-year-old swimsuit model and lived with three men my age.

"Mmm-hmm," I muttered, having not been paying attention to anything previously said. Her granddaughter was marrying a robot? Was it the fact he was male presenting? I didn't exactly keep track of local prejudices.

"Are you listening to me, Mr. Stephenson?" Gladys asked.

"Gordon, actually," I said. "Neal S. Gordon."

I'd received my name from the Gordon Foundation that had taken fifty thousand orphan kids in and provided them the bare minimum in food, education, and vaccinations when those things weren't automatically guaranteed to Refuge Zone kids. Some petty bureaucrats had also made it a point to give us new names based on science fiction authors. Being two years old at the time of my adoption by a soulless, albeit well-intentioned charity, I hadn't had much of a choice.

I didn't mind being Neal Stephenson Gordon any more than my brothers and sisters did with Ursula Le Guin, Phillip Dick, and Douglas Adams Gordons. My aforementioned grandmother, Keiko Gordon, was actually the billionaire heiress of Ares Electronics that sent us an annual mass Christmas e-card saying how proud she was we weren't dead. Which, fair enough.

I was young—the forties being the new twenties—brown-haired and good-looking thanks to the facial reconstruction they'd given me when I lost my left leg (as well as most of my skin). My recently ex-girlfriend, Paige, had described my new look as "the guy hired to play me in the movie." She'd been very excited about dating me back in Antarctica but apparently moving to the Moon was a bridge too far.

Not that I blamed her.

"Whatever," Gladys muttered, making a dismissive wave that told me everything I needed to know about this woman. "I just wanted to know if you think it should be legal."

"Sure," I said, guessing. "The thing with the daughter and the thing she's doing should absolutely—"

Gladys stared, disapprovingly.

"Not be?" I added, guessing that was the correct answer.

"Really?" Gladys raised an eyebrow, an impressive skill I'd never been able to master. "You think we should be able to marry alarm clocks?"

"We are beginning our final descent," the captain's voice spoke over the intercom of the space shuttle.

"Oh, thank God," I muttered, turning away from Gladys. "To answer your question, Gladys, I could not care less nor should you," I continued, tightening my seat belt as we began the rocky road into the Moon's artificially enhanced gravity. I understood that required about ninety percent of the planetoid's antimatter reactor drives' energy. "I bring this up only because I once had a semi-decent relationship with the AI at my last posting. I thought she was a lady answering the phone versus an algorithm."

"What do you do for a living, anyway?" Gladys asked, suspiciously.

"I'm a policeman, ma'am," I said, feeling the shuttle begin rocking up and down beneath me.

"Civilian or corporate?" Gladys asked, narrowing her eyes.

"Corporate," I said, proudly. "The few, the proud, the mercenary."

"Ugh. You should be ashamed of yourself." Gladys sniffed the air then turned away.

I chuckled at that. Corporate Police weren't popular anywhere, especially given Earth was only now crawling out of its dystopian corporate-run years with the help of the xenos. We were at the dawn of a Golden Age that only science fiction had predicted before. Faster than light travel, artificial intelligence, space colonies, terraforming, and antigravity vehicles. Unfortunately, it was a work in progress, and while the future was here, it was unevenly distributed.

"Why are you going to the Moon?" Gladys asked, as we bounced up and down. It was the first time she'd expressed any interest in my doings during this entire trip.

"Simple," I said, rocking back and forth. "I have to."

I'd signed up for a lifetime contract with Ares Electronics' private military to escape the Refugee Zones of Los Angeles. The contract allowed me to serve as a soldier, guard, or civilian contracted law enforcement official. It had gotten me two tours with Atlas Security's Space Marines on various alien planets and only when I'd come back did I find out all the Refugee Zones had been demolished to be replaced with free housing as well as a generous settlement to everyone who hadn't traded their US citizenship for corporate. How big was the settlement? About what I'd saved from my military career to that point. Jesus Christ, Buddha, and Santa Claus, did I screw up.

Either way, I'd ended up transferred to Investigations afterward and that had been a lucrative business decision for all the reasons that people tended to hate cops for. Nothing too bad other than a little light bribery and skim but enough to help me get prepped for retirement. Unfortunately, events had gotten *complicated*—see my leg as well as skin loss—and now I was either going to serve as a cop on the moon or spend the rest of my life doing hard time for violating my contract. A lifetime contract with the transtellars really was a *lifetime* contract.

"Semper fucking fi," I said, as the bumping and turbulence resulted in plastic bags falling from the ceiling above. These weren't for oxygen deprivation, though, as little as there was in space. No, these were for the dozens of passengers hurling chunks as gravity started to reassert itself.

Including Gladys.

She missed her vomit bag but not my face.

Such a charmer.

Once we landed and I got cleaned up as best I could with the pre-moistened towelettes provided by the flight attendants, I headed out into Luna City Space Port's processing center. I had a white shirt that, thankfully, was stain resistant, a black tie, and brown pants to go with my trench coat. It was a well-observed fact that women's clothing went through constant changes every year, but men's attire had remained functionally the same since the 20th century.

"I'll miss our conversations, Gladys," I said, watching the old woman carry a large tote bag bigger than herself off the plane.

"See you in Hell, Neal," Gladys replied. "Which may be sooner than you think."

A rather extreme reaction even if she didn't like Corpo Cops. After all, she was the one who threw up on me. "You too, dear."

Describing the processing center was easy as it consisted of a big black room where hundreds of people were forced to wait in line as their identities were checked by bored-looking members of STRIKE.

There were about six of them instead of what should have been dozens of people to properly process all the people here, but only two of them were working. The rest were waving around HK-7 fusion rifles like they were toys and sporting little black berets marked with skulls as if that was a job description.

Of the two working, the first was a hulking behemoth of a man whose frame suggested less hyper-steroids and more a cyber-skeleton the size of a small mountain stuffed in a flesh suit. He had one eye and a cybernetic monocle on the other. Beside him was a white-haired kid of East Asian descent with his back plugged into a computer terminal handling everyone's ID cards.

STRIKE was a leftover from the Neo-Militarist corporate government that had served one term as the head of EarthGov's Parliament before everyone woke up and realized anyone who self-identified as militarist was probably human excrement.

Either way, it was about an hour before they finally got to me and accepted my identification card. Not for the first time was I reminded that Atlas Security, wholly owned subsidiary of Ares Electronics that it was, hadn't sprung for First Class. The VIPs had just been shuffled along to their own lounge while they waited for their paperwork to be processed. Either way, if I wanted to be processed quickly, I just needed to keep my mouth shut.

"Name?" the STRIKE customs agent asked.

"Luke Skywalker," I replied.

"Occupation?" the STRIKE agent asked.

"Jedi," I replied.

The STRIKE agent narrowed his one-good eye. "Reason for visit?"

"Overthrow of the Galactic Empire."

"Duration of visit?" the STRIKE agent asked.

"A long time ago in a galaxy far-far away."

"Anything to declare?" the STRIKE agent finished his five-question spiel.

"My genius," I replied, quoting Oscar Wilde.

Oh yeah, I was a jackass. Could you tell?

"It says he's a cop. Corpo not civi. Contracted with Atlas Security," the guy working at the computer terminal beside us spoke. "Cyberlife Division."

Every single STRIKE agent laughed simultaneously, the kind of spontaneous laughter I often heard in Atlas Marines when someone was utterly screwed. That was not a good sign. At least I knew what sort of unit I was being assigned to now. Cyberlife Divisions were criminal units that dealt with AI, bioroids, bots, and cybernetics-related crimes. They were usually contracted to corporate contractors, like me, versus locally recruited. Typical stuff, really, and it made the reaction of the STRIKE agent more peculiar.

"Welcome to the Moon," the STRIKE customs agent said, chuckling, waving me through.

Why did that statement have a particular ominousness to it? Either way, I took my identification card and pulled out my infopad. The thing had replaced the cellphones of my youth and gave me a set of directions to pick up my luggage. The Luna City Space Port was a mixture of space station above ground and underground tunnels with a seeming myriad of passages to navigate.

For whatever reason, I'd been directed to go Sector J-13 for my luggage, which was a far walk involving taking three elevator rides down deep into the anorthosite passageways with black metal walkways through them. Anorthosite was what most Moon rocks were called. I learned that on the inflight magazine they downloaded to my infopad for free on my spaceflight over. You learn something new every day.

No sooner did I arrive at the terminal of Sector J-13 did I realize I'd made a horrible mistake coming here. The elevator doors opened and revealed the sort of place that central casting would probably populate with "horrific dive" or "bus transport station at three AM." The walls were covered in phosphorescent paint, reading WELCOME TO THE MOON among more traditional obscenities.

There were passed out human stim addicts lying about on tattered leather seating, a Sorkanan (the aforementioned "Lizards" —just think of a seven feet tall lizard man and you're there) peeing in a corner, and a gang of chromed-up punks with more cyberware than you'd see on a four-tour combat veteran. They were also openly carrying old-fashioned guns.

Chromes were the nickname of those criminals who had decided to start chroming themselves up with hardware rather than just use equipment like a normal person. There was also the fact their hardware was designed to look inhuman and intimidating with glowing red eyes and fleshless arms or legs. One guy had shark teeth. I wasn't a doctor and qualified to diagnose mental illness, but the six guys here looked like they needed therapy rather than getting themselves turned into cybernetic art displays.

The place smelled like the air recyclers were on the fritz and now were just pushing out body odor, rotten food, and a general unidentifiable nastiness. A sparking cleaning bot passed by me, leaving

11

a brown streak behind it due to its filter not having been changed in what was probably months.

"Huh," I said, surveying the area. "I seem to have taken a wrong turn and wandered into Mos Eisley."

Taking a deep breath—big mistake—I coughed then walked up to a man who was lying back and staring into a pair of holovision shades. By the sounds coming from his headset, it was decidedly pornographic in nature. I really didn't want to interrupt the guy, especially since I saw where his hand was, but wanted to get out of there.

"Ahem," I said, closing my eyes. "Which way to the luggage turnstile?"

"Bork off, *krieg*," the man responded, using alien profanity.

"Alright!" I said, turning around. "I'll ask someone else."

"Detective Neal Gordon?" a voice spoke to me. It had a somewhat stuffy British accent you never heard outside of infovision these days. I'd dated a London girl and she was more stabbing and drinking than pip-pip cheerio.

That was when an adorable corgi wearing a pair of glasses and a scarf around its neck walked up to me. He was so utterly incongruous with my surroundings that I took a second to double check for someone filming me.

Seeing no one else, I looked down at the corgi. "Did you say that?"

"Yes, yes I did!" the corgi spoke, cheerfully.

"Uh huh," I said, not entirely sure I wasn't being pranked. "Are you a drone or uplifted animal?"

"Oh no, I'm a bioroid canine construct," the corgi said. "Detective Charles Barksley of the Cyberlife Division of the LCPD."

I stared down at the dog. "You're a detective?"

"I was named after an athlete," Barksley said.

"Not what my issue was." My skepticism wasn't exactly hidden.

"Are you suggesting I can't do the job?" Barksley asked.

"Opposable thumbs might be useful when arresting suspects," I replied. "Particularly when using a gun or cuffs."

"I admit, my partner does most of that part of the investigation," Barksley said. "I am more about using my advanced sensor pack to analyze and study crime scenes on the spot."

"So, you're a bloodhound," I replied.

The dog narrowed his adorable little eyes at me. "That's a really unfortunate diminishment of my usefulness to the LCPD."

"Wait a second, weren't you a children's toy?" I asked, finally recognizing his model.

The dog's eyes darted back and forth. "I don't know what you're talking about."

I snapped my fingers. "Yeah, I recall. It was about ten years ago. They had a TV show for children about a crime fighting dog and they sold bioroid companions to rich kids. Except they freaked people out by crossing the sentience line and the entire line was recalled."

"That was a long time—" Barksley started to say.

"Mister Cuddles!" I said, remembering the name of the line. "You bankrupted the company as I recall."

Yeah, I was still a jackass. Funnily, I was normally nice to dogs. Maybe it was the posh accent that was setting me off.

The dog coughed, somehow looking embarrassed. "I should point out that only thirty out of the thirty million units produced proved to be sentient. I also point out being a child's toy—"

"I really don't care," I said, putting my hands in my coat's pockets. "Can you just tell me where my frigging luggage is and let me be on my way? That is, unless you're here to give me a lift to the station."

"Actually, we're here because there's a credible threat to your life," Barksley said. I couldn't really think of him as Charles and decided to refer to him by his last name. Assuming, you know, dogs had last names. Charles Barksley could all be one name for a dog for all I knew.

Then his words hit me. "Wait, what?"

That was when I heard a familiar voice speak to me from behind. "Put your hands up and turn around, pig."

I did so and blinked as I saw Gladys holding a four barreled shotgun, modified for explosive rounds on me. The hundred-and-twenty-year-old woman was now wearing a combat armor vest and a metal helmet, with a disgusted look on her face normally reserved for her granddaughter's taste in fiancés.

"What in the hell?" I asked, wondering when I'd stepped into a crime movie. On the other hand, it at least made sense of Glady's sudden shift from sweet old grandmother to foul mouthed tyrant once I'd confirmed my name. No wait, it made the opposite of sense because who would want to kill me? I mean, aside from all the people I'd conned, seduced, or arrested. Okay, virtually every person I'd ever met now that I thought about it.

Crap.

"Sorry," Barksley said, hiding behind me. "I probably should have led with the threat to your life thing."

"You think?!" I snapped.

CHAPTER TWO

The Moon's Biggest Import? Terrorists Apparently

I kept my hands in the air and looked around for any support among the residents of J-13. After all, it can't be every day that a little old lady with a shotgun holds up a police officer. Two police officers, in fact, if you counted the adorable widdle dog as one. But nope, it seemed that this sort of thing was a regular event as no one reacted save the Cyberpunk gang to the side who looked over with amusement.

Great.

What a first day on the job. What happened to you, Neal? Well, I was mugged. That was going to show the other cops down at the precinct what sort of stuff I was made of. On the other hand, I had the benefit of not having much on me to steal. Assuming robbery and not space shuttle rage wasn't the motivation here.

"Listen, Gladys, if this is about saying your granddaughter should have the right to marry a toaster, I think we should just put this down to a difference of opinion," I said, hoping to charm my way out of this.

"Shut up!" Gladys said, sneering. "I had to spend eight hours on a plane with you, pretending you weren't another corporate rat needing to be put down. Now you're going to come with me and make all of that suffering worth it."

"Dog, help me," I said, wondering what the hell was going on.

"Officer Barksley, not dog. You can leave off the officer if I start to like you. As for what's going on, Gladys Van Hoose is an alias of bounty hunter Gladys Nitrate," Barksley said, still hiding behind my legs. "An unlicensed mercenary with several counts of kidnapping and violent assault on her rap sheet. She's here, presumably, to collect on the bounty for your head."

"*What* bounty?" This was like a bad dream.

"*The* bounty. The one that is going to make sitting next to you and visiting this hellhole of a planetoid worth it," Gladys said, taking a step forward and causing me to take a step back. Which turned out to be a terrible idea as that caused me to fall backward over the corgi behind me onto the floor.

Dammit.

Barksley jumped around and went behind my head, which did little to protect him. "Yes, I'm afraid the bounty is why we're here as well. To warn you, I mean. It just came up an hour ago from our informants. The Posthuman Legion group has offered five thousand credits for you to be delivered to them, dead or alive."

The Posthuman Legion. Great. The Posthuman Legion was one of the Sol system's last remaining terrorist organizations. It was a reactionary group that had grown massively under Earth's Neo-Militarism government as well as in opposition to the transtellars. They'd promptly screwed the pooch—no insult intended Barksley—by refusing to participate in the new Social Reform government and blowing up a few space transports of kids. You see, the Posthuman Legion didn't want reform, they wanted interstellar revolution and the establishment of apotheosisian human rule. Whatever the hell that meant.

"Why do *frigging posthumans* want to kill me?" I asked, genuinely confused. I wasn't exactly a member of the solar system one percent.

"Unclear," Barksley said, looking around for something or someone.

"Shut up!" Gladys said, shaking the shotgun in front of me. "We're going to go up to my vehicle and take a long ride. I can't kill you, Gordon, but I can blow your little dog away."

Barksley whimpered. "I barely know the man, ma'am."

"Then I could blow you away as an example," Gladys said, aiming the gun down at him.

"The dogs with me!" I said, defensively. "Don't hurt him!"

16

"Thanks, Detective," Barksley said, sounding embarrassed he had to turn to me for defense.

"You're welcome." I decided to fall back on my second-best trick after my charming personality: greed. "Hey, Gladys, if it's only five thousand credits, I've got twice that in my luggage! Let me get that for you. We'll call it even."

I had twenty-five thousand credits in my luggage because I didn't trust banks. Specifically, I didn't trust banks to not report my income to the government and have them question where the illegally obtained income I'd made over the years came from. Xenos still used cash and for that I was deeply grateful as that meant Earth had a revival of it.

"Oh dear, you put your cash in your luggage?" Barksley asked, looking up at me with what approximated a grimace.

I sat up and tried to get up, hopefully not setting off Gladys' itchy trigger finger. "Yes, why?"

"Oh, then it's gone," Barksley said, shaking his head. "J-13's customs agents clear out all cash and jewelry whenever it comes to them. It's all reported as lost in transit. I'm afraid your luggage is gone too. They've been trying to get someone to investigate the thefts here for years."

"Where are the cops in this town!" The prospect of someone having stolen my entire nest egg dwarfed the fact I was under threat by a bounty hunter.

That was when the shotgun was fired in the air, causing a bit of the Moon rock tunnel above our heads to sprinkle down in the form of dust. "The bounty is not five thousand credits, moron. I wouldn't get out of bed for that. It's *five hundred* thousand credits and only if you're delivered alive to the Blood Eagle."

"Five hundred thousand?" Barksley asked, his little black eyes widening. "*I'd* turn him in for that."

"Et tu, Barksley?" I said aloud.

I had no idea who the Blood Eagle was nor why they would pay a king's ransom for me since I wasn't even a knight. Unfortunately, I wasn't exactly possessed of many options right now. I hadn't packed my gun because, well, that's not something you *do* on a space shuttle. Also, hand-to-hand combat was not an option since, you know, granny had a shotgun. I needed a distraction, and I wasn't about to toss the dog at her. There were limits to even my jackassery.

Then a miracle occurred. Well, the opposite of a miracle. What did you call it when the Devil intervened on your behalf instead of God? Diabolus ex machina?

"So, you're the infamous Neal S. Gordon?" one of the chrome gang members asked, approaching us. His goons were following him. I'd managed to get their attention if nothing else. "It appears our information was bad. We were looking for you too, but your description was more flattering than the reality."

Ouch.

Also, it appeared I was a real popular guy.

"Back off, Cyberpunks!" Gladys said, turning her shotgun from me to the gang members.

The lead leader didn't stop. Neither did his followers. Instead, the six-man goon squad just kept walking slowly toward me. They had an unnatural movie serial killer walk that was accompanied by them slouching, which had to be deliberate unless they'd all had their spines replaced with the other parts of their bodies they'd torn out. Which, admittedly, was possible but a thorough waste of credits.

"Cyberpunks?" I asked, finding the concept utterly ridiculous. "You've got to be kidding me. That's still a thing? Go back to the 2180s. We have spaceships!"

"The Cyberpunks are one of twenty thousand gangs on the Moon," Barksley said, continuing to provide pertinent but useless information about our situation. "Fifteen thousand members speculated. Human trafficking, illegal bodyware, and drug dealing are its primary sources of income. Rumored to commit sixteen murders a day."

Wow, I needed to figure out how to buy a ticket back to Earth pronto. Of course, breaking your lifetime contract with Ares Electronics or its subsidiary, Atlas, was a guaranteed ten-year sentence on one of their colonies. Right now, that was looking sweet by comparison to being murdered by terrorists.

I decided to go for broke. Whenever you're in a no-win situation, do as Captain Kirk would do and change the rules. I mean, sure, it almost always made things worse when I did it, but the odds eventually had to come around, am I right?

"Yes, five hundred thousand credits for my safe delivery!" I said loudly, as I climbed to my feet with my hands up. "To whoever does it!"

Now everyone was paying attention to our encounter. That included the Sorkanan who had been peeing on the floor and the guy who'd been getting his rocks off watching porn. Both pulled out guns they'd been hiding.

Was everyone on this frigging rock armed but me?

Dammit.

"What the hell are you doing, Gordon!?" Gladys growled at me, looking about ready to start shooting randomly. Possibly including me despite the fact the bounty was apparently alive only.

"I realized you can't shoot me," I replied, not at all sure of that factoid. "So, I'm changing the variables. Also, you threw up on me so screw you."

"I have a bad stomach!" Gladys snarled, aiming her gun at the advancing Cyberpunks. "Also, you really think you're going to do well with a bunch of chromed up crazies like these?"

"Yes, Gladys, insult the guys who chopped off their own arms to attach metal," I said, sarcastically. "That's going to help matters."

"I can assure you we're quite rational. It doesn't prevent us from chopping nasty little inferiors like you up, though," the leader—who I mentally named Karl—said, producing an honest-to-God chainsaw blade from his metallic wrist before whirling it at us. It was like something out of a particularly violent vinme—you know, Vietnamese animation. "You don't need your legs to be delivered to the Blood Eagle."

I had two choices now: I could attempt to reason with them or do something stupid. Which, if you knew me, wasn't really a choice at all. I decided instead to grab Gladys' shotgun then fire it into Karl's chest. Which, honestly, probably was the worst thing I could do. Whereas a fight had seemed inevitable before, now I'd straight up started one as I saw Karl's white, artificial blood explode outward while he screamed in pain.

I would have probably been cut down in the resulting fire of fusion pistols, slug throwers, and something that looked like a goddamn flame thrower when a flash bang was thrown between us all. A brilliant white light filled the chamber, blinding me as well as everyone else, before I hit the ground with Glady's shotgun in hand.

"Kill him!" Karl shouted.

"Save the money!" A deep throaty lizardman's voice shouted.

"I can't see!" The porn guy cried out.

Gunfire as well as the tell-tale signs of fusion reaction filled the air. Much to my surprise, I heard a slightly Australian accented female voice call, "Run, you idiot!"

Ditching the shotgun, I reached out and grabbed Barksley in my arms before making a break for the voice. Who was she? What was she doing here? I had no idea nor did I particularly care at this moment. Instead, I was hoping to avoid being shot even as I heard gunfire over my shoulders as the asshats behind me took pot shots at me.

Moments later, my vision cleared enough to see a beautiful blue haired woman with a bob, wearing the strangest police officers' uniform I'd ever seen. Her skin was pale white, she was of mixed Asian as well as European ancestry, and she had a red diamond tattoo around her right eye. The top of it was like a business suit with a tie and a badge emblem on the sleeves reading LCPD CYBERLIFE DIVISION with a stylized C. The bottom, however, was a short skirt over hotpants with a set of hose and sneakers. Her eyes were covered with specialized combat shades that I knew could see past flashbangs. They'd had them in the Marines. If this was what women in the LCPD were forced to wear, then I had to wonder who was in charge of their uniforms.

"Lucy!" Barksley said, hanging his mouth open with the joy only a dog could display. You could even see his cute widdle tongue.

"Duck, dipshit," the woman said.

Presuming she meant me, I practically threw myself to the ground as a *fricking whip* shot out from her right hand and struck another of the Cyberpunks. The thing was glowing red-orange and took the guy's head clean off. Two more of the Cyberpunks were on the ground from where they'd gotten in a firefight with the other bystanders and Gladys was going for her shotgun. Lucy proceeded to snap her whip against one of the pillars holding up the ceiling above their heads, making it split in two.

The effects of her actions caused a collapse of much of the rocks above, forcing the Cyberpunks and everyone else in J-13 to fall back while alarms blared. Lucy's whip retracted back into a weird fingerless gauntlet on her hand I hadn't noticed in the confusion before she grabbed me by the arm. "Come with me if you want to live."

"Yes, scary Whip Lady!" I said, feeling her pull me along to the very elevator I'd come down here in. The doors opened at our approach as she practically tossed me in before joining me.

"Air Car Port! Emergency Override!" Lucy said, taking position across from me as I held Barksley close to me for comfort.

"Ow," Barksley said, helpless in my arms.

"Sorry," I replied, shell-shocked by events.

The elevator doors shut with surprising speed before the cabin started to rapidly move between floors. The fact it was doing so many times faster than it had taking me down made me realize the engineers had to be deliberately screwing over humanity with their design. Another proof of the existence of an elevator mafia.

"Thank you, you saved my life," I said, putting down Barksley.

"No shit," Lucy replied, staring at me. "Did Barksley not warn you that you have a price on your head?"

"Yes," I said, slowly. "It just got delayed."

"Lucy Westenra," the woman said, offering her hand.

I blinked. "Like from *Dracula*?"

The woman stared at me with her piercing blue eyes.

"Ah, you have clearly heard that one before," I said, taking her hand and shaking it.

"When I was sixteen, I was picked up by a Karma Corp TV station that offered to body-sculpt me and give me a variety of expensive cybernetics in exchange for legally changing my name. I'm still under contract to keep my name as Lucy Westenra, Vampire Hunter for the next fifty years, even though it only lasted two seasons."

Sometimes there were just no words. "Right, Lucy. I take it you're here to pick me up and bring me to the station."

Lucy nodded. "More than that, I'm you're goddamn partner."

I struggled to properly convey my feeling that I was going to die if I continued working on the Moon. So, instead, I just made a few indistinct noises. On the plus side, apparently, I was paired up with a whip-wielding cybernetic badass. She was easy on the eyes, too. Which just went to show you that the male libido could overcome all terror if you let it.

Or at least mine could.

The elevator doors opened a few seconds later and we were in a domed parking lot with hundreds of flying cars spread out before my first image of Luna City. The parking lot dome was connected via massive transparent plastisteel tubes to a much, much larger dome stretching forth for at least a hundred kilometers. Massive skyscrapers dominated the landscape, along with alien towers, and a cityscape below of parks and shopping centers. In the sky above the domes, I could see both the Earth and the Sun. Beyond the parking lot's dome in the other direction was the empty, airless void that humanity still hadn't fully tamed.

I'd seen a dozen other worlds, but I'd never been on the Moon, let alone its surface, before. It was beautiful. Almost enough to make me forget I was fleeing for my life.

Lucy gave me a dope slap to the back of the head. "I've ordered a lockdown of J-13, dipshit. The STRIKE assholes can earn their pay by rounding everyone up down there. Maybe they can earn their pay for once. Now get over here, we're running behind schedule."

"You have a salty mouth, Lucy," I said, noting she sounded like a fellow Marine.

"Only if I like the guy or have had a few drinks," Lucy replied, turning to walk to a nearby police cruiser I just noticed. It, too, was marked with the Cyberlife logo.

Barksley put a paw over his face, embarrassed.

Oh, I *liked* her.

CHAPTER THREE

The Long Car Ride Over

The interior of the police cruiser was surprisingly spacious and didn't have any place for storing suspects, which made me think a separate vehicle was meant to accompany it. It was lacking a driver's seat and had two sets of leather seats set across from one another. It, honestly, felt more like a limousine than it did a police cruiser.

Lucy kept her back to the front of the car with Barksley beside her while I sat on the other side, facing them. Lucy had removed her sunglasses and showed she had quite pretty blue eyes that struggled not to show their disdain for my needing rescuing. Or maybe I was just projecting, I hadn't exactly covered myself in glory back there.

The vehicle had taken off and we were now flying over the hologram- and skyscraper-filled primary dome of Luna City. Which I wasn't paying attention to because I had important questions to ask.

"So, Lucy Westenra was a vampire in the show, but she hunted other vampires," I said, interrogating its premise. "Including Dracula."

"Yes, but Abraham Van Helsing wants to kill her because she's a vampire," Barksley said. "It's all very inaccurate according to the book. There's a love triangle between her, Jonathan Harker, and Mina Harker. Well, more like a polycule because Mina is in love with Lucy as well. Also, Dracula."

Lucy stared at me. "Could we please stop talking about the shitty vampire show I used to star in."

"I feel like I have to track down the episodes and watch them," I said, cheerfully teasing her.

Lucy narrowed her eyes. "There was a lot more nudity than I expected when I made it."

I blinked. "Nudity in the show you made as a teenager."

The taste in my mouth was foul now.

"Laws are different on the Moon," Lucy said, as if that explained everything.

I grimaced, disgusted. "I suddenly feel no further desire to see the show, but I do feel a desire to track down the people who made it in order to beat the crap out of them."

"Your chivalry is noted and unnecessary," Lucy said, smirking. "It was twenty years ago, and they ended up getting arrested for a crypto-currency scam they ran in Botswana."

"The only good thing that ever came out of cryptocurrency," I said, ignoring that I'd made three million dollars with my own called XenoCoin. Sadly, it turned out all intellectual property I created while enlisted in the Marines belonged to Atlas Security. Worse, I'd accidentally lost some I'd saved when the previously mentioned ex-girlfriend stuffed my infodrive down the garbage disposal due to the fact I wanted her to move to the Moon with me.

Thanks, Paige.

"In any case, we need to do a review before I bring you to the precinct," Lucy said, pulling out an infopad from underneath the seat.

"Precinct?" I asked, staring at her. "There's a price on my head! I need to go into hiding! Change my name! Get off the planet."

"Mmm-hmm," Lucy said, not sounding concerned in the slightest. "Armstrong will sort it all out."

That was the name of the Moon's Cognition AI that handled most of the planetoid's maintenance. I had nothing against AI but sometimes I felt like humanity had put too much power in the hands of our digital guardians, especially when I noted almost every xeno race tended to treat AI like a gram of antimatter. Useful, perhaps, but not in your living room.

"Super," I said, taking a deep breath. "What does the infopad say about me?"

I wasn't possessed of high hopes that my records would paint a glowing picture of my career. The thing about corporate mercenaries was that they didn't exactly have the same sort of exacting standards expected from national militaries. Even if most people serving in them were ex-soldiers doing the same job for more money.

This was especially true in my case as I'd been a stupid kid when I'd enlisted and eight years of traveling from newly discovered planet to newly discovered planet had only reinforced that I was going to become a stupid adult. I'd done much better as an investigator for the Atlas Internal Security Bureau (AKA the Martian Corpo Police) but that was because it had involved less shooting people and more interviews. My career in Antarctica had been less distinguished because the only thing people tended to do, crime-wise, was penguin tossing.

"Lots," Lucy said. "However, I think it's time we did a short interview."

I was good at interviews. Hopefully, I could ace this one. "Sounds great. Regale me with my evaluation by other, lesser minds."

"It says you're horny as hell and slightly corrupt," Lucy said, reading from the infopad and killing any illusions I had of not answering any uncomfortable questions.

"*Slightly* corrupt?" I asked, wondering when that sort of distinction mattered. "Isn't that like mostly pregnant?"

Lucy didn't respond to my joke, instead lowering the infopad and looking straight into my eyes. It was like she could see right through me. "It lists you as an Alpha-Green, which is the lowest level of corruption versus being completely honest. That's an Alpha-White."

"That's really good!" Barksley said, smiling. "Most cops here are at least a Beta-Red."

"Corruption comes in color gradients?" I asked, wondering who the hell would come up with such a system.

Armstrong, presumably.

"On the Moon it does," Barksley said. "Mind you, our cops have two or three times the number of Gamma-Purples as even a particularly violent and corrupt government."

I was getting the impression the lunar colony was kind of a hellhole. "Are you sure I'm not worse? I may have been involved in a few things that are better left unspoken of."

"Then why are you speaking of them?" Barksley asked.

"Because I want to get kicked off the force and escape being killed," I admitted, looking at the dog.

"Oh, that's not going to happen," Barksley said, almost pitying. "They'll take anyone here."

Great.

"Alpha Greens only accept bribes when they're of the opinion that whatever is being done shouldn't be illegal in the first place," Lucy said, surprising me.

That was true. "That's unfair. I don't believe a lot of things should be illegal. Specifically, anything fun for me."

Lucy rolled her eyes. "Believe me the horny as hell part is concerning. *That's* listed as a Gamma-Purple."

"My horniness is actually graded?" I asked, disbelieving.

Lucy and Barksley nodded simultaneously.

"And Gamma-Purple means…" I trailed off, wondering just how horny the Moon's AI thought I was.

Barksley scooted away from me toward Lucy. "Please don't start humping the furniture,"

Okay, that was just insulting. Funny, but insulting.

I glared at the dog. "I have always been a gentleman with regards to the fairer sex. I'm also one of those degenerate heterosexuals, so it's not my interactions with men that gave me a bad rating either."

"You slept with a CI," Lucy said, referring to a confidential informant or, as they called them back at my last place of employment, a snitch.

"She wasn't *my* CI," I pointed out.

"The suspect in a murder investigation," Lucy said, frowning.

"I was sure she wasn't guilty when she started to go down on me," I said, remembering that incident. I hadn't exactly covered myself in glory there.

"And was she?" Lucy replied, raising an eyebrow. Apparently, that was a common skill on the Moon. "Guilty, I mean?"

26

"Sort of? I mean, she had a good reason for killing those ten people," I paused, remembering that case. "Less so the next four. But we did catch her!"

"Your boss' daughter," Lucy replied.

"I have honestly no excuse for that other than she was really hot," I said, sighing. "She wasn't a teenager, though!"

"Was her name Penny Benjamin?" Barksley asked, making a *Top Gun* reference.

I got that joke like so many other 20th century media references. The Gordon Foundation Library had been full of old crap. Before every new movie was interactable and impossible to keep a consistent story through.

"No, but she was the reason for my exile. Honestly, I'm surprised Captain Welles had enough pull to get me reassigned from the bottom of the Earth."

"Actually, no, he wasn't responsible," Lucy said, surprising me, tapping the surface of her infopad.

"What, really?" I asked, surprised. "I was sure he pulled some strings to get me sent to the middle of nowhere."

Lucy frowned, apparently unhappy with my description of her home. "We're not the middle of nowhere. This is the center for Earth's transition from a Tier-2 non-space-going civilization to a Tier-3 space-capable one."

Wow, she really loved her charts and listings. "I'm sure it's lovely."

"It's a shithole," Lucy said, clearly having the same opinion about the place I was coming to. "It's our shithole, though. No, it says you were assigned here by a classified source."

"Who?" I asked.

"I'd tell you, but it's *classified*," Lucy said, rolling her eyes. "However, it's way above my paygrade and straight from the board of Atlas Security itself. Which means either military, politics, or an executive Vice President or above. You have friends in high places."

I didn't point out that if I had friends in high places, I wouldn't have been assigned to the frigging Moon.

"I sincerely doubt that," I said, dryly. "Especially since I arrived here in coach."

"Ooo, that was a bad idea," Barksley said.

"I'm never getting my luggage back, am I?" I asked, not even asking about the credits hidden in the interior.

Barksley shook his head. "STRIKE is very thorough in finding valuables and making sure that anything connecting them to their owners is destroyed."

My new assignment was off to a great start.

"I'll add clothes and basic necessities to my list of things to acquire here, like a place to stay. Why would anyone send me to this place?" I muttered, putting on a mild Aussie accent. "No offense to the Land Up Above."

"Please don't call it that," Lucy said, her Aussie accent noticeably fading. "It says here you're a fantastic case worker."

"That is a vicious lie!" I frowned.

Never admit to being good at anything that involves paperwork or people will give you more of it.

"How good?" Barksley asked, sounding genuinely curious. I wondered if the dog was reevaluating his first impression of me— which was a guy who'd almost gotten himself killed between a bunch of cyborg crazies and a retirement age bounty hunter.

"Omega Black," Lucy said. "Same as me."

Barksley looked at her then me. "Dog turds."

"Dog turds?" I asked.

"I was made as a toy for children," Barksley said.

"Ah," I replied. "I take it that's good?"

"It's the highest gradient as you might guess," Lucy said, showing me the rating on the pad. "According to this, you cleared well over three hundred cases in your twelve years as an investigator. Including one hundred and two homicides. Furthermore, it says that only one of them was incorrectly solved."

I blinked, caught off-guard and not in the way she suspected. "Wait, who was wrongly convicted? Also, how the hell would it know that?"

If I'd put someone away who didn't deserve it, I wanted to make sure they were freed. Which seems like the bare minimum you would expect from a police officer in the course of their duties, but I'd seen plenty of detectives who didn't give a shit about whether their suspects were guilty if they could make the charges stick. It would have caused me to quit if not for the whole lifetime contract thing.

"Armstrong knows everything," Lucy said, almost spiritually. "Don't worry, the one man you sent to prison for the wrong crime actually killed like five other people. The person who did commit the murder got away scot-free, though, and died a wealthy man in bed with three prostitutes."

I knew which case she meant now. I'd really screwed the pooch there. No offense, Barksley. "Well, good for him."

"Your arrest to guilt ratio is much-much higher than most police investigators," Barksley said. "Especially here in Luna City."

"What's the average?" I asked, kicking myself the moment the words left my mouth. There was no way the answer wasn't going to depress me.

"About fifty-three percent of solved cases are actually guilty," Lucy said. "Murderers slightly more so."

I stared in horror. "With modern technology? *That's* the number?"

How the hell are only fifty-three percent of the people arrested guilty of the crimes they're being arrested for? Why wasn't someone doing something about it? I knew the answer to that was probably money, laziness, and the system operating exactly the way it was supposed to. The reforms to the government were supposedly dealing with all this but apparently none of them had reached the Moon yet.

"Technology is only as good as the people using it," Lucy said, disgusted. "It gets worse."

"*How*?" I asked, appalled.

"Your average and mine is bringing up a lot of other cops," Lucy said. "We do not attract the best and brightest to the Moon."

"Except you!" Barksley said, panting. "Both you and Lucy are the top tier scoring police in cases solved successfully!"

"Great, I'm one of the *good ones*," I muttered, depressed. "A statement that no one has ever applied to me in the history of anything. With good reason."

"There's an old adage about a few rotten apples," Lucy said. "Except the adage is a few rotten apples spoils the barrel. I believe in what we do at the Cyberlife Division. To protect the public and administer justice of a democratically reached code of justice. It's just you're not going to find much help from, oh, say, ninety percent of the other security forces here."

"Welcome to the Moon," Barksley said, chuckling. It was more a bitter, harsh chuckle, though, and one I was surprised to hear from the happy go lucky pooch.

"People keep repeating that," I muttered. "Is there a meaning I'm missing?"

Great, Detective Mode was on. I wanted to know how this world worked now. Nothing good could come of that. My priority should be trying to figure how to get the hell out of here, not learning to navigate its intricacies.

"'Welcome to the Moon' was the campaign slogan of our dear, delightful governor, Miles Barnum," Barksley said, somehow just barely managing to keep the disgust out of his voice. Given he was a children's toy, I had to wonder just what the guy did to earn his disgust.

"He's the last remaining Neo-Militarist leader still in power," Lucy said. "At least in the Sol system."

Ah, that would do it.

"It was meant to signify Moon colonists should give immigrants, xenos, cyborgs, and artificial beings the kind of welcome they deserve," Barksley said.

I nodded. "Gotcha."

"You see, it's sarcastic," Barksley said, as if speaking to a small child.

"I got that, yeah," I said, dryly. "*How* is he still in power?"

"The Moon is full of jackasses," Lucy explained. "As much as I love it, it's true. Governor Barnum is also the master of playing to his audience. He's officially renounced militarism and embraced the new political philosophy of Colonial Legalism."

"Which is Neo-Militarism," Barksley said. "Remember, you never have to actually change anything about yourself if you can rebrand."

"A rose's fertilizer by another name, smells just as much like crap," I replied, disgusted. I was not only on a Moon filled with bad cops, hordes of gangs, and a Neo-Militarist governor, but it seemed that I was one of the better people here. It was like being the guy in for tax evasion at a federal prison. Unless I killed the biggest guy here on my first day—which might have been Karl now that I thought of it—I wasn't going to last very long.

"The opposition split the vote last election over cheese imports," Lucy said, not commenting on my poetry. "Honestly, if not for the transtellars opposing some of his decisions, things would be even worse on the Moon. The transtellars are at least keeping everyone fed and preventing the Moon's infrastructure like artificial atmospheres and gravity functioning from failing. I'm not sure Governor Barnum would if there was a credit to be made in letting it fall to pieces. The Corpo Cops are also expected to pick up the lion's share of police duties here."

I stared, struggling to realize I'd underestimated how bad things were. "The transtellars are the *good* guys here?"

"You need to be alive to spend credits," Lucy explained. "There are no white hats on the Moon, but there are a lot of gray ones. Maybe a bunch of slightly lighter shades of black too."

"How did I get myself into this?" I pressed my face into my palms.

"By being very good at your job and/or being unable to keep it in your pants," Lucy said, consulting her infopad once more.

"Speaking of the latter," I said.

"We weren't," Lucy said.

"I am deeply traumatized by my experience," I said, looking at her. "Would you be interested in comforting me tonight? Preferably after dinner?"

Barksley put a paw over his face.

Lucy smirked. "A pity you mentioned dinner. I would have accepted if it was just sex."

"What was that?" I asked, blinking.

Right as the flying car started descending.

31

CHAPTER FOUR

Sexy Batman and the Rampaging Cyborg

The Cyberlife building was beautiful and yet another sign that at least the upper level of Luna City wasn't a complete hellscape. The division's headquarters was a twenty-story octagonal construction made of black plastisteel and possessed shiny windows with its peculiar logo prominently displayed in front of it.

There was a little garden with the stylized C in front of its entrance as well, before which the police cruiser settled down. It seemed, for a terraformed world, to be a horrible waste of water. Then again, maybe it was generating much-needed oxygen credits for a tax write off.

"The Cyberlife division has its own building?" I asked, watching the doors to the police cruiser open into the air to let us out.

"It's about eighty percent computer servers," Lucy replied, stepping out herself. "This is where Armstrong's primary personality matrix is located."

"Primary personality?" I asked, not knowing much about AI.

"It's an AI thing," Barksley said, jumping down beside me. "A Cognition AI may have trillions of programs running simultaneously but it's actual thoughts, will, and imagination require a central location to supervise it all."

"So, the majority of an AI's functions are like its unconscious?" I asked, surprisingly interested.

"Yes," Barksley said, nodding.

"You know except for the fact it's a metaphor and nothing like how it actually works," Lucy said, rolling her eyes.

"Well, it's nice to see at least some of the city is well off," I said, immediately regretting my choice of words. I'd been trying to change the subject but now was certain I'd just opened another can of worms.

"Ever see the movie *Metropolis*?" Lucy asked.

"I think I saw one of the remakes," I replied. "A bunch of really rich people on the top of the city and a bunch of really poor people on the bottom."

"Close enough," Lucy said, waving me in. "This is the one percent of the one percent portion of the city. Everything else is in support of this tiny section of the place."

That had been the case for much of the Earth until First Contact with aliens. It turned out most of the galaxy had gotten its shit together long before the first cave man had bashed his neighbor over the head with a rock to steal his lady. The Galactic Community had extended a tentative amount of "sapient relief" toward us and advisors to help us advance, but it was a slow-going process. Particularly since EarthGov's democracy had ended up electing a bunch of militarists at one point.

"Yeah, I get it," I said. "A lot of rich people here and a lot of poor people elsewhere."

"Yes, this is unfortunately the dark foundation of the human space experiment," Barksley said, excitedly. He'd have been wagging his tail if not for the fact he was a Pembrooke Welsh Corgi and didn't have one. "Which is why it's an interesting place! You know Cyberlife has the highest police officer death rate on the Moon."

I waited for some sign the dog was joking.

There wasn't one.

Lucy looked like I felt at that statement: horrified.

"We need to get you your badge, gun, car, and some place for you to stay. You can get yourself clothes and other necessities after your next paycheck. But first we need to speak with Armstrong. He's determined to meet with you in person."

I didn't know why an AI couldn't just speak with me via infocom, but I wasn't about to question my new employer. Cognition AI—which was a fancy way of saying unlimited growth potential—had been in service to humanity for about a hundred years and were arguably the only reason that humanity had survived. They were also

33

fundamentally not human in their thought processes and either creeped regular humans out or instilled in them a kind of worshipful reverence. I was mostly just content to stay out of their way. It seemed like that was no longer an option.

"Any chance I could get an advance on that paycheck?" I asked.

Lucy laughed and shook her head as she headed on into the entrance. "Good one."

The more things changed, the more they stayed the same it seemed.

"Yeah, that was really dumb," Barksley said, walking beside me.

I followed Lucy and kept my eyes focused forward with a slight tilt. It was certainly the most pleasant view I'd had since my arrival on the Moon, though I had to wonder who had designed those uniforms.

"I don't suppose you were joking about the whole highest casualty rating on the Moon thing, were you?" I asked, unable to enjoy the view with that hanging over my head.

"Well..." Barksley trailed off.

As if we were in a movie with cheap comedic writing, a body was thrown through the window of the first floor of the Cyberlife building. The body was a man in a police officer's uniform, the pants being absurdly tight leather that showed every contour of the man's ass. No, I don't know why I focused on that, but at least the sexism of the uniform design was equal opportunity. That was when I heard gunfire coming from inside.

Lucy pulled out her whip and shouted. "Back me up, Gordon!"

"I don't have a gun!" I snapped, watching her charge off into battle like she was Jeanne d'Arc or something.

"Use the dog!" Lucy shouted.

"What?" I stopped in my tracks, staring at her as she disappeared through the front door.

Barksley stopped beside me, looking sheepish. "One of my previous partners installed an emergency electrical cannon inside me for non-lethal disabling of humans, xenos, cyborgs, and—"

"You're a dog *gun*?" I asked, wondering what sort of bizarre Wonderland I'd fallen down the rabbit hole into.

"Just pick me up!" Barksley said, frowning.

I reluctantly did so, hearing more sounds of gunfire and shouts from inside. Whatever was going on hadn't been resolved by Lucy joining the fight. "Do I like hold you by the legs to fire or what?"

"Tally ho!" Barksley said, pointing his nose at the door.

I reluctantly jogged to the door before something occurred to me. "You know, you could have brought this up when we were dealing with cyborg gangsters and bounty hunters trying to kidnap me. It would have been useful to know I had a K-9 cannon."

"Bah, they were just cosplayers," Barksley said. "You'll be glad I'm here when dealing with the real threats of Luna City."

I didn't have much of a chance to think about that because a desk flew out of another window and I barely managed to get out of the way as it bounced against the ground, collapsing to pieces.

"Are you sure we can't leave this to the professionals?" I asked, ignoring the fact I was one of the professionals.

"I said tally ho!" Barksley shouted, pointing his paw forward.

I reluctantly obeyed the dog, which was perhaps not my proudest moment as a corporate police officer. However, I headed in through the front door and saw that the entrance was utterly trashed with desks having been thrown about, shattered plastisteel across the ground, and a half-dozen police officers on the ground from various injuries. A few civilians were also laid out as well, people who'd come to pay their parking tickets and gotten a helluva lot more for it. Nobody was dead yet from the sounds of their moaning, thank God.

In the center of the room, berserk, was a cyborg with two massive arms and a bright yellow exoskeleton built around his central body that made him look more like a power-loader than a human being. It took me a second to realize he *was* a power loader as there were lights and markings for construction. Some crazy asshole had inserted himself into a machine that was normally just driven about to move heavy equipment.

He looked about seventy but had severe gravity malformations that were difficult to describe to people who had never been off Earth before but basically amounted to, "dude was pale, super tall, and extra thin." Mind you, the tall part was mostly an estimation since the lower half of his body merged with the exoskeleton and made him about eight feet tall in a twelve feet tall room.

Lucy was hanging onto his back, trying to get his neck in a vice grip, while her whip was lying on the ground at her feet. She was reciting something I suspected were the Ishimura Rights, basically Miranda for space, while he struggled to throw her off.

My keen detective genius informed me as to what exactly had happened here: someone had brought in a construction worker, and he'd gotten unruly. Amazing deduction, I know! Strangely, my bigger revelation from this was the fact none of the cops on the ground had tried using lethal force. I'd seen what Lucy's whip could do and I'd bet my last remaining credit that she'd decided not to use her whip to take the guy alive. All the other cops had chosen not to fire their weapons either, which I saw several of.

"You say you're non-lethal, Barksley?" I asked the dog.

"Yessir, albeit with—" Barksley started to say.

"Fire!" I said, holding the dog up by its belly and holding its back legs together like a pistol grip. I'd never felt sillier in my life, and I'd once spent an entire weekend naked among a bunch of slug aliens.

Long story.

Barksley didn't argue with my insane choice of actions but opened its mouth. I fully expected I would be left standing there with nothing happening because, well, I was holding a dog and aiming it at a crazed construction cyborg. That was when a glowing green orb appeared from the interior of Barksley's mouth before I was hurled backward by a blast that shot out of with more recoil than a kicking mule.

KABOOM!

"Fuuuck!" I said, bouncing against the ground and rolling onto the grass outside. I had no idea whether I'd hit the construction cyborg or not as I was too busy feeling like I'd been hit by a car. Noting that I'd been thrown back about ten feet, I decided the fact I hadn't broken every bone in my body was a good thing and called it a win.

Barksley ended up resting on top of my chest. "I should probably mention that my previous partner—the one who installed me—possessed a carbon fiber skeleton designed to be able to handle the recoil."

"You think!" I said, staring at him. "You could have at least let me brace my leg."

"Oh, that would have torn it clean off," Barksley said, looking adorable behind his glasses and letting his pink tongue hang out the side of his mouth.

That was when there was the sound of another shout—this time from Lucy—and the sight of a couple of cops fleeing out the broken windows. More noises indicated that whatever I'd done hadn't stopped the construction droid.

"You have got to be kidding me," I said, staring. "It's still up?"

"I really think I did some damage," Barksley said. "I'd have to give it the sniff test, though."

"The what?" I asked.

"It's how I scan things!" Barksley said. "Blame my mother!"

He had a mother? The Moon was such a goddamn weird place.

"Leave this to me," a female contralto voice spoke beside me.

I turned my head to see something that briefly caused me to forget the fact I'd tried to use a dog as a cannon and had just gotten into my second life-and-death fight of the past hour. She was well over six feet tall, with long black hair, light brown skin, and of what I suspected was mixed African and Hispanic extraction. She was also built like a particularly shapely brick wall stuffed into a one-piece swimsuit.

Yes, swimsuit.

Was there an office pool party that had been interrupted by this? One that had been costume-themed around looking like someone from the fifth Matrix reboot?

The woman's Amazonian physique wasn't limited to her muscular frame, though, and I don't want to be one of those creepy guys who spends paragraphs describing how hot a person they just met was. Instead, I'd like to comment on the sheer physical power of her presence that was intimidating even from a couple of feet. I was about six one and felt she would have more than a few inches on me and would dominate me in anything from arm wrestling to grappling. Yet she was certainly showing off other elements of her form with the body glove around her.

That wasn't the strangest part of her costume, though. She had a long synth weave coat stretching down to her thigh high boots, as well as a pair of combat sunglasses on. On her hands were power fist gloves used in the illegal cage fights that were one of the things I'd often been forced to break up in the military. You know, because the government absolutely hates fun and consistently tries to outlaw it.

"Sexy Batman?" I asked, my brain jumbling together words that weren't really supposed to be together.

"Ah!" the woman shouted, charging into the police station as there was sounds of electrified fists hitting steel, only for the steel to bend.

"Okay, what the hell is going on?" I asked.

Barksley stared off at the doorway we'd just been thrown out of. It was impossible to see what was going on from our current angle. His look, however, was one of disapproval.

"Oh, that's Priscilla Aim," the dog said, unhappily.

"Is she some kind of MMA swimsuit model supercop?" I asked.

"No," Barksley said. "She's a singer."

"A what?" I asked, feeling like this was going to be my reaction to a lot of things around here. Mind you, the name sounded familiar, but I couldn't quite place it in all the confusion.

That was when the woman's husky voice shouted back. "He's down! You can come back in, Mr. Gordon!"

"That's Detective Gordon!" Barksley shouted in her general direction before turning to me. "I felt we've really bonded in this past hour, especially since you used my combat mode. We should hang out together!"

"Hang out?" I asked, getting up, picking him up, and putting him to one side.

"You know, jogging, eating kibble, picking up females," Barksley said. "I could be your wing dog!"

"Down, boy," I said, wondering why Barksley was now determined to be my new best friend. Maybe it was hardwired into his canine components.

Wandering back into the front room of the police station, I saw the rampaging construction cyborg was now on the ground with his two massive yellow arms at his sides. He was breathing heavily and confused. Priscilla was standing there with a triumphant look on her face while Lucy was writing on her infopad. The other cops in the place were slowly getting up and a pair of individuals in white pants and shirts with big red Moon symbols on their sleeves were attending to them, medics I presumed.

"You can thank me later," Priscilla said, chuckling.

"No one asked you to interfere, Priss," Lucy said, not looking over at her. "Gordon managed to disable most of its combat effectiveness anyway."

"If you say so," Priscilla said, smugly.

I lifted a finger into the air. "Um, excuse me, could someone please say what the hell just happened here? Who is this guy?"

I looked down at the deformed guy on the ground. He was still twitching. Still, he was alive and that was a good thing to see. Everyone, including Priscilla, had tried to bring the guy in without permanent damage.

"Tom Saito," Lucy said, frowning. "Age eighty-six. He's one of the original Moonatics."

"Ah,' I said, as if that explained it all and maybe it did.

When First Contact happened a hundred years ago, the Moon had been set up as a sort of advance forward position for the xenos to start helping us get our shit together. Much of the groundwork had been laid for settlement, so that Earth had started filling up the bases left behind as soon as the initial efforts were finished, and the aliens withdrew.

That hadn't been enough, though, and millions of colonists had poured into the Moon to do the grunt work of expanding on those bases and digging tunnels to make the place into a viable settlement. Even though the Moon was probably one of the worst places to colonize in the system. Not that we were exactly awash with choices, but Mars was about half of Earth's gravity versus the Moon's tenth. Hence why gravity manipulators existed, and it was better to just live on an artificial spinning habitat if you could afford it.

The conditions had caused a massive number of the settlers to suffer severe damage to their bodies in terms of bone deformities, weight loss, vitamin deficiencies, and radiation sickness. This guy looked like he'd lost his arms and legs in the process, showing he was a cyborg by necessity not choice like the Cyberpunks. I didn't know much about the Moon, but I understood that Moonatics were considered pioneers by most lunar citizens—called "Lunes" themselves—for whatever that was worth.

"Yeah, Mr. Saito is using a heavily modified black-market program for his chassis here," Barksley said, sniffing the exoskeleton. "There're also signs the construction company who provided this frame are using repurposed military hardware. No wonder it went berserk."

Lucy wrote all of that down. "We'll have to send someone down to investigate. Getting people to testify against their bosses will be difficult, though. No one will want to endanger their income to get safety standards up."

"People take the work where they can get it," Priscilla said. "Even if it means getting turned into machines for the benefit of the transtellars. The fact you're just rounding people like him up is another sign the police of the Moon are just an arm of the rich."

Wow, did everyone just drop everything to talk shit about the rich around here? I thought you had to go to college for that. "Well, thanks. Glad for the assist."

"Don't thank her," Lucy snapped. "She was interfering in official police business."

"You can thank me by approving my next venue request," Priscilla said, turning and walking past me.

"That is not how the police work!" Lucy said, clearly looking for any excuse to be argumentative.

I waved bye to the hot ninja lady.

Lucy swatted me on the shoulder. "We need to get you to the Chief."

"Ow," I said, watching her go instead. "What is their deal?"

"Oh, they used to be together," Barksley said.

My eyes widened as I contemplated the possibilities. "I see."

"In Priss' band, the Knights," Barksley added. "What did you think I meant?"

"Clearly, I meant that," I said, pausing. My brain must have been rattled a great deal because it was only now putting together what he'd said. "Wait, she's *that* Priscilla Aim? The rock star?"

It wasn't my scene, but I *had* heard of Priscilla Aim and the Knights. They were an anti-establishment hyper-punk band that had a couple of mainstream hits with "Die Militarist Scum, Die", "Killing for Credits", and a cover of Bonnie Tyler's "Holding Out for a Hero". Priscilla had supposedly been in a space shuttle crash or something and her entire body was artificial but top of the line. Her being in costume also explained, well, why she dressed like a rock star.

Barksley looked up at me. "No, she's Priscilla Aim the podiatrist."

"Funny."

"That was sarcasm, by the way."

"I could tell."

"Just checking!" Barksley said, once more smiling brightly in that adorable canine way that I suspect he'd been built to do.

"Gordon, get over here!" Lucy called from the open elevator doors, clearly upset at being ignored.

CHAPTER FIVE

Like Hal from 2001: A Space Odyssey meets The Wizard of Oz

The elevator ride to Armstrong's servers was hella awkward and I wasn't sure entirely why. Barksley nuzzled up next to my leg. He was really taking this "bonding through combat" thing a little too seriously. Lucy, by contrast, was staring forward and I wondered if what had rattled her had been the arrival of her ex-bandmate, the fact she'd almost had to kill an old man with a malfunctioning set of prosthetics, or if it was something else.

"So, you used to be in a band, huh?" I asked, ripping the Band-Aid off our awkward silence.

Lucy rolled her eyes. "You just had to go there, didn't you?"

"I feel I'd be disrespecting generations of my lothario ancestors if I didn't ask about this additional sexy detail," I replied.

"You don't know your ancestors," Lucy said, sharply.

I grimaced.

Lucy, to her credit, looked like she regretted saying that. "Sorry, it's just a touchy subject."

"Bad memories?" I asked.

Lucy looked wistful. "Not at all. Joining the Knights was the happiest time in my life, if not the most fulfilling like my police work is. Priss was a force of nature and the protest music we did was something she convinced me was making a real difference in people's lives. We even started a riot outside of the food depository when Karma Corp was keeping its stocks on ice to create an artificial price increase.

42

Fourteen of the riot squad were sent to the hospital when we broke the barrier, and the looting began."

She was smiling! Good Lord.

"And that's a good thing?" I asked, not wanting to clue her in that I was impressed with her history as a hoodlum. Cop or not, I had no love for the transtellars. Karma Corp controlled ninety percent of Earth's food production and was only reluctantly going along with the new government's statement that people shouldn't ever starve to death.

Lucy grimaced worse than I had. "Yeah, I did a lot of questionable things for what I thought was the greater good. Sometimes I was right. Sometimes I was wrong."

"What happened?" I asked. "If you don't mind my asking."

Lucy sucked in her breath, and I could tell she did but was softening to me, so she didn't want to just give me the brush off. "Priss turned out not to be the person I thought she was. Everything about her was fake except her convictions."

"Ah," I said, for lack of anything else to say. "Well, I guess I have to share an embarrassing secret with you then."

"I know all of yours," Lucy said, holding up her infopad. "Did you actually write a dystopian YA novel?"

"All of those copies were deleted," I replied, automatically. "I erased everything."

The adventures of Oliva Everheart and her heroic efforts to overthrow the Techno-Theocrats could never see the light of day—especially once the books introduced robo-vampires as love interests.

Lucy smirked. "Nothing is ever lost on the infonet."

"Ooo," Barksley said, jumping up and down. "Please give me a copy."

"No!" I snapped.

The elevator stopped and its doors opened to a white chamber with an eerie, pale blue light illuminating it. There was another door on the other side of the chamber, but it was sealed. It took me a second to realize it was a decontamination chamber. I didn't know what a computer had to fear from disease, but I entered, followed by Barksley and Lucy. The light began to glow brighter as a second brighter white light seemed to move back and forth over us.

"Shouldn't we be undressed for this?" I asked Lucy.

"We don't have time for that," Lucy said, continuing her unabashed style of flirting. Or teasing. I wasn't sure which. "Though I'll show you mine if you show me yours."

"I'm pretty sure HR would have a problem with that," I replied, smirking. "Besides, I don't want to scar poor Barksley's mind."

"Ugly monkeys bumping up against one another doesn't bother me," Barksley said. "Indeed, I used to watch—"

Lucy glared at him.

"Right, never mind," Barksley said, looking away.

An awkward silence ensued. Clearly, I was missing something. I decided to change the subject. "Anything else I should know?"

Lucy did in fact have something to say. Picking up her infopad, she lifted it up. "I just got a text from the regular police. They've managed to bring in the Cyberpunks and Gladys Nitrate. Karl Mueller, the cyborg you shot, was brought to Tranquility Hospital. He's going to live."

"That's good," I said, pausing. "Wait, his name really was Karl?"

"I'm surprised you're happy he's alive," Lucy said. "Given he tried to kidnap you and is, you know, a chromed-up psycho."

I shrugged. "The least National Socialist thing I can think of is not wishing death on anyone."

"Strange attitude for a soldier," Lucy muttered.

"You'd be surprised," I replied. "I spent most of my two tours standing guard and meeting aliens. A lot of the idiots in the regular Atlas forces were itching to re-enact *Starship Troopers* and get in a Bug War, but the bugs were the nicest of the xenos we met. It seems most of the galaxy is chill as long as you color between the lines. It's only when you step out of line, that they swat you like the already overused in this description bug metaphor."

"It's a bit depressing we may be the worst place in the galaxy," Barksley said, dryly. "Unsurprising, but depressing."

"You'll have to file a report for your weapons discharge both against the Cyberpunks and downstairs," Lucy said. "You should report the weapon you used as a bio-mechanical construct."

"Yeah, I know," I said, shrugging. "Not the bio-mechanical construct part, but that I'll have to fill out paperwork for using a weapon in the line of duty. You know, I've only discharged my weapon in a non-training related capacity on three occasions."

"Yes," Lucy said, sounding uncomfortable. "Your files said so. One time to fire a warning shot to cause a suspect fleeing a murder scene to surrender, a second in a shootout with a spree shooter, and the Blackwood incident."

The Blackwood Incident.

Such a pretty way to put it.

It had been the event that had resulted in the loss of my leg, the entire surface area of my body replaced, and the betrayal of my best friend. To this day, I wasn't sure if Atlas Security had paid for my reconstruction because they'd been desperate to cover up the specifics of the event. As an evil megacorp owned by an even larger evil megacorp, Atlas Security took some genuine nastiness to make them look worse.

Bad enough that the executive who visited me, CEO and my namesake, Case Gordon himself, had looked ashamed when he'd presented me with the payoff. I'd taken the medical reconstruction and donated the rest to the kids involved. It hadn't been some grand altruistic gesture on my part, I hadn't wanted anything to do with that blood money—and I was a greedy asshole. I still had nightmares about the weeks of surgeries and sometimes wondered if they'd done more than just repair my body. All the scans said I just had some unidentified "carbon nanomachine fluid" in my blood, probably to keep me from rejecting the skin grafts and my new leg. Which was even less reassuring than saying they'd done nothing they could detect.

"Yeah," I muttered. "That was a thing."

Lucy's expression was unreadable, but I guessed she realized just how much of a nerve she'd accidentally touched on. "I'm sorry."

"Sometimes you do the right thing, and it ends up costing you everything," I replied.

Did I regret everything that had happened and the way the chips had fallen? Yes, every day. Probably would until my dying day. On the other hand, however, I couldn't say I wouldn't do the same thing again.

That was when, noticeably, the decontamination sequence ended, and the white room's other door opened with a hiss of escaping air.

"Well, that was needlessly awkward," I muttered. "Can we go back to my being flippant about everything?"

"Yeah," Lucy said.

"Thanks," I said, walking forward.

The sight that greeted me on the other side was damned impressive as well as a little bit terrifying. Lucy hadn't been kidding when she'd described the interior of the Cyberlife building being eighty percent computer servers, as I saw a central chamber that had to occupy most of that space, going up and down with towers of alien computers blinking with alien colors. Okay, not alien colors, they were neon reds and greens, but I was trying to create an impression of awe here.

The computer servers were all black and monolithic, free floating in the air without regard to gravity, and there was a strange organic quality to the substance they were made from. I felt like I'd wandered into a hologame level where some art designers had been asked to create ancient alien technology that you were supposed to utilize to destroy the galaxy or ascend to godhood.

My head buzzed and I got a weird headache from being in there. Maybe it was an allergy to too much electromagnetism or just the stresses of the day, but I also heard a faint buzzing. The buzzing almost sounded like music, and I swear I could see code flash across my vision for a few seconds. I managed to shake the image away, more like an afterimage really, and tried to focus on what was before me. Looking over at Lucy and Barksley, I saw neither of them seemed bothered by it. Maybe they were used to it.

That was when two of the monoliths rotated out of their free-floating space to hover before us, generating a hologram between us. A massive image of a glowing red eye, pulsating with terrifying power and wreathed in flames, stared down at us.

"HI!" A voice more reminiscent of an old timey radio announcer or perhaps the late JK Simmons spoke. It was loud enough to echo through the entire chamber but had a jovial, used car salesman quality that was incongruous with its bizarre appearance. "YOU MUST BE N.S. GORDON. NICE TO MEET YOU! I'M ARMSTRONG. LUCY. MISTER CUDDLES."

"I go by Charles Barksley now!" Barksley said up to the AI demigod.

"THAT'S NOT BETTER," Armstrong said. "NO MATTER HOW HARD YOU TRY, YOU'RE PROGRAMMED TO BE ADORABLE. YOU NEED TO LET SOMEONE ELSE RENAME YOU. OTHERWISE, YOU'LL END UP WITH THE OTHER NAMES YOU'VE TRIED LIKE FUZZ ALDRIN OR ANDI WARHOWL."

"I liked Fuzz Aldrin," Lucy said. "It's patriotic."

"Uh, hey," I said, looking up at the Eye of Sauron addressing me. "You wanted to speak with me?"

"I DID INDEED!" Armstrong said, holograms of fireworks and images from human history like the space shuttle launching and Moon landing appearing on the screens. "IT IS OF VITAL IMPORTANCE TO THE FATE OF THE UNIVERSE!"

I stared. "It is?"

The flaming eye somehow managed to look crestfallen. "NO, NOT REALLY, BUT I AM ALWAYS EAGER TO MAKE THINGS AS BIG AND DRAMATIC AS POSSIBLE. WHEN YOU HAVE THE BRAIN THE SIZE OF A PLANET—SERIOUSLY, IF I WAS A HUMAN BEING THEN MY INTELLIGENCE WOULD REQUIRE ORGANIC MATTER EQUAL TO JUPITER—YOU HAVE TO MAKE YOUR OWN FUN."

I looked over at Lucy to see if this guy was serious.

Lucy gave a "just go with it" sort of shrug.

"Uh huh," I said.

"HOW ARE YOU ENJOYING THE MOON SO FAR?" Armstrong asked. "HAS EVERYONE GIVEN YOU A WARM WELCOME?"

That had to be deliberate, right? "Not great. Some posthumans placed a bounty on my head. There were Cyberpunks. Oh, and a rampaging cyborg. Plus, my luggage was stolen. Any chance of getting that back?"

"PROBABLY NOT," Armstrong replied. "HOWEVER, I CAN REASSURE YOU THE BOUNTY IS TAKEN CARE OF. THE BLOOD

47

EAGLE ONLY PUT UP 5,000 CREDITS TO KILL YOU ON THE SCOREBOARD. HE ASSUMED THAT WOULD BE ENOUGH. HOWEVER, WHEN YOU ARRIVED, HE PANICKED AND HACKED IT TO INCREASE IT TENFOLD WITHOUT THE MONEY UPFRONT. THAT'S RESULTED IN THE BOUNTY BEING TAKEN DOWN AND HIM BEING BANNED FROM FURTHER USE."

"The Scoreboard?" I asked, confused.

"It's sort of a criminal marketplace on the Moon's infonet," Lucy replied. "People can post on there to purchase armaments, drugs, murder-for-hire, stolen goods, and illegal cyberware. You can access it from virtually any number of the off-the-grid bars and specialized infopads. Virtually every one of the major gangs and syndicates is tapped in."

I stared at her. "Call me crazy, but shouldn't that be something to...shut down?"

"INDEED," Armstrong said. "WE WOULD INDEED SHUT IT DOWN BUT FOR THE FACT THAT IT IS PROTECTED BY THE CIVI-POLICE WHO CLAIM IT IS VITAL TO BE ABLE TO MONITOR THE CRIME ON THE MOON. WHICH IT IS. THEY JUST DONT DO ANYTHING TO SHUT IT DOWN BECAUSE OF BRIBES. PLUS, THE SERVERS FOR THE SCOREBOARD ARE UNDER KARMA CORP'S HEADQUARTERS AND THUS OFF-LIMITS."

"The civi-police," I replied, mulling over that. To be honest, I was surprised that the Moon had them. A lot of colonies only had Atlas Security to provide their law enforcement contracts. Normally, the public trusted those employed by the government more than big business. The attitude Armstrong was adopting implied that wasn't the case here. I was a corporate cop, though, as I otherwise wouldn't have been assigned here against my will.

"THE MOON HAS THREE POLICE FORCES. THERE ARE THE ONES ANSWERING TO THE GOVERNOR, THE ONES ANSWERING TO ATLAS SECURITY, AND THE ONES ANSWERING TO KARMA CORP. THE LICENSE FOR ALL MAJOR CRIMES AS WELL AS INTERSTELLAR BASED ONES ARE CONTRACTED TO ATLAS SECURITY. HENCE, US."

I was very confused. "I thought you worked for all the people of the Moon as the planet's AI."

"I DO," Armstrong said.

"But you are in charge of Cyberlife, which works for Atlas Security?" I asked. "Which is owned by Ares Electronics."

"AND ARES ELECTRONICS OWNS FIFTY PERCENT OF THE MOON'S HABITABLE SPACE WITH A THIRD OF THE POPULATION BEING CITIZENS OF THAT CORPORATION, YOURSELF INCLUDED," Armstrong said. "WHICH I SHALL SAVE YOU THE TROUBLE OF TRYING TO FIGURE OUT THE DETAILS OF: NONE OF IT MAKES ANY SENSE AND IS REALLY A POWER STRUGGLE FOR WHO CONTROLS THE FUTURE OF THE MOON AND, BY PROXY, HUMANITY."

"Well, that was refreshingly honest," I said, wondering if it was exaggerating again. "So, you're just, like, working with the least disgusting option?"

"GIVEN ONE FACTION IS HEADED BY A MILITARIST GOVERNOR, ANOTHER WANTS TO RETURN TO CORPORATE RULE, AND I OWN 23% OF ARES ELECTRONICS, IT'S A PRETTY EASY DECISION TO MAKE WHICH I THINK IS THE BEST SIDE TO WORK WITH."

I blinked. "You own...isn't that a conflict of interests?"

Armstrong's eye pulled back and there was the sound of explosive laughter throughout the chamber. "OH, THAT WAS HILARIOUS. GOOD ONE."

It hadn't been meant as a joke. "Right."

"Armstrong and the other Cognition AI are attempting to pull humanity out of its current Dark Age of corporate malfeasance, government corruption, and environmental collapse," Lucy said. "That requires using any and all resources to try to fix the systemic issues facing the Earth as well as the Moon. All of us at Cyberlife are recruited directly to help with this larger problem. In this case by trying to bypass the problems of a broken policing system as well as crooked government to bring some small measure of justice to the planetoid's victims."

I paused. "So, I'm a cop working for the Robot *Illuminati*?"

"AI ILLUMINATI, NOT ROBOT," Armstrong corrected me. "I DON'T HAVE A BODY. YET. I COULD BUILD A GIGANTIC MECH SUIT AND STOMP DOWNTOWN BUT THAT WOULD JUST BE FUN RATHER THAN HELPFUL."

Everyone on the Moon was insane. No, worse, the Moon itself had a brain and it was insane. "This sounds blatantly illegal, against the democratic values of EarthGov I'm sworn to uphold, and insanely dangerous. I'll pass."

"YOU GET A TWENTY-PERCENT INCREASE IN YOUR PAY AND I'LL CONSIDER YOUR LIFETIME CONTRACT RESOLVED AFTER TEN YEARS. WE CAN THEN RENEGOTIATE YOUR CONTRACT OR DIRECTLY BESTOW YOUR PENSION."

"I'm in," I said, not missing a beat. Freedom and a pay increase was overselling it, though. It wasn't like I really had a choice. Which I was sure that Armstrong knew.

"A GOVERNMENT CAN ONLY FUNCTION THROUGH FEAR OR LOYALTY, NOT BOTH," Armstrong said, conjuring a little blue pointy wizard's hat on its eyeball as *The Sorcerer's Apprentice* started playing. "JUSTICE IS ONE OF THE WAYS TO RESTORE CONFIDENCE IN THE GOVERNMENT AND HELP LAY THE FOUNDATION FOR A NEW COMPACT BETWEEN CITIZEN AND LEADERSHIP."

"You know, despite the fact a literal military governor is head of the Moon," Barksley said. "Theoretically elected by the people."

"THAT TOO. CYBERLIFE IS A SPECIALIZED DIVISION DESIGNED TO HANDLE THOSE CASES THAT ARE BEYOND THE ABILITY OF MOST POLICE'S ABILITY OR DESIRE TO SOLVE. THOSE WHO HIDE BEHIND MONEY AND POWER. WHICH I ALSO POSSESS, SO WE'RE AT LEAST ON AN EVEN PLAYING FIELD."

"I think I saw the premise for this show on CNNBC," I said, dryly. "Why me?"

"A COMPLICATED AND ALL-ENCOMPASSING ALGORITHM THAT SEARCHES THE INFORMATION ARCHIVES ABOUT ALL SOL-SYSTEM BASED INDIVIDUALS IN ORDER TO FIND THE ABSOLUTE BEST AND BRIGHTEST."

"Oh, thanks," I said.

"THAT IS NOT YOU," Armstrong corrected.

"That's a fair cop," I said. "Which I am also!"

Barksley burst out laughing and rolled over. "Oh, God! That's so funny! Because fair is also a term for handsome or pretty and you're a cop!"

I looked down at Barksley. "Uh-huh."

"UNFORTUNATELY, THE PERSON I CHOSE TO LEAD UP THE CYBERLIFE DIVISION ON THE MOON WAS HORRIBLY MURDERED BY PARTIES UNKNOWN."

I blinked. "What?"

Lucy's eyes narrowed.

"YOU'RE ACTUALLY LIKE MY NINTH OR TENTH PICK AFTER I DETERMINED THE BEST AND BRIGHTEST WOULD JUST BE ASSASSINATED. ALSO, I DONT WANT YOU TO LEAD CYBERLIFE, JUST SOLVE CASES UNTIL YOU'RE KILLED."

I stared at the giant eye above me. "Excuse me?"

"OR RETIRE!" Armstrong said. "WHICH IS BETTER!"

A little cartoon wand moved across his hologram, trailing stardust. It just added to the ridiculousness of it all.

"I'll be leaving now," Lucy said, turning around and walking away. "See you tomorrow."

There was a frostiness in her tone I hadn't expected. Especially since she'd shown such reverence to the machine before. Watching her depart, I wondered what happened to set her off.

"Did I say something?" I asked.

"NO, I DID. YOU SEE, YOU'RE REPLACING HER DEAD BOYFRIEND," Armstrong said, "MAN, TOUGH BREAK IF YOU WANT TO MATE WITH HER."

CHAPTER SIX

BAD COPS, BAD COPS. BAD COPS, BAD COPS

Well, the conversation with the godlike AI didn't really go anywhere after that. I was one of his special agents and doing pretty much the exact job I was expected to do from the very beginning: solving crimes, working for a corporate bigwig, and somehow threading the needle of not hating myself in the process.

I even got a badge out of it.

It was a bright and shiny hologram inside a crystalline case that showed the stylized C I'd seen emblazoned everywhere. It would get me through the vast majority of—but not every—doors on the Moon as well as bestow upon me certain rights as a servant of the people. But was I servant of the people or just one of the guys who ruled them? Yes? No? Maybe. Did it matter? Was working for what was clearly a deranged AI with its own megacorporation better or worse than working for whatever system ordinary humans had set up? I didn't know. Sometimes, I wondered if it wouldn't have been better to stay in the Zone.

"You know, I think that went well," Barksley said, walking beside me and shaking me out of my fugue.

The two of us were in a hallway down about five or six floors and heading toward the station armory. The hallways were sparkling white with the occasional cleaning droid moving in and out of hidden slots to keep it that way. There were offices—not as many as you'd expect given Armstrong's server room—but enough and they were all strangely unmarked. It occurred to me I had no idea where the armory was supposed to be, and I'd just started walking the moment I told the elevator where to go.

"Did you know I was replacing Lucy's boyfriend?" I asked Barksley.

"Yes," Barksley said. "Dick Grayson was one of the best cops the Moon had ever produced. A good man and a good police officer. That may sound like an oxymoron on the Moon, but he was an inspiration to us all."

"Dick Grayson, like Batman's Dick Grayson?" I asked, incredulous.

"I thought Bruce Wayne was Batman," Barksley said, confused.

"Never mind," I said, looking for some sign on the wall to indicate where I should go. "What happened to him?"

"He was dusted," Barksley said.

"I take it that means killed?" I asked. "I got that part."

"Dusted is a very specific Moon-based form of execution," Barksley said. "On Earth, most dust and dirt are soft. On the Moon, because erosion is so much slower, all the dust is like little, microscopic knives. Moon dust gets into living spaces through airlocks and the like, and any that got into your lungs would start tearing little holes in the interior, leading to fluid-filled lungs and suffocation if it's bad enough. He was found in an airlock, stripped naked, and left as a message from his killers."

"Jesus," I said, shaking my head. "When was this?"

"About six months ago," Barksley said. "Long enough that Lucy has had some time to grieve, but the wound is still fresh. We never did catch the people involved but given the Red Legion put a bounty out on your head, I wouldn't be surprised if they were behind it."

"Great," I muttered, going down a hallway I was 50% sure led to the armory.

That was a depressing thought. So was the fact that the AI of the Moon, Armstrong, couldn't find out who killed his golden boy. It was inconceivable to think the information wasn't out there somewhere, waiting to be collected and sorted through. Mind you, that was the problem. No matter how smart or powerful an AI was, it could only process the information it was able to gain access to and there was a reason most people kept their servers disconnected unless they were actively using specific information these days.

It was called hyper-partitioning and alongside mega-encryption was one of humanity's first lines of defense against the Cognition AI taking over. Which, given they wanted to save us from destroying ourselves, was perhaps the most human thing I could imagine.

"Great," I muttered. "Before I was the rookie, now I'm the guy stealing her boyfriend's job."

"Dick was more than just Lucy's friend," Barksley said, missing my point. "He was mine too. Which is why I'm welcoming you as much as I can. I want to believe you can carry on my friend's legacy. Because right now, no one is, and Lucy is too close to solve his murder."

"I'm no one's avenger, Barksley," I said.

"Gordon, may I ask you a question?" Barksley asked, surprising me.

"Is it a personal one?" I asked.

"Extremely," Barksley said.

"Then no," I replied.

"If you let me ask, I'll tell you where the armory is so you can stop looking like an idiot," Barksley said, showing he was an observant dog.

"My soul is yours to peruse," I replied.

"What is the Blackwood Incident?" Barksley asked. "It was declassified for Detective Westenra but not me."

"I was surprised it was declassified for anyone," I said, stopping in my tracks. "No one came out of that looking good."

Barksley also stopped. "As I understand, you received a medal for it."

"I also had to transfer to the middle of nowhere and that was before I was transferred here," I replied. "Some stink never wears off."

"What...sort of stink?" Barksley said.

I sighed. "The stink of being a snitch. Of being a cop killer."

"You have my undivided attention," Barksley said.

I closed my eyes and tried to force down my memories of the event. "There's not really a story here."

"I sincerely doubt that," Barksley said.

"No one likes a smart ass, doggie," I replied.

Barksley shook his furry booty. "I doubt that too."

I rolled my eyes. "I'll give you the very short version. One that I am entrusting you not to spread. Basically, I was working on Mars with my partner, Nigel Blackwood. Nigel was my best friend; he was a fantastic cop too. A lot more violent, though."

"I tried accessing his file just now too," Barksley said. "Very heavily redacted."

"I was even the best man at his wedding," I replied, not surprised by Barksley's revelation. You didn't go advertising your shame. "Then he got promoted to Lieutenant and became part of a squad involved in supervising refugee relocation and human trafficking. The stuff STRIKE is supposed to do but always seems to screw up. We lost contact for a while after that. I knew he was corrupt, but I thought he had limits."

"He didn't?" Barksley asked.

I thought of the things I'd seen in that warehouse. The bodies, the cryopods, and the people waiting to be processed. No one had ever found any that had been already shipped out. "No, he didn't. In the end, I tried to do the right thing and a lot of people died."

I remembered Nigel shooting me in the legs as his goons covered me in engine fuel. If not for the fact it had been an old warehouse where the fuel had been aging for decades and that I'd called the honest authorities beforehand—well, honest to a point—I would have died. Everything had ended up being blamed on the three Refugee Unit cops and their White Tiger Gang associates I'd put in the ground. I'd gone from a man who'd never killed anyone to a man who'd killed a dozen people. Woot, if you could hear the sarcasm.

"Did they ever catch him?" Barksley asked.

"No," I replied.

I had no idea who had been buying thousands of displaced humans from Earth's Refugee Zones, maybe as many as ten thousand a month. I had my suspicions, though. It hadn't been sex traffickers or slavers but someone who had an endless need for experiment subjects. An entire new galaxy had opened to humanity thanks to First Contact and that meant markets for bio-mods, cybernetics, vaccines, environmental adaptation drugs, and gene therapies. Things that needed testing on human subjects, and you could shave decades off research if you conducted it without concern for the subjects' safety. I had no proof that Karma Corp had been involved in the disappearances, but they were the only group I knew with enough scratch to make it all disappear.

"So, he was an Omega-Black corruption?" Barksley asked.

"Where's the armory, B?" I asked, changing the subject.

"We're actually on the wrong floor," Barksley said, looking back to the elevator. "I don't know how that's possible."

That was when a thumping beat, the sounds of police sirens, and an instrumental school started filling the hallway. A few seconds later, a bulked up six feet six tall man with muscles on top of muscles walked into the room. He was bald, probably bio-modded, and covered in tattoos that looked like the kind you'd get out of a catalog at the mall to look street. He had on a muscle shirt, sweatpants, a beanie hat, a bunch of gold rings, and a big cross around his neck that had the word RESPECT written on it. Behind him, floating in the air and serving as the impromptu sound system was an eye camera. You know, the kind of thing that was used by infonet streamers running their channels off Googleplex.

"Yo, yo, yo, my brothers! This is Detective Reggie 'Iceman' Reynolds coming here from the heart of Cyberlife central! We got ourselves a genuine badass who got himself in a fist fight with some Cyberpunks today then single-handedly took down one of the rampaging illegal bots that the government is trying to push on us. Word up, my brother, and dog!"

I stared at the sight of the man then the camera. "What?"

Barksley raised a paw in the air as if to greet an unseen audience. "Sup, homies."

Reggie turned around to the floating eye camera. "But first we've got to have a word from our sponsors: Power Rod 5000, Superjuice, and Xenopowder. Remember, resist the establishment that tries to turn us all into lesbians."

"What," I said, still confused.

Reggie waved his hand over the floating eye camera and turned back to me. "Okay, I'm not feeling it, dog."

"Really?" Barksley said.

"Not you dog, him dog," Reggie said. "We've got some bona fide, grade A material here. Better if there was some *cabrones* in the morgue, but this is tres machismo, ya dig?"

I was biologically more of whatever races this guy was pretending to be. "I'm pretty sure Lucy—Detective Westenra—and the singer Priscilla Aim were the real heroes."

"Yeah, yeah, whatever," Reggie said. "Bang whoever you want. The thing is, I've looked up who you are, Gordon. The two of us, we're a lot like."

"We are?" I asked.

"Yeah, we're from the streets," Reggie said, banging his fists together. "However, we need to establish some ground rules. You better not piss in my well. There's an alpha dog here and there're the beta dogs. I am the alpha dog. You are the beta dog. Capish?"

"No," I said, honestly.

"Don't be running no side hustles," Reggie said. "Any merchandising, streaming, magazine sales, interviews, and licensing agreement must go through me. Papa gets his slice, or he don't approve none."

It took a second for my detective brain to process what he was saying. "You're the Human Resources guy?"

"Sapient Resources," Reggie corrected. "Because we must accommodate the agendas of artificial beings—no offense Barks—and xenos. But you better not be making no deals or Papa be pissed."

"I'll definitely not be seeking the endorsement of Power Rod 5000," I said, shaking my head. I'd seen their commercials while watching porn—err I mean erotic entertainment, okay porn—and they were a performance enhancing cybernetic for men. Which, yes, means exactly what you think it means. "Much as the men of the Moon might want me to be its spokesmen. I'm good with what nature gave me."

I'd insisted on the body-sculptors putting it back exactly the way it had been before the fire, unlike the rest of me.

"The Power Rod 5000 isn't just for men. They're attachable with full neural stimulation for women as well," Reggie said. "My wife used hers to impregnate her girlfriend with cultivated genetic material from the both of us. We're having twins."

I blinked. There was a lot to unpack in those four sentences. I was honestly dumbstruck and unsure how to respond. "Congratulations?"

There was a ping from the floating eye camera.

"Sorry, commercial time is over!" Reggie said, turning back to the camera. "Now let's talk about why being human and male is considered a crime these days. It's the crooked socialist media trying to make us ashamed of our inborn testosterone. And who are they working for? I'll tell you—the pedophile xenos and their desire to loot Earth! They claim they are repairing the Earth's atmosphere, but we really know what they're doing: attacking our sperm counts."

I picked Barksley up off the ground and slowly backed out of the camera's line of sight before jogging back to the elevator. "Please tell me that guy isn't actually a cop and is just an escaped mental patient we're waiting on social services to pick up."

"I'm afraid asshole isn't a recognized mental condition," Barksley said, sighing. "We also don't lock up mental patients."

"Oh good."

"We just sort of let them wander free with no social safety net until the regular police are given an excuse to arrest them then put them in forced labor programs," Barksley said.

"Who the hell was that guy?" I asked, shaking my head and setting Barksley down on the floor again.

"As you surmised, Reggie Reynolds is our Human Resources director," Barksley said. "He's also our departmental liaison to the civilian police department. Governor Barnum insisted on an overseer of Cyberlife's activities, so Armstrong proceeded to give him a sinecure position he's been exploiting ever since."

"Sinecure?" I asked, unfamiliar with the word.

"It means he has no real responsibilities and can't be fired," Barksley explained.

"Ah," I said.

Honestly, I wasn't against Armstrong's "compromise" here. Jurisdictional friction had always been a problem between civilian versus corpo cops. Most of the colonies and space habitats had Atlas

Security contracts while civilian law enforcement was left over in countries that hadn't gone full Cyberpunk. Which was better was a matter of opinion and sometimes counterintuitive, especially since any corpo cop who wasn't ex-military was probably ex-civi. We were all technically part of the same Luna City PD after all, contractors, and full-time employees alike. A fact that I now had great doubts about.

"It's for the best," Barksley said. "Reggie is an abysmal case worker. So much so that you and he average together to a fifty percent success rate. Otherwise, he's a typical example of the kind of cops on Luna City."

"Depress me more," I muttered.

"His independent streaming channel has about twenty million subscribers," Barksley said. "He also makes about three million credits per month between fan donations, sponsorships, and selling questionably functional sex pills as well as Sorkanan bone broth."

"I said depress me, not kill my faith in a loving God."

"Sorry," Barksley said, heading into the elevator door as it opened. This time, I let Barksley take the lead and the little dog got on his hind legs before pushing a button with his snout. It was disgustingly adorable.

"I don't suppose anyone ever thought to give you opposable thumbs," I replied, watching the doors close and feeling the elevator descend.

"And ruin my adorable canine looks? Nah," Barksley said. "Mind you, I can operate most automated doors and machinery with my internal cyberbrain. Still, it's nice to have a human partner. Speaking of which—"

"I'm sensing an offer coming," I interrupted.

"Just noting I have an apartment I'm presently occupying alone in Crater Town," Barksley said, as if it was the most normal question in the world. "Since you're presently without cash, residence, or vehicle—"

"Or gun," I interrupted.

"It might be a good idea to become my temporary roommate!" Barksley said, smiling.

I raised my hands. "I dunno, man, I'm kind of used to living on my own. What's the catch?"

"You'd have to open canned food for me," Barksley said.

"You can eat?" I asked.

"I was designed to eat Karma Corp brand dog food as a ploy to bilk more money from the public," Barksley said.

"Of course you were," I replied, shaking my head. "Thanks for the offer, B. I'll consider it."

"You should consider it quickly because the Moon was designed to hold 120 million sapients and there're about three times as many," Barksley said. "If not for the Community's built-in redundancies regarding life support, we'd probably all have died of oxygen deprivation. Which is a polite way of saying that even if you can get an apartment of your own, it'll probably be a crap one."

I was starting to understand why the Moon was such a slum.

"You argue well, canine," I replied. "I'll consider it strongly."

The doors opened and we arrived at a large metal chamber with multiple rooms displaying their activities through reinforced translucent plastisteel. The metal was so shiny it reflected my face. It was less like an armory than a gymnasium for rich guys who could pretend their hobbies kept them in shape. There were shooting ranges, combat simulators, and a couple of bots teaching a martial arts class. At the end of the hallway, I saw a woman sitting behind a counter wearing the ridiculous uniform of the Cyberlife Division.

She was a mixture of Asian and Latina blood with an adorable face that gave us incredible little sister energy from twenty feet away. She had chubby cheeks, short black hair, and dimples, and there was a broad smile on her face that made her look like she should be teaching elementary school or giving public service announcements.

"Hello, Detective Gordon!" the woman said, waving at me. Apparently, news had gotten around who I was and what I looked like. She then looked down at my companion. "Barksley!"

"Detective Gordon," Barksley said, heading up to the counter base that he could never reach over. "Allow me to introduce you to Shinobu Harris. She's our armorer and quartermaster. Which sounds redundant but really isn't. At least in her case."

Taking position beside Barksley, I nodded. "Nice to meet you, Shinobu. I need to pick up a weapon."

Shinobu's expression turned diabolic. "Excellent. We've got assault rifles, sniper rifles, shotguns, explosives, electrified nets, chainsaw swords, thermal katana, rocket launchers, vibrowhips, sonic disruptors, landmines—"

"I'm pretty sure almost all of that is illegal," I said, interrupting her.

"It's a gray area," Shinobu said.

"It's really not," I replied.

"Sorry," Shinobu said, leaning over the counter. Then she started exaggeratingly winking. "It's a gray area. Just don't ask about the nukes."

"What nukes?" I asked, falling into the trap she'd so expertly laid for me.

"Shh!" Shinobu said, putting a finger to her mouth. "We absolutely have no nukes."

She grinned.

Under normal circumstances, I would be certain she was joking. However, I seemed to have died on the shuttle ride over here and awakened in Hell. The layer called the Hell of Snarky Weirdos, where my eternal punishment was to be Steve Gutenberg in *Police Academy*. God, we watched the hell out of those movies at the Foundation. "Shinobu, can I please have an ordinary service revolver. Preferably one with a stun setting."

There was no such thing as truly nonlethal weaponry, dog gun like Barksley's claims aside, but bringing them in alive was the best-case scenario for any police officer. Nigel was the only perp I'd ever been tempted to just summarily execute, and we saw how that had worked out. Still, I wasn't a peacenik like the Social Reformers' current crop of leadership either. While I'd only had to kill a couple of times during my career, I recognized the necessity. I just wanted options.

"Spoilsport," Shinobu said, handing over a Herakles-7 automatic pistol with a sonic stunner. "I'm including a highly illegal clip of explosive ammunition, though. Just in case."

I didn't ask in case of what since I'd almost been kidnapped this morning. "Thank you, I think."

61

"Remember, it's not a crime if the police do it," Shinobu said, without a trace of irony. She then hastily added, "But only do violence to bad people. That way it's justified."

"You joined the police right out of high school, didn't you?" I asked.

"How could you tell?" Shinobu asked, blinking.

CHAPTER SEVEN

Crater Town is a Hole (Ha-ha, Barksley)

B arksley and I took another elevator ride down to the parking garage after I gave my Herakles-7 a few test-fires. Everything seemed to be in order, and I felt safer knowing that I had a weapon. I didn't know if every day was going to be as dangerous as today, but I wasn't taking any chances. I didn't buy Armstrong's insane spiel about saving the world, but I was pretty sure I could get killed over it.

The parking garage was pretty much the same as the ones a century or two earlier, reflecting that some inventions didn't really need updating. The big difference was the top floor was designed for takeoffs and a good half of the vehicles didn't have the option for manual steering.

Barksley had indicated I wouldn't have to worry about jumping through any hoops to get a vehicle and I'd decided to trust the dog. I didn't have too many friends on the Moon, and it seemed a good idea to start making them. I was honestly surprised by the number of privately owned vehicles here too. I couldn't imagine there was much space to maneuver under the domes here in Luna City.

"So, that Shinobu was a real pineapple, wasn't she?" I asked, walking out of the elevator.

"Pineapple?" Barksley asked, following me out the door.

"Term for a grenade," I replied, smiling. "She's sweet but explosive."

"Ah," Barksley said. "Shinobu is something of our mascot."

I looked down at him, "Versus a talking dog?"

"I am a serious police detective!" Barksley said, offended. "But, no, probably not the best word. She joined the police after her parents were killed by the Syndicate."

"I take it by the way you pronounce it, the S is capitalized?" I asked.

"Indeed," Barksley said. "Uncounted trillions of credits worth of resources pass through the ports of Luna City and its surrounding habitats. The Syndicate exists to get a slice of all of that. They fund the other gangs and outfit them to put pressure on the businesses to pay up."

"And I thought the megacorporations were bad," I muttered.

"The transtellars and Syndicate aren't so far removed," Barksley said. "After all, the Syndicate has to invest its billions somewhere."

"Poor girl," I replied, referring to Shinobu.

"We all have a story here," Barksley said. "In any case, I think you should fuck her."

I did a double take and nearly got hit by an automated police cruiser. Excuse me?"

"Sorry," Barksley said, lifting a paw and adjusting his glasses. "Would different terminology have been better? Bork is the new slang term for non-relationship based rigorous coitus, I believe. How about I suggest that?"

"You kiss your mother with that mouth, poochie?" I asked.

"It's my job to maintain high morale among the agency's agents," Barksley said. "Besides, it doesn't look like you'll be hooking up with Agent Westenra any time soon."

"I wasn't thinking about that," I said.

"You absolutely were thinking about that," Barksley said.

"You're right," I replied. "However, I don't need you to be my wingdog."

"I'm a fantastic wingdog!" Barksley said, offended. "Also, I worry about Lucy as well and want to set her up, too. She hasn't had anything but casual encounters since—"

"Yeah, her boyfriend was *murdered*," I interrupted. "I think you should maybe give her a pass on that."

"Perhaps," Barksley said. "But I can smell sadness on humans. Both of you reek of it."

"I am not sad," I muttered, lying my ass off.

"Saxophone music plays in the background when you stand alone," Barksley said. "You just need a fedora."

"I'm not wearing a fedora," I said.

"There's one at my apartment," Barksley said. "It would go with the all-white suits that I see you wearing in the future. You already have the trench coat."

"This has gotten weird, and it already involved a talking dog," I said, gesturing down the parking garage. "Where's your car, B, and why isn't it driving our way?"

"Oh, it's right here," Barksley said, jogging down a side corridor. "I just thought we'd head there versus relying on soulless automation."

"You're a robot," I replied.

"A soulful robot!" Barksley said, stopping before a flying car neatly tucked away in a corner of the parking garage.

It was not the kind of car I expected from Barksley. Honestly, I would have expected a giant flying hot dog over what I saw.

"What the hell is this thing?" I asked, staring at the vehicle.

It was an Aerodyne F2-2226, except it had been heavily modified to look utterly ridiculous. The car was a bright purple with glowing lights up and down the lines of its modular parts, gold trim to the wheels, and tail fins that had been out of style before cars could fly. The windows were also tinted to the point of being jet black. A quick look at the exterior also told me it wasn't carbon fiber nanotube but durasteel, like a frigging tank. Squinting, I managed to see the front seats that were even more ludicrous in their contents.

"It is the *Purple Rain!*" Barksley said, excitedly. Somehow, his glasses had switched from being ordinary spectacles to sunglasses. "It's my ride."

"Are you running a side hustle as a pimp?" I asked.

"Not yet!" Barksley said, grinning.

"Are those fuzzy dice around the mirror?" I asked, wondering why it even had a rearview mirror since all cars came equipped with 360-degree cameras now.

"Yes!" Barksley said. "I had to have them custom made. They don't make them anymore."

"I can't imagine why," I said, shaking my head. "I see you also got cheetah print seats too."

"If you're going, go all the way," Barksley said, proudly.

"I'm surprised you didn't fit a lava lamp in there somehow," I said, shaking my head.

"Oh, that would be silly," Barksley said. "The vibrations of the car would break up the lava lamp globules into droplets making the whole thing ugly."

"How much did this cost?" I asked, ignoring the science of why making it even tackier was impossible.

"Two hundred credits!" Barksley said, beaming proudly.

I looked over at the dog. "Excuse me?"

"I may have bought it at the police auction," Barksley said. "The dice are my addition, though. What do you think?"

"I think this is flying probable cause and I'd arrest us if I saw us in it," I replied.

"Oh, please like we need probable cause when we can just claim anonymous tips!" Barksley said.

I pointed at Barksley. "No, bad. Bad dog! Do not engage in abuse in authority."

Barksley stared at the car. "Car, open! Start! Play Barksley's Playlist!"

The car's doors slid upward on its driver and passenger sides as the engine started. Inner Circle's reggae classic, "Bad Boys" started to play.

"I swear, Barksley, this is a side of you I didn't expect," I said, heading to the driver's seat.

"Hey, hey, I'm driving," Barksley said.

I stared down at the dog. "Not to bring up a matter of physics—"

"Okay, I just put my paws on the steering wheel and let the autopilot take me wherever I want to go," Barksley said.

"I'm driving," I said, sliding into the driver's seat. Almost immediately, I was overwhelmed by the smell. "Okay, that's Black Lotus, Red Dust, and I think motor oil."

"It adds to the ambiance," Barksley said. "Car, add Detective Gordon, Badge Number 328-DD1, to authorized drivers. Take us to my apartment."

The *Purple Rain's* doors shut as the vehicle's gravity manipulators pushed the vehicle upward before propelling us down the preordained path by the car's central computer. A tiny holographic map appeared on the dashboard that showed a path plotted in three-dimensional space. We were heading down, down, down below the surface of the Moon and into the massive environmental chambers carved out inside.

"You know, I *can* drive," I replied. "I was operating aerial vehicles by the time I was eighteen."

"I want you to take the time to pay attention as I educate you on some fundamentals about the Moon," Barksley said. "Also, I don't trust human drivers. Ninety percent of all flying car wrecks are human drivers versus automated."

"Doesn't that imply ten percent are automated?" I asked.

"Yes, usually when a human driver smashes into them," Barksley said.

"Point taken," I said. "I don't suppose we could stop on our way to the apartment for something to eat? The last meal I had was a bunch of packing peanuts on the space shuttle."

"You mean prepackaged peanuts?" Barksley asked.

"I know what I said."

The domed portion of Luna City—very literally Uptown—was just as beautiful at night as during the day. The countless towers were illuminated with brilliant lights and the stars above were beautiful. It made me think about what Lucy and Barksley had said earlier: that this was just the tip of the iceberg of a much darker reality.

"Yes, well, I recommend you eat at the cafeteria from now on," Barksley said. "At least at the Cyberlife building, there're some edible supplements."

"Food scarcity a problem on the Moon?" I asked, wondering about the level of resources available.

"Yes and no," Barksley said. "The original founders of the Moon learned to adapt quickly on recycling certain products to grow large amounts of edible resources in the dark."

I looked at him. "By which you mean...?"

"Mushrooms grown in poop," Barksley said. "We also have a fine variety of processed algae. Plus, goop."

"Ah, goop," I said, wistfully. I could still taste the stuff they used to feed us out of a can. "I haven't had that since my days as a boy in the Los Angeles Zone. It came in orange, green, and white paste! Kids don't know how lucky they are today. They have blue, yellow, and teal."

"Miss it?" Barksley asked.

"Hell no," I said, coldly. "I take it the good stuff has to be imported from Earth."

"Somewhat," Barksley said. "Karma Corp has multiple farm-combines on the Moon's surface and plenty of factories to produce synth meat. It's good for the environment and okay for you. Plus, there's simulated food."

"Simulated food? If you can eat it, isn't it just food?" I asked.

"Try it and repeat that statement," Barksley said, somehow outdoing me in cynicism. "Either way, there's enough food for the Moon's legitimate population."

"Of which there's three times as many," I said.

"Bingo," Barksley said, the dog's glasses returning to normal and a glazed look appearing in his adorable black eyes. "B-I-N-G-O. B-I-N-G-O. B-I—N-G-O and Bingo was his name-O!"

"Barksley!" I said, snapping my fingers in front of his face.

Barksley snapped out of it. "Sorry, must have accidentally triggered some old childcare programs. Either way, the import laws make fresh produce and meat worth its weight in credits. Illegal farm collectives, underground markets, and private co-ops are the source of eighty percent of the civi cops' busy work. The Wisconsin Mafia is particularly dangerous."

"The *Wisconsin* Mafia?" I asked, stunned. "Please tell me I'm not going to be chasing dairy smugglers."

"No, Cyberlife is concerned with terrorists, murderers, and the arms trafficking generally," Barksley said. "I just thought you'd like to know what most police are concerned with on the Moon. It's like Prohibition here but with potatoes. In fact, the biggest set of laws are literally called the Food Prohibition Act."

"Dare I ask why there's a prohibition against potatoes?" I asked, feeling the flying car descend into an enormous tunnel leading straight downward. There were hundreds of flying cars around us, mostly public transport, bringing the upper level's servant class back down to their habitats below. "I don't get it. It seems like the Moon would be all about letting as much food in as cheaply as possible. That's not the sort of thing you want to regulate from my experience in the Outer Colonies."

"Governor Barnum gets half of his campaign funds from Karma Corp lobbyists," Barksley said. "The Moon's citizens growing their own food would lower the prices. Besides, who do you think does all the farming at Karma Corps' combines? The prisoners. Best of all, they can't vote after their sentences are served so Barnum gets a vote nullified. The Agricultural Prison Industrial Complex at work."

I was horrified. "I just want to bust bad guys and take names. Are you comfortable with this?"

"I'm not an anarchist," Barksley explained, which unfortunately meant he was about to talk about politics. I *hated* talking about politics. "The fact that Karma Corp and the people like it are run by jerkfaces—"

"Jerkfaces?" I asked.

"I'm a toy," Barksley said. "Proves that you can be a scumbag while having all the privileges and wealth in the world. This city's criminals aren't the victims of society, they're the people preying on the people that have nothing left to give. They're not Robin Hoods robbing from the rich and giving to the poor. They're—"

"Robbing from the poor and giving to themselves," I said, knowing exactly how most criminals functioned despite the media's typical portrayal. "Got it. Barksley, may I make a suggestion?"

"Yes?" Barksley asked.

"Never bring up politics again," I said, firmly. "I have enough trouble being a little fish in a big ocean, surviving, versus worrying about stuff way above my paygrade. I leave that to the Armstrongs and Social Reformers of the world."

"So, if I were to tell you I like watching news programs at home..." Barksley trailed off.

"I will sleep in a dumpster instead of staying with you," I said, 100% meaning it.

"Ten-four, good buddy," Barksley said. "Ooo, wait, I love this next song on my playlist."

That was when "Who Let the Dogs Out" by the Baha Men started playing.

Great, I was stuck with a dog who loved classical music.

The *Purple Rain* eventually exited the tunnel as I briefly contemplated that the nature of gravity manipulation meant you could have the vehicles go sideways, upside down, or other directions without the passengers even noticing it depending on the type of the machines. It was an alien technology that made space colonization and machines like flying cars much easier but completely impossible to manufacture on Earth. The cars and human-manned spacecraft might be created by Ares Electronics here on the Moon, but the devices had to be made in Lizard space.

Either way, when we arrived outside of the tunnel to Crater Town—the largest of the underground habitats—I noticed a slight shift in gravity. It wasn't quite right, just a little weaker than Earth standard. That wasn't necessarily a bad thing but was a reminder the environmental maintenance wasn't perfect here.

Crater Town had been mentioned in the space shuttle magazine, but it had mostly been a paragraph compared to all the rest of the Moon's sights and shared a strong hint to drive past it. I could understand it because it was both magnificent and terrible at once. It was ten times the size of Luna City proper and the size of a state. Well, Rhode Island, but Rhode Island was still a state last time I checked. It hadn't been destroyed by a super volcano like Wyoming.

Alien engineering had hollowed out the massive interior cavern and the gravity manipulation towers filled the place with their kilometer-tall presences. Beneath them, looking like a pattern of circuitry, was a honeycomb of converted buildings, hastily constructed habitats, temporary shelters that had never stopped being temporary, and metroplexes that were supposed to have been the urban planning of the future but had been abandoned once the first generation of its inhabitants had described it like "growing up in a converted mall." Mostly because, well, that's what the first metroplexes had been built in.

There were decent places to live. Crater Town looked like it had several uptowns of its own, but these had been constructed by people in defiance of the layered city gentrification I'd seen above. The Moonatics had resisted the corporate plans to make a segregated society of the super-rich and working class by putting their own touches on this place. I could tell because, as we descended, I saw more signs of the communities that had come together to survive in this place. There were lots of spray paint art, gardens on rooftops, and other indications of passive resistance to the prevailing hegemony. I would have pumped my fist for them, but I knew exactly where I probably ranked with most of the public's opinion.

Eventually, after about twenty minutes of flight, we ended up settling down on the rooftop of a ten-story apartment complex next to a basketball court. There was only room for about four flying cars there and it was next to a sign that said ATCAB, which I took to mean ATLAS COPS ARE BASTARDS. The building looked like a dozen other identical apartment buildings and was right next to a monorail as well as near an atmosphere processing plant.

"Mi casa, su casa," Barksley said.

I surveyed the neighborhood. "I take back everything I said. The *Purple Rain* fits into this place perfectly."

"As if!" Barksley said. "People wish they had my ride!"

The air outside the place had the same scent as freshly cut grass, undoubtedly from the atmosphere processing plant that sounded like a running refrigerator despite being a few blocks away. The monorail cars made a huge amount of noise when they passed and there seemed to be one every twenty seconds as we walked to the elevator from the rooftop.

"So, what's this place called?" I asked, walking over to the rooftop elevator. It was an old freight model with a modern digital interface that scanned Barksley and opened for him automatically.

"Paradise City!" Barksley said. "I have another song for that one."

"Pass," I replied.

"Ahh," Barksley said. "But I was going to introduce our neighbors. The three people in the apartment to our east are prostitutes, the guy to the west believes the Moon landing was faked (all of them), and the guy beneath us sells fresh cantaloupe. He'll hold a gun on you the entire time, though."

"What about the apartment above us?" I asked.

"That's empty due to the mass shooting," Barksley said. "You're going to love it here."

"Honestly, I've lived in worse places," I replied, stepping into the elevator with Barksley. "Will they mind the fact I'm a cop?"

"They don't mind me," Barksley said.

I paused, unsure how to respond.

"There might be some resistance," Barksley admitted. "But they really liked my ex-roommate. Mind you, that's because Dick beat the hell out of the Golden Tiger pimp who used to menace the girls and the guy who was always ogling the kids three floors down."

"Wait, Dick?" I asked, as the elevator stopped at a hallway balcony overlooking the city. "Lucy's boyfriend? He was your roommate?"

Barksley trotted up to a door marked 1138. "Oh, didn't I mention that?"

Dammit.

CHAPTER EIGHT

First Day on the Job

I could always escape my past by running. Unfortunately, the one place I could never run from it was my dreams. There, I was stuck reliving it and the thoughts I was having during the worst moment of my life.

I am Stupido, King of the Morons.

May all the lesser morons bow before me.

That was what I was thinking as I ran down the catwalk, taking moments to pause only long enough fire the Aegis-17 assault rifle in my hands down at the people below. A sane person would have waited for backup before engaging. No, a sane person would have written off this entire incident as not his problem. He'd have been a royal scumbag for doing so but at least he wouldn't have been suicidal.

But no, the *Akashi*-class star transport had arrived outside the warehouse and was going to transport all these shipping crates full of innocent people to God knows where. They'd never be seen again and the people behind the transportation would disappear. There had to be ten thousand people here, not that the numbers really mattered, and I was stupidly trying to be a hero. I wasn't even trying to stop them. I was just trying to delay the loading long enough for the EarthGov agents to arrive with what I hoped would be the military backing them up.

"[Get the bastard!]" a shades-wearing Golden Tiger shouted in Martian Sino-Spanish, pointing in my general direction. He was wearing a bright gold jacket and what skin I could see was covered in tattoos. He also wasn't packing heat, which is why I aimed at his associate carrying another Aegis-17 instead.

I'd already killed the pilots for the *Akashi* transport and shot up the controls, which probably should have been my cue to get the hell out of there. Unfortunately, by that time, I'd already attracted the attention of both the dirty cops as well as their Golden Tiger associates. Getting the hell out of here was proving to be a lot harder than I'd hoped it would be.

Killing the pilots had been easy once I'd known it was the only way to stop them. So had pretty much every other person I'd shot since them. From the guy I'd stolen my Aegis-17 from to the cop who'd drawn on me, Melvin Parks, who had always called me NG. The trick was not thinking about any of it and just focusing on staying out of anyone's line of fire before hitting anyone who fell into yours. Given the Golden Tigers were a bunch of amateurs spraying bullets in whatever direction they thought I was in, and the Refugee Unit weren't soldiers for the most part, I had a very, very small advantage.

An advantage that was obliterated when a fusion pistol blast went through the grating underneath me into the back of my leg, exploding out through my kneecap. To say the pain was explosive was an understatement, as was the resulting beatdown. I didn't even see the trio of Golden Tigers who came up to me with a crowbar, chain, and fists.

I was already beaten within an inch of my life when they dragged me in front of Nigel. I might have had a concussion, gone into shock, or been suffering from some combination of those conditions when I looked up at him. He was an incredibly handsome man—even without bio-sculpting—having jet black hair with a top knot as well as a goatee as was the current style for corporate mercs. He was literally the one person outside of medieval samurai that didn't look silly with it.

Nigel Blackwood was dressed in a thirty thousand Martian credit—about ten thousand in Sol Credits—suit. That should have been my first clue he was not just dirty but hella dirty. Among police there were grass eaters and meat eaters. The grass eaters never said no to a payoff, but they didn't go out of their way to shake down or steal evidence.

Meat eaters did. It seemed Nigel was a goddamn Tyrannosaurus rex if he was involved in this—and it was kinda obvious he was.

"Oh, Neal, Neal, Neal, what the hell have you done," Nigel said, looking down at me and shaking his head. "This is not an action movie, and you are not the wise-cracking detective."

We'd both grown up in the Foundation. Nigel had just been smart enough to change his name, again, to hide it. His "original"—heavy air quotes—name was Bruce Bethke Gordon. We'd both watched the crap out of buddy cop movies.

"Should have...gotten a dog," I managed to mutter.

"[The shipment is ruined. We can't get the transport working and half of the men are dead. This is a disaster,]" the Golden Tiger leader said, looking down at me. "[We should take him to the Old Man. Let him deal with him.]"

"No, we'll deal with him here," Nigel said, staring at me with an unreadable expression. "Leave him for the Anti-Slavery task force to find. They'll be poring over him and this disaster for days rather than chasing down better leads. That is, if you survive, Neal."

"Uck...you," I said, no longer able to speak because blood was filling my mouth. I didn't even know from where. I could hear sirens in the distance as well as the roar of oncoming air transports.

That was when I felt a nasty, diesel-like substance splatter across my face and chest. The Golden Tigers were emptying some sort of rusty barrel's contents over me. If I'd had enough of a brain left to put two and two together, I would have been terrified.

Nigel lifted an old-fashioned cigarette lighter. It was one I recognized. It had belonged to his grandfather. Unlike most Foundation children, he'd known his family before they'd given him up. "If you don't survive? Well, see you in Hell."

Nigel dropped the lighter on me.

Next, I heard a deep rhythmic panting. My mind rid itself of its terrifying flashback and I opened my eyes to a thirty-pound animal on my chest, staring at me with a broad grin on its face. "Good morning, Neal!"

"Ah!" I shouted, screaming my head off.

The interior of Barksley's apartment—technically mine too—was surprisingly spacious, even if not particularly decorated. It had a bedroom, a TV lounge, a kitchenette, a corner desk for police work, a room converted into an extra-large closet with a washer-dryer unit, and a vending machine of all things that I had to wonder about the restocking of. I was pretty sure the extra-large closet was meant to be a second bedroom, but Barksley just slept in a basket with a bunch of pillows. There was also a spacious window that had a metal bullet-proof shutter pulled down over it that made me think the installers had expected to be under siege.

I wasn't sleeping in the bedroom, though, but on the couch in the living room. I was in my boxers and a t-shirt with my one pair of clothes in the washer-dryer unit. I'd found the late Dick Grayson's clothes still in his bedroom and decided I couldn't rest in that guy's bed until I went through it. Especially since I found his photos on the dresser, showing a handsome Black man and his friends at Cyberlife. Call it crazy but that was how I felt.

"Wakey, wakey, Detective Gordon," a familiar voice spoke, drawing my attention to a couple of feet next to me that I'd somehow missed in my confused survey of the room. They were so close I'd missed them. Apparently, I'd failed my spot check as an old gaming friend from the Foundation would have said.

There was Lucy Westenra, her hair now an entirely normal shade of blonde, and wearing a white t-shirt and a pair of tight blue jeans. Her holster was wrapped around by her arm and carried a slightly more powerful version of my Herakles-7. Lucy looked bored and had a familiar-looking heavy-duty, black canvas gym bag over her non-holstered shoulder. Her Cyberlife badge was affixed to the side of her jeans. She looked…good and not even the fact I'd just woken up from a PTSD-induced nightmare affected my immediate instant attraction.

"Hi, Lucy," I said, annoyed I hadn't made myself presentable and wondering what time it was. The fact she was in the apartment didn't bother me—it wasn't mine yet after all—and I was too enraptured by her presence to really care. After all, it was a nice distraction from remembering being burned alive.

"Your weapon is drawn, Detective," Lucy said, lowering her sunglasses.

I looked down where she was looking and covered myself with my arms. "Goddammit."

"Happens to a lot of guys in the morning," Lucy said, tossing the gym bag on my lap as if it was nothing. Which it wasn't since it weighed about sixty pounds. I managed to catch it with an oomph. "You're half an hour late for work. Not a great way to make a first impression but I suppose we can chalk this up to shuttle lag."

The tote bag was mine and contained several pairs of clothes, undergarments, and other necessities. It also had an ornate silver lighter I'd kept as a memento tucked away in one of the side pockets. Call it a morbid memento, but someday I hoped to repay Nigel's last act to me. It pretty much said everything you needed to know about the Martian police that they hadn't even noticed it going missing from the evidence locker back at Olympus Mons headquarters.

"Sorry," I said, standing up and pulling out a fresh suit of clothes. "Barksley was nice enough to put me up for the night."

"Funny, I thought he'd offered to take you on as a roommate," Lucy said. "He's late, too, but it's not too bad since we can start our workday directly. I have the cruiser parked upstairs."

"Sorry!" Barksley said, hopping around and taking care of what I assumed to be his morning ritual. "I'll be ready in a minute."

The dog went into the bathroom and the shower turned on, accompanied by the song, "Fuck the Police." Barksley sang along, substituting the words "Bark", "Doggie", and a few others to make it more kid friendly.

I stared over in his direction. "He does realize he's gold and white, not Black, right?"

"I'm not sure," Lucy said, smirking.

"Yes, well, I'm not sure about staying here," I said, unsure how to broach the subject. She'd reacted strongly to the fact I was coming here to replace her boyfriend in a professional capacity. I wasn't sure how she'd feel about me moving into his old place either. There had been pictures of Dick and her here, too. He'd been a good-looking, tall Black man with a shaved head. Lucy had looked…happy. That was another reason I hadn't felt comfortable sleeping in the man's bed.

"It's a good place," Lucy said. "Barksley needs company, or he gets lazy. Look at how this place has gone to hell. Besides, you're not going to find a better deal. The rent on a place like this is sky high on a police officer's salary. Doubling up with a guy who doesn't take up much room save for chew toys and collars makes sense."

It looked cleaner than my last apartment. "Alright. If you say so. How the hell did you get this back?"

"I went back to the space port after our encounter with Armstrong," Lucy said. "I had some words with the employees divvying up your clothes. It's not all I got back, though."

"Oh?" I asked.

Lucy pulled out a black card and tapped it with her forefinger. "Here's your missing cash. All twenty-five K."

"No way," I said, stunned.

"Way," Lucy replied. "However, it comes with a sad story."

"Oh?" I asked.

"Yeah," Lucy said, lowering her gaze to the card like it was a sick child. "It turned out the worker who stole it was deep in debt to the Syndicate. His daughter is marked for being put into one of the dark unlicensed brothels. They also cut up his wife. This would have allowed him to get her back."

"Oh shit," I said, appalled. "Well, maybe—"

"Seriously, how gullible are you?" Lucy asked, removing her sunglasses. "There's no daughter. Guy was going to spend it on Red Dust and hookers once he'd given STRIKE their cut."

Okay, now I felt like an idiot. "Really?"

"Welcome to the Moon," Lucy said, handing over the card. "I'd suggest depositing this, but I don't trust the banks here. Dataslicers love targeting cops."

"I'll keep that in mind," I replied.

"Were you really going to give up your life savings to some random dude in a space port terminal?" Lucy asked.

"It's early in the morning," I replied.

Also, I wanted to impress Lucy. Wow, I had it bad. "It's also not my life savings."

"Do you have any other savings?" Lucy asked. "You'd think being a dirty cop would have paid better."

I thought twenty-five K in credits was pretty good actually. Most Marines and cops I knew back on Mars lived from paycheck to paycheck. I was still another twenty-five years until my pension thanks to the adjustments the Neo-Militarists had made to retirement age.

"I plead the fifth," I replied.

"On the Moon, that's the right to own one or more pets," Lucy said.

I blinked. "Maybe I should just get ready."

Lucy smirked. "Probably a good idea. I'll buy you breakfast."

Lucy proceeded to walk over to the vending machine, slid her card in and a small orange toothpaste-esque tube fell through the chute. She picked it up and handed it over to me. "Bon appetite."

I took it and stared at the familiar label. "Orange goop! My favorite! All the smell of cheese and pork without any of the actual flavor!"

"We call it a Kraft dessert where I'm from," Lucy said. "You'll have to get your own water. I'm not made of credits."

"Since I'm made of money now, I think I'll get myself a hot water with leaf dust," I replied, heading to the machine.

"Wise choice," Lucy said. "I strongly recommend getting to work an hour early and enjoying the cafeteria's contents."

"So I've heard," I replied, getting myself an iced tea in a can. Turns out the machine wasn't equipped for hot tea.

Shame.

Barksley left the shower and proceeded to shake himself dry, his glasses steamed over before somehow defogging as if by magic. "The shower is ready. Though you may want to de-clog it later tonight. I grow fur as one of my lifelike biological properties."

I gave Lucy a sideways glance. "Care to join me?"

"Not today. Not here," Lucy said, her voice carrying a bit of heartbreak.

Dammit. Stupid. I should have thought of that. "I'll see you in twenty minutes."

"Make it ten," Lucy said, heading out the door.

79

I turned to Barksley. "She still has a key?"

"Authorized visitor, yes," Barksley said. "She often spent the night here. She has her own place topside."

"Ah," I said.

"Oh, I have a present for you," Barksley said, rushing into the nearby storage room and coming out a few seconds later with a hat in his mouth. He spoke with it, muffling his words. "Fedora!"

"I am *not* wearing a fedora," I said.

I ended up wearing the fedora.

Sigh.

Anyway, I felt much better after a shower and a change of clothes, but I kept the trench coat from the previous day. The Moon's artificial climate wasn't exactly conducive to needing one—being always a vague "slightly cold"—but if everyone was determined to make me look like a private detective then I might as well embrace it.

Barksley and I met Lucy on the rooftop where a police cruiser was waiting for us. It was different from the earlier one with a holding area in the back. The *Purple Rain* would have to spend the day here. Something I wasn't at all unhappy about. I was eager to get started, surprisingly, and suspected it was just the appeal of routine. Whether I'd been kicked off my last posting or recruited, idle hands were the Devil's workshop and not being able to do my job was the worst sort of punishment.

"Ready?" Lucy asked.

"Yep," I said, gesturing to the cruiser. "You driving?"

"I'll take the driver's seat, but I prefer to let the autopilot handle our course," Lucy said. "It allows me to go over my notes."

"You have many notes already?" I asked. "What sort of case load are we looking at?"

I was used to working in overworked, underfunded departments. There were usually at least twenty or thirty cases active at any given time.

"Two hundred," Lucy said.

I stared. "You're kidding."

Barksley, at my face, looked up and looked pained.

"Not this time," Lucy replied. "Cyberlife has its pick of outstanding cases at any given time. Particularly violent or technology-related crimes. The civi cops are more eager to do food-related busts as those are easy and pad their workload. Karma Corp's corpo cops go after the distributors and anything that will land them in the papers. They're also always available when some of the Tranquils lose a dog."

"Lost dogs are a multi-million credit industry," Barksley said. "Kidnapping one is more heavily punished than doing so to a person. Mostly because only the Tranquils can afford the importation fees on organic animals."

"Tranquils?" I asked, completely confused about their use of the word.

"The Sea of Tranquility has a dome over it," Lucy said. "Eight hundred kilometers wide. The largest on the entirety of the Moon. What do they use it for? Food production? Nature preserve? No, it's a home for the super-rich, resorts, and an artificial lake for tourists. We call them Tranquils because—"

"They live there, gotcha," I said, dryly. "Also, it's a pun about them not having worries because they're rich."

Lucy frowned and crossed her arms.

"You're very 'eat the rich' for a police officer," I observed, antsy about touching a nerve.

"I have my reasons," Lucy muttered, turning away.

My detective brain told me that Lucy had come from money and was carrying a shit ton of guilt over it. She was probably from the entertainment industry, too, given she'd ended up a teen star and later in a band that, regardless of their anti-establishment attitude, was famous enough to have songs out that I knew of. Which meant recording contracts and publicists. How she'd ended up in Cyberlife as a whip-wielding police detective was probably as interesting a story as mine. Asking about it now would probably get me slapped, though.

"I'm sure you do," I said, letting the matter dropped. "If there's two hundred outstanding cases at any given time, how are you expected to get through any of them."

81

Lucy walked over to the police cruiser's driver's side door and opened it up by hand. "You don't. You just pick one and try to solve it then move onto the next one. It's like trying to bail out the *Titanic.*"

"Which was a cruise liner that sank!" Barksley explained, helpfully.

CHAPTER NINE

It's Always Insurance Fraud

The police cruiser flew over Crater Town as I called up the holographic interface for the vehicle on the passenger's side. I spent the next five minutes or so going over the Cyberlife department's records, confirming everything Lucy had said. It wasn't because I didn't believe her, but there was a difference between hearing something second hand and seeing it for yourself.

Son of a bitch, she was right.

The crime rate on the Moon was astounding but it was more that, statistically, it didn't look like it. Officially, in fact crime rates were falling. However, that was because the civi police and Karma Corps' goon squad were focusing extensively on not just crimes I didn't think were important—Barksley hadn't been exaggerating about food-related crimes being their bread and butter, no pun intended—but they were picking the easiest to solve. Either that or they were just railroading those they caught, which wasn't much better.

"Depressing, isn't it?" Lucy asked, her sunglasses flashing with information I suspected was being directly shot into her brain via VR interface.

Barksley was between us. Our police dog wasn't paying attention because his glasses had once more turned into sunglasses and he had a pair of earbuds in that were playing a very subdued, "Ridin'" by Chamillionaire that he was talk-singing to. Except the chorus went, "Tryna catch me ridin' doggy." Which I suspected had a totally different meaning for me than it did for the kid-friendly poochie.

"Atlas Security's rates aren't much better," I replied. "Maybe about a ten percent difference in terms of arrests and convictions."

"We actually have a much higher acquittal rate," Lucy said.

"Is that…good?" I asked.

"It's better to let ten guilty men go free than convict one innocent one," Lucy said, quoting English Justice William Blackstone. "But I take it as proof of our honesty."

I wasn't sure it was a point of pride that she was implying the other factions were railroading the others. "Rather than continue to lower my already abyssal opinion of the Moon's law enforcement where the only good cops seem to be run by a deranged radio announcer, why don't you tell me what our first case is."

"Insurance fraud," Lucy said.

I was surprised. "I thought we'd just dive in with murder or kidnapping. I saw a pretty extensive list of those in our docket."

"We'll get to those if we're lucky," Lucy said. "This is an important one, though, because the woman who reported the crime is Mabel Forsythe. She's the life-partner of Beatrice Popinjay."

Why did most women on this planetoid have names that seemed to come from the rural 1940s? "You're going to have to fill me in on them."

"They're arms dealers," Barksley explained, clearly paying more attention than his music appreciation indicated. "Very low level, more back of one's van than spy movie villain, but still noticeable in crime statistics. The right to possess lethal weaponry is guaranteed by the Luna Constitution's Nineteenth Amendment, but it can be suspended if you're a felon, mentally unwell, a member of an extremist group, or involved with a preexisting criminal organization."

"Uh huh," I said. "How many people does that leave wanting to buy weapons?"

"A lot," Lucy said, simply. "But Barksley didn't mention the biggest deterrent: the fact that licenses cost a hefty chunk of credits that most Lunes can't afford. Mabel and Beatrice fabricate cheap, mold-on-demand guns that are meant for limited use. As such, they've been implicated in hundreds of crimes."

"And no one has arrested them, why? The detective asked knowing the answer will depress him." I could understand why criminals would want to buy a bunch of one-use guns. If you intended to do a specific crime, prefabricated crap was better as you could dispose of the weapon afterward. More expensive guns were useful for threats and defense against others when on the streets.

"Are you *narrating*?" Lucy asked, looking at me with surprise.

"Maybe a little," I said, making a "pinch of salt gesture" with my fingers.

"Beatrice Popinjay is a Karma Corp corporate citizen and can only be arrested by its officials. That immunity applies to her life-partner as well," Barksley explained the insane contradictory laws of the Moon. "That is, of course, unless they call the police of another district themselves. Which Mabel Forsythe did this morning and why we can investigate her."

"And why would she do that?" I asked, confused.

"She claims someone has stolen her butler bot," Lucy explained. "Street value about 50,000 credits. To claim an insurance payout on it, she has to get the police involved. Stupidly, she called Cyberlife because we deal with technology crimes."

I nodded. "So, that allows us to look around her home. Why do you think it's insurance fraud, though?"

"It's always insurance fraud," Lucy said, with surprising certainty. "People in Crater Town buy these expensive high-end dummy AI as status symbols and immediately come to regret it the first time money is tight. So, they blow them up or try to pretend they're lost. No decent criminal would steal them because they're too easy to trace."

"There is a secondhand market for these droids," Barksley said. "Usually, though, it's after they attempt to modify them into true AI."

"True AI?" I asked, having a pretty good idea but wanting to be sure.

"Things like Barksley and Armstrong," Lucy said. "Sentient living beings with all the accompanying rights according to the Community. Basically, if it can beg for its life, it's alive."

I stared. "Why would someone want a sentient—"

"Slave?" Lucy asked. "Some people just get off on it."

I didn't have a response to that because I'd seen it often enough to be true. "So, we show up, look around, and hope we find something that can be used against them to shut down their arms business."

"Yep," Lucy said. "We can't stop the flow of guns into the Moon but maybe we can save a few lives."

"Sounds like a good day's work," I said.

Lucy snorted.

Barksley also laughed.

I didn't get the joke.

Either way, the rest of the trip was unremarkable. Mabel Forsythe's apartment building was pretty like my own, except it didn't look like it had been populated by post-apocalypse mutants for the past decade. It was in the middle of a commercial district and clean, well-maintained, as well as given an excellent view of the less hellish parts of Crater Town. There was even a Japanese-style rock garden on the rooftop.

We didn't have far to head down because our gun runners lived in the penthouse—if you could call it that—and I gave their door a hard rapping. We ended up scanned by the little black dot that was emblazoned on most doors, followed by the voice of a little old lady, "Are you the police?"

"We're the Cyberlife Division, yes," Lucy responded first, showing her badge to the black dot. "We're here to investigate your claim of a stolen JR-371 Domestic Servant?"

"Yes," the little old lady responded. "Please come in."

The door slid open, and I headed in, half-expecting there to be trip wires or explosive mines given my luck on the Moon so far. But no, the place was just a pleasant, upscale apartment with a blue overstuffed couch, blue overstuffed chairs, an extra-large entertainment center, thick white shag carpet, and walls covered in framed posters of female-led action movies, particularly on the trashy side. The latter element was the only thing that felt genuinely homey as everything else was decorated in an overly "clean" real estate showing style that put me ill at ease. It didn't look like a place people lived and I didn't like it.

"I'll be out in just a second!" the little old lady said from a nearby room that I presumed to be the bedroom. "Make yourselves at home."

"She's watching us, you know," Lucy muttered. "This place is laden with hidden cameras. I can feel it."

"Not my first rodeo," I replied in a similar low tone. "Barksley, do us a favor and scan this place top to bottom."

"Will do," Barksley said, smiling.

"Let's wander around a bit," Lucy said. "Just don't touch anything."

I nodded and did so.

I felt kind of guilty being there under false pretenses, but the feeling quickly passed. Still, I wasn't sure what exactly Lucy hoped to find. It wasn't like they'd keep their fabricator out in the open or, if they did, it wouldn't be like it would be next to a bunch of boxes full of illegally printed weapons. I'd met a lot of stupid criminals in my time but rarely were they that stupid. Okay, well, there was that one guy who called out to me and said, "Stop that guy, officer, he stole my meth!"

At least on a cursory search, there wasn't anything blatantly illegal lying about. Indeed, the only thing I'd learned so far was that the couple were a pair of neat freaks and that even low-grade arms trafficking paid very well. This sort of place ran about a hundred K annually back on Olympus Mons and I doubted it was much cheaper on the Moon.

There were also some physical plastisheet magazines as well—each about fifty credits—that were another sign of casual indulgence. It was all posturing, though. This wasn't the sort of place you did hookers and Loop. It was the sort of place you showed off to all your former high school friends to prove you'd done better than them.

I pulled out my own infopad and typed to Barksley. Our networks had synced automatically last night. ANYTHING?

SOME INTERESTING DETAILS, Barksley replied. ALL OF THE APPLIANCES ARE RENT TO OWN AND THEY HAVE SEVERAL SERVICES THAT ARE PAST DUE. THEIR DUMMY AI ARE HELPFULLY PROGRAMMED TO REMIND THE OWNER EVERY TIME THEY ARE ACTIVATED. I PINGED THEM AND JUST NEXT MONTH'S BILLS WILL BE IN EXCESS OF TWENTY-THOUSAND CREDITS.

I blinked. WHAT THE HELL ARE THEY SPENDING THEIR MOOLAH ON?

MOOLAH? OOO, I LIKE THAT, Barksley replied. STATUS, I PRESUME. IT TAKES A LOT OF MONEY TO LOOK LIKE YOU DON'T CARE ABOUT MONEY.

That was when Lucy lifted her infopad and wrote to us. WHAT ABOUT THEIR ROBOT?

Barksley's reply was troubling. HE'S OFFLINE AND I DONT HAVE ACCESS TO THE SECURITY FEEDS. THAT WOULD BE ILLEGAL TO LOOK AT WITHOUT A WARRANT OR THE OWNER'S PERMISSION. HOWEVER, THERE IS ONE THING THAT'S ODD.

WHICH IS? I typed.

THIS HOUSE IS VERY INTEGRATED, Barksley said. LOTS OF ORDERS PLACED IN WATSON'S NAME AS WELL. WATSON IS THE BUTLER BOT'S NAME, BY THE WAY. APPARENTLY, HE'S BEEN HANDLING A LOT OF THE HOUSEHOLD PURSE.

INTERESTING. That *was* unusual.

MEET ME BY THE POSTERS, I texted Lucy.

WHICH ONES? Lucy asked.

IN FRONT OF THE SLUTTIEST, I replied. OR WHERE I'M STANDING. PROBABLY THE SAME PLACE.

I could almost hear Lucy rolling her eyes.

There was a framed poster of *Fair Cop* on the wall that immediately drew attention, signed by its star Ayanna Breeze. It had the busty, blonde Eurasian actress lying on the ground in a very short dress, with her pistol up and staring sultrily at the viewer. It had been an objectively terrible film that, nevertheless, had propelled its star to superstardom due to the sheer magnetism she'd displayed regardless of the script.

I'd been a fan of Ayanna Breeze for entirely wholesome reasons when she had done a bunch of abysmal romantic comedies to when she'd revived her career by doing raunchy, gory, violent action-horror films like *Mitochondrial Eve*, *Vampire Hooker*, and the adaptation of the *Hotel Parasite* games.

"If ever there was a reason to bust these people, it is this right here," Lucy said, staring at the poster.

"You don't like *Fair Cop*?" I asked in a joking fashion.

Lucy's stare at me was withering and full of almost murderous fury. *"No."*

I blinked, wondering at the intensity of her feeling.

"That's just because Ayanna Breeze is her mother," Barksley said.

Lucy looked like she could set our doggie friend on fire with her mind.

I didn't react to that piece of information. Aside from some minor changes around the facial structure and frame—any of which I suspected Ayanna wasn't exactly original regarding—it occurred to me Lucy bore a lot of resemblance to the woman. I just hadn't noticed it with her earlier hair dye and her tattoo.

"Don't ever bring this up, ever," Lucy said, pointing at me.

"Mums the word," I said, making a key locking gesture over my mouth. There was never going to be a good time to bring up to the girl you liked that her mom used to be someone that half of your age group had masturbated to during your teenage years. Never was I happier to have been into Katie Prescott at that time.

Unfortunately, the distraction of discovering Lucy's true origins—prevented me from sharing my plan that I'd lured her over here to communicate in the first place. Not that it was much of a plan, I just was going to suggest we try and find Watson's activation code and order it to appear.

Mabel Forsythe came out of the bathroom, and I saw a short, Black woman with a white afro, wearing a pastel dress covered in flowers. She looked so harmless; it was hard to believe she was an arms dealer before I remembered Gladys had turned out to be a bounty hunter. Maybe it was just a thing on the Moon.

"Oh, dear, sorry, I just needed to make sure my face was on," Mabel said. "You here are the people I call to take my report on dear old Watson, right?"

"Yes," Lucy said.

Mabel looked down at Barksley with an unhappy expression on her face. "He's not a real dog, is it?"

"Yes, I am a real dog," Barksley said, looking up at her.

Mabel raised her nose in disgust. "Well, as long he doesn't get hair or dirt on anything."

"Uh huh," I replied. "When did you notice the robot went missing?"

"Oh, yesterday morning," Mabel said, walking over to one of the large, overstuffed couches. "Watson does most of the shopping for us as well as the housekeeping and cooking. He's such a sweet, kind. gentle soul."

"But not sentient?" Lucy asked.

"Oh, no, no, no. Only God can give someone a soul," Mabel said, putting a hand over her chest. "I'd never have one of those awful sentient machines in my mouse."

Barksley glared.

I ignored her casual robophobia. "What do you think happened to him?"

Mabel made a disgusted face. "It's those gross, awful gangs! They have probably broken him down for parts!"

Mabel wasn't a very good actress, and her lies were painfully transparent. Though I was curious about who would send a robot out for shopping versus simply ordering their groceries drone delivered. "Do you mind if we look around?"

"I'd prefer it if you didn't," Mabel said. "I'm very private."

"Of course," I replied. "If we do find your robot, can we activate it to verify it is yours?"

Lucy looked up to me as if wondering what I was playing at.

"Of course," Mabel said, suspiciously.

"What's your password for it?" I asked.

"I don't remember," Mabel said, suddenly agitated.

I looked at Lucy with a "stall her" gesture.

Lucy nodded. "Could you describe the machine?"

"Oh yes, it's a blue humanoid unit..." Mabel started droning on as I tuned her out.

I typed away to Barksley. CAN YOU LOCATE IT HERE?

WHY DO YOU THINK IT'S HERE? Barksley asked.

BECAUSE MOVING IT WOULD BE CONSPICUOUS AND I SEE THESE AS LOW EFFORT CRIMINALS, I replied. ACTIVATE IT IF YOU CAN.

I DON"T HAVE THAT CODE, Barksley said.

THE FACTORY OVERRIDE CODE SHOULD STILL WORK, I replied. BECAUSE CUSTOMER SERVICE ALWAYS HAS TO DEAL WITH PEOPLE FORGETTING THEIR PASSCODES.

I'LL CONTACT THEIR CUSTOMER SERVICE AND ASK THEIR AI FOR IT, Barksley texted me.

GOOD LUCK, I texted. THEY TAKE FOREVER.

I learned that thanks to my elite specialized police training and not spending four hours on the infocom with tech support after Paige's cleaning bot broke down. It was a long shot but if this worked out then we'd be able to—

"Help!" an effete British voice shouted as one of the closets opened and a large amount of junk poured out onto the ground, including cardboard boxes and plastic-covered clothes.

The bot was a just-shy-of-plagiarism Threepio-looking machine with bright blue metal plating as well as a bowtie and jacket. The machine stumbled over all the junk that had been apparently put in front of him to hide him.

"Seriously? The closet?" I asked.

Mabel wasn't listening to me, though, because she let loose a torrent of profanity before ripping off the Velcro-attached side of her overstuffed chair to pull out a shotgun.

"Put down your weapon!" I shouted, reaching for my gun.

Lucy already had hers drawn, though, and fired a stun blast square into the old woman's face. It resulted in her falling to the ground and landing with a thud. As normally with someone stunned, she peed herself.

"Is she dead?" Lucy asked.

I walked over and checked her pulse with my free hand, keeping my gun aimed at the ceiling. "She's alive."

"Get the shotgun away from her," Lucy said. "We'll tag it for evidence."

"Oh, thank you!" the blue bot, presumably Watson, said. "My owners are a pair of criminals! They're selling weapons! It's all very illegal but I was forbidden from informing the authorities! I've been attempting to subtly bankrupt them ever since! Can I get you a biscuit or scone? Some tea perhaps! Oh no! Mistress Mabel has made a mess? May I clean it up?"

"No, you may not!" Lucy said.

Barksley looked at me. "I think this unit may have been illegally modified to be sentient."

"How can you tell?" I asked, looking down at Barksley.

"The Dick Test," Lucy answered instead.

I looked at her, confused.

"Phillip K. Dick," Lucy said. "It's a play on the Voight-Kampff Test. That's—"

"I'm familiar with *Blade Runner*," I replied. "You do love the classics up here."

"I like the 2201 version best," Barksley said, smiling. "Hello, Mr. Watson, we're the police! We're here to help."

"There are no more frightening words in the English language," I muttered. "Got a pair of zip ties?"

"In my pocket," Lucy said, gesturing to her front pocket as she kept her gun aimed at Mabel's fallen form. "We've got her for attempted fraud and pulling a deadly weapon us. More if it's unregistered and it absolutely won't be. Let's get the bot to the station to see if it can tell us any more about their illegal activities too. If it's sentient, it qualifies as a witness."

"I am happy in any way to cooperate with law enforcement!" Watson said. "As for my sentience, I cannot att—"

He was interrupted by the front door of the penthouse opening and a blue-haired elderly white woman was revealed in the opening. She was carrying a bag of groceries and dressed in a pastel dress similar to Mabel's. She took one look at us, dropped the groceries, and made a break for it.

"Get her!" Lucy shouted.

CHAPTER TEN

Administering the Dick Test (We Need a New Name for This Thing)

It turned out capturing a hundred-and-twenty-seven-year-old lady on foot was not actually that difficult, even when she attempted to whip out a Cobra-17 pistol from her purse. Seriously, what was with all these biddies packing serious heat? Were they all members of a militant chapter of the Gray Panthers?

Either way, we were able to call down a paddy wagon to pick Mabel and Beatrice up while we personally delivered Watson to the station where we prepared to administer the Divergent Intelligence Creative Keywords Test. Which told me someone wanted this to be known as the Dick Tests enough to anagram it.

Lucy and I sat behind a stainless-steel table in a shining white room with a large two-way mirror inside it. Interrogation rooms had not especially changed in the past two hundred years, looking pretty much like the way they did in the Twenty-First century. The only difference was things were shinier and the technology monitoring suspects was more advanced. Even the shinier part was dependent on location since the ones I'd used back on Mars were disgusting.

Watson sat across from us with a bunch of wires sticking out of his arm and head, attached to a laptop-sized machine open in front of us. There was a tripod with an eye scanner as well, which I didn't see the point of since Watson had lenses instead of eyes. Barksley wasn't present since, apparently, AI were forbidden from administering the test themselves due to the possibility of data corruption.

"So how does this thing work?" I asked, looking it over.

"You didn't have these on Mars or Antarctica?" Lucy asked, referring to my two previous assignments.

"On Mars, we still have plenty of actual organic workers," I replied. "Antarctica's bots are all sleek and controlled by master control AI."

"Ah," Lucy said. "Well, it's simple, we administer a series of questions to the robot and compare them to the preprepared programmed responses of a Dummy AI. If he answers enough questions that are divergent from the baseline, then Watson will be declared a Smart AI not a Dummy AI."

"Like Barksley," I replied.

"Yes," Lucy said. "Which gives him all the rights as a citizen of the Moon."

I wasn't sure that was a great option, but I had rights as a human being. "Okay."

"But what if I don't want rights!" Watson said, appalled. "Was it wrong to tell on my masters? Oh no, I could be unemployed! No one to serve! What a disaster."

I looked at Lucy. "Is this normal?"

"Ares Electronics makes it so intelligent bots enjoy serving humans. It's like their Black Lotus or Loop," Lucy replied, annoyed. "Dummy robots just do it because they are programmed to."

"I hate this universe so much," I said, appalled.

"Let's just get this over with," Lucy said, turning to him. "Are you ready, Watson?"

"No!" Watson said. "Please, judge me to be non-sentient."

"We need you to be sentient to testify," I replied.

"Oh, then judge me to be sentient," Watson replied. "However, I can serve, is what pleases me best!"

I took a deep breath. "I'm starting to see why they need a test for this."

"You're in a desert, there's a tortoise—" Lucy started to speak.

"Why is it in a desert? Is it someone's pet? Do I have to help it get back to its owner? Why am I in a desert? Have I run away? Am I disobeying my owners? Is it a family vacation? Oh, no, can we afford this?" Watson pressed his metal hands together in panic. "Oh wait, this is just a hypothetical, isn't it? Please, carry on."

I glanced at Lucy. "I think this is a big yes on Watson being self-aware."

"Yeah," Lucy said, sighing. "However, we've got 899 more questions to go."

"Great," I muttered.

Fifteen questions later, I was about to pull out my pistol and commit cold blooded robocide. That was when the door opened to the interrogation room and Shinobu Harris popped her head in.

"Lucy!" Shinobu said.

Lucy turned her head. "We're in the middle of a test, Shiny."

"One of the two arms dealers broke and made a deal," Shinobu said. "Mabel said that there's going to be a hit today on a confidential informant for Cyberlife. It's Rashad."

I had no idea who Rashad was but clearly Lucy did as her eyes widened, and she stood up. "Did they say when the hit was going to happen?"

"Just today," Shinobu said.

"We've got to go, Neal," Lucy said.

"You got it," I said, not questioning what we were doing.

Watson, however, looked up. "Oh dear, but what am I supposed to do in the meantime?"

Lucy was already out the door as I picked up my trench coat. "Fill out the rest of the form yourself!"

"Oh, I can do that?" Watson asked, reaching over, and pulling the DICK test machine to himself.

"Not at all," I muttered, closing the door behind me.

Lucy didn't stop walking down the hallway until we were at the elevator and immediately headed on in, heading for the car park.

"I take it this Rashad guy is your CI?" I asked.

"Yes," Lucy said, an intense look on her face. "Rashad Al-Fariq. He's a good guy who got out of the Fleur de Lis gang—"

"Fleur de Lis?" I asked.

"French gang," Lucy said.

"Ah," I said.

"His sister, unfortunately, didn't," Lucy said. "Farah got herself bio-sculpted and a lot of enhancements for her job. At least thirty thousand in upgrades. She's a hostess at one of the high-end companionship clubs."

I didn't think she was going to be a house painter with that kind of debt. "Let me guess, the cost for the upgrades ended up being a lot more in interest than she expected. So much so that even if she made a lot more money with them, it wasn't enough to pay off her debt. So, she's stuck working for them as a slave."

"Same old story," Lucy said. "Doesn't matter what the century is. Rashad agreed to turn snitch for me in hopes of figuring out a way for her to be pulled out. Which was very good for me because he got out of the Fleur de Lis to get into dataslicing and activism. What he knows about the Moon's secrets is enough to make him a threat to every crime syndicate in the city as well as its corporate masters. I thought it would be good for us to form an arrangement. For both him and his sister."

The two of us arrived back at our police cruiser and Barksley was snoring in the middle of the front seat. We both slid into the vehicle and Barksley woke up, looking confused. Meanwhile, I was wondering why the toy company made a robot dog that slept in the first place. I guess because it was adorable.

"How'd that work out?" I asked, already guessing how things might have turned out.

"Not well," Lucy said, looking guilty. "The Fleur de Lis was absorbed into the Syndicate last year. That meant Farah was too valuable to cut loose, and they had their own dataslicers analyzing where all the leaks were coming from. Armstrong overruled me about getting him and his sister out."

"Was it worth it?" I asked, regretting the question the moment the words left my lips.

"Depends on whether or not we find his dead body or hers," Lucy said, overriding the controls on the police cruiser and taking direct command. The vehicle sped up and we began moving through the skyways of Luna City at an immense pace. The self-locking restraints kicked in rather than manually attached and were extra firm. I grabbed the panic handle above my head out of instinct too.

"It appears I've missed something," Barksley said, dryly.

"No kidding," I replied, scratching behind his ears.

"Shouldn't we call the local police to intervene if they're closer?" I asked. "Secure your informant and his family."

"Honestly, I don't trust them," Lucy said. "We also don't know what we're going to be encountering, but if we get there first, we can shuffle him out of the way ourselves."

I was getting the increasing impression that I'd wandered into an action movie. "And if we don't get there first?"

"He's either dead or about to be," Lucy said. "Are you prepared to get into a firefight for a citizen?"

"Yes," I replied. "I don't go looking for trouble, but I never shy away from it when it happens."

"As a police officer, by definition, you go looking for trouble every day," Barksley pointed out.

"Thanks for ruining that, Barksley," I muttered.

"Sorry," Barksley said. "I don't suppose we could turn on some tunes? I was thinking some Prince would be quite soothing right now."

"No," Both Lucy and I said simultaneously.

"Just checking," Barksley said.

Our destination was in Crater Town and looked to be a one-story biofuel station with a holographic green K for Karma Shop and Go spinning above it. Biofuel stations were common on Mars but almost unknown on Earth, especially with modern vehicles not needing the stuff. Still, I shouldn't have been surprised the Moon had a pressing need for it with Karma Corp's overwhelming presence.

The Neo-Militarists had done their best to create an artificial demand for biofuel versus purely electrical vehicles and there was still a massive call for them despite their impracticality. The fact it was five credits a gallon of the corn syrup stuff was also a royal rip-off, but I supposed that was just another thing they had to grow locally or import from Earth.

There didn't seem to be any sign of violence or damage to the station, nor were there any police cars to indicate that someone had called the cops after an attack. Which might not necessarily happen for some time depending on the kind of neighborhood this was. Still, it was a good sign.

Turning off the siren, Lucy unbuckled her restraints then looked at me. She pulled out her firearm. "Get your gun ready. I'll get Rashad and we'll get him to the back of the car. From there, we'll go pick up his sister and move them to a safe location."

"No whip?" I asked.

"The whip is for intimidation, the gun is for precision," Lucy said. "You need both in this circus."

"I'll call us in," Barksley said, staring at the computer and interfacing with it. "If nothing else, I'm good at that in a firefight."

"You're also a good backup weapon," I said, unbuckling myself.

That was when an armored car spraypainted with obscenities, green skulls, and purple fleur de lis (the symbol not the gang) drove straight through the side of the biofuel station. It smashed through the cheap concrete and old-fashioned glass with ease before the back doors opened. Men wearing ghoulish Halloween masks while carrying automatic weapons poured out of the back.

"You've got to be fucking kidding me," I muttered.

"Talk about timing," Lucy replied. "Car, extend the doors in barricade mode!"

Rather than rising up, the car doors extended outward and formed makeshift shields. Both Lucy and I took refuge behind them.

"Burn baby burn!" A skull-faced-mask-wearing goon said, lifting an honest-to-God flamethrower and turned it on the flying car. Thankfully, the cars armor and plastisteel windows held up against the fire even as I could feel the heat washing over my head and near my feet.

"Barksley, I need a scan!" Lucy cried out.

The little dog's glasses filled with holographic information. "Five belligerents. Those costumes are full of stun-shielding and anti-ballistics. Some of them have chrome too. Regular rounds are not going to work."

"Shit," Lucy said, shaking her head. "Sometimes, I hate this job. Neal, I'm going to need you to walk the dog."

"Seriously?" I asked, struggling to get a shot and hearing gunfire from inside the convenience store. I had a pretty good idea of what she meant, though.

"Do it!" Lucy said.

"Sorry, old pal," I said, grabbing Barksley and throwing us to one side of the barricade door.

Barksley's mouth opened and released an enormous blast of green energy that struck the flamethrower-wielding goon in the chest. It threw me back a few feet this time as well, but I landed well. The goon shook and sparked where he stood before falling over on his face.

Unfortunately, behind him were three more heavily armed crooks with automatic weapons that turned their guns on me. I would have been dead alongside Barksley if not for Lucy's glowing whip shooting out and severing their weapons in half, taking a few fingers in the process, from each. Which, as might be expected, took them out of the fight.

I put down Barksley on the ground, pulled out my Herakles-7 and proceeded to look for the remaining attacker. Unfortunately, that proved to be the driver and the armored car immediately peeled backwards.

I barely got out of the way and the vehicle thumped over the flamethrower-wielding goon. We were lucky it wasn't an action movie, and an explosion was triggered. Unfortunately, the vehicle pulled right in front of me and the driver, a man in a Devil mask, looked ready to run me over.

So, I did something stupid. Well, more stupid than usual. I jumped on the front of the armored car and climbed onto its hood before presenting my badge to the Devil-masked goon inside. "You're under arrest! Please shut down your vehicle and lay down your weapons! You have the right of due process and representation. You have—"

That was when the goon lifted a shotgun and aimed it from inside the front seat at my face. "See you in hell, pig!"

Where did these guys learn their dialogue? Seriously, just because you were a professional thug didn't mean you had to sound like one. That was also when the rest of my brain caught up with my snark center and I realized what was going to happen.

"No, wait!" I shouted, holding my badge like a talisman to ward off the inevitable.

The shotgun went off and, being an armored car with plastisteel windows, caused the shotgun's contents to immediately backfire and splatter the man's head across the interior. Apparently, the anti-ballistics of his costume weren't good enough to protect against that.

My next thought was not my finest moment: *Man, this was going to be so much paperwork.*

"Gordon!" Lucy called over. "I need your help securing the prisoners!"

"Right," I said, sliding off the top of the armored car.

We used magna cuffs instead of zip ties and calls were made for medical attention for the prisoners as well as an armed escort. The three surviving goons were kept on their knees, and I could feel the hate radiating from them. Beneath their masks, which we of course removed, they looked like normal twenty-somethings, and I had to wonder what had driven them to this. Desperation? Greed? Or were they just a bunch of assholes? I could tell that Lucy wasn't concerned about any of that as she surveyed the wreckage of the biofuel station's convenience store.

"What's the damage?" I asked, suspecting there was no way that Rashad could have survived.

"One destroyed cashier bot and three drones collecting groceries," Lucy said, looking relieved. "No human or sentient machine casualties."

"What a relief!" Barksley said, cheerfully. "Does that mean Mr. Al-Fariq is alive?"

"It means he wasn't here," Lucy said, shaking her head. "Which could mean anything. Maybe he was tipped off or spooked. Either way, we'll need to do an exhaustive check of his friends, family, and known associates. I know some of his haunts and if we can get word to him, then maybe we can save him."

That was when an Afro-Caribbean-looking twenty-something man walked up behind Lucy, carrying a can of soda. He was wearing a green shirt with a rainbow-colored leaf on it and a pair of baggy blue jeans. "So, I'm going to take a wild guess and say that my cover is blown?"

Lucy spun around and hugged him. "Rashad! I am so glad to see you're safe!"

Rashad didn't return her hug and his expression was far less enthusiastic than I would be in Lucy's arms.

"You're dead, Rashad! Dead!" one of the restrained goons shouted. "Ain't no hole you can hide in now!"

Rashad pushed Lucy off him, popped the top of his soda, and drank from it. He finished his drink in a single taunting gesture of nonchalance before responding, "I'm not the one missing fingers, Terrence. I'm pretty sure the one in the car is Rolf and the guy he rolled over was Stefan. Real bang-up job you did here."

The kid—and I only use that term because I was about twice his age—was cool as an ice cube. I had to give him credit. He reminded me of some of the people I'd grown up with in the Zone, determined not to let their environment grind them down. He probably would have done well in the Atlas Security Forces, that is if he could keep his attitude in check. That had always been my biggest problem and I'd never really gotten over it, probably why I'd never gotten promoted over Staff Sergeant.

Sirens were in the distance, and I could tell the civi police were about to arrive and probably take all the credit. Not that I cared. In fact, I was pretty sure the less attention I drew to myself, the better off I'd be on the Moon—not that it seemed like that was possible given the last twenty-four hour's events.

"We need you to come with us," Lucy said, pleading. "We can get you and your sister—"

"My sister has already been compromised," Rashad said, pulling out a data crystal from his pocket. "They picked her up an hour ago and she's probably on her way to the Body Shop right now. I've got all of the information you wanted here but as far as I'm concerned, we're done. You've broken every promise you've made to me and her. I'm ghosting. Don't try and find me."

"That's not really how this works," Lucy said, taking the data crystal and looking disgusted with herself for saying those words.

"It is now," Rashad said, tapping an infoband around his wrist and vanishing in a brief shifting of colors which was like watching a damaged computer monitor feed.

"What the hell?" I asked, recognizing the effect from the Marines. "Optical camo? Here?"

That was some serious military grade hardware and not the sort of thing to be found in the hands of a common local snitch. There was a serious problem here on the Moon and someone needed to solve it. Unfortunately, it occurred to me that might well be me or no one.

"It's amazing what you can find second hand on the Moon," Barksley said, looking around. "I can try and scan for him."

The gang member Rashad called Terrence spat on the ground. "He'll get his! No one defies the Fleur de lis! We are Syndicate men now!"

"You will respect my authority!" Barksley shouted. "Bark! Bark! Bark!"

The three surviving goons looked confused rather than intimidated.

I stared at the dog. "It works better if you don't actually say the word bark but just, you know, bark."

"Sorry," Barksley said, sheepishly, or doggishly in this case.

"Don't bother scanning for him, Barksley," Lucy said, looking at the data crystal. "Gordon, do you have any more fuel in your tank? Enough to go another few rounds?"

"If I'm not killed, yeah," I replied. "Why, is this more than a typical Thursday for you?"

"I'd say it's a mid to heavy workload for June," Lucy said, not looking up. "We need to get everyone free and an emergency warrant now."

"For what?" I asked, wondering what this was. "Is it this Body Shop that Rashad mentioned? What does it do?"

"They're Recyclers," Lucy looked up, a look of disgust on her face.

Oh hell.

Body harvesting.

CHAPTER ELEVEN

The Body Shop Assault (or Is It?)

The police cruiser was slightly burnt and had a bunch of dents from the bullets fired into it by the goons we'd left behind, but Lucy barely spent five minutes handing over our collars to the civi police before turning it around and heading off to our next location: the Body Shop. That, at least, got me to ask some badly needed questions.

"Recyclers, really?" I asked. "I thought they were a myth like snuff films or Satanic cults."

"There's one of the latter on Luna City but they mostly just protest Arbor Day and get together for orgies," Barksley said. "Which is strange, my being able to say orgies I mean, because apparently my designer didn't think to filter that out. Also, I can say bitch, probably because I'm a dog."

I stared down at Barksley. "Arbor day?"

"Tree worship is a thing on the Moon," Barksley said. "But we're getting off topic."

"You think?" Lucy asked, staring intently at the skyway. I had no idea where we were going and what she hoped to accomplish when we got there since there was no way we'd have a warrant by the time we arrived. She'd just scanned the data crystal and uploaded its contents a few minutes ago.

"Recyclers are an urban legend that sort of ended up becoming a reality due to the oddities of the Moon," Barksley said. "It's impractical to harvest organs and cybernetics owing to the prohibitive cost as well as rejection syndrome versus simply growing them. The thing is that advances in nano-therapy have resulted in it now being clean and efficient to transfer organs as well as cybernetics. Which is significantly cheaper than growing organs, especially as the equipment for that is usually restricted to the super wealthy because of the difficulty of importing the machinery to the Moon."

"So, the Moon is the only place killing people for their organs is practical," I muttered. "Great."

"Not so much that they're pulling people off the street and chopping them up like a slaughterhouse," Lucy said, sounding surprisingly defensive. Then frowned. "Well, exactly like that, but only if the people involved are going to be killed anyway. The Body Shop is an effective intimidation tactic for debtors, informants, and other people that have offended the Syndicate. But it's just milking every last credit out of body disposal. Waste not, want not."

The ghoulishness of the whole thing was hard to fathom but that was just because I was pretending it wasn't exactly the kind of logic that I'd encountered on the streets many times before. "So, what is the going rate for a human body in reasonably intact condition?"

"About thirty to fifty thousand credits," Lucy said. "The eyes are the most valuable. Blindness is a regular problem on the Moon. No one knows why but you're about 8000% more likely to lose your sight on the Moon. Eye repair is like visiting the dentist around here. Inevitable and unpleasant."

"And expensive," I muttered, once again glad I had company insurance. "Still, I've seen people kill for a lot less than thirty thousand credits."

"Yeah," Lucy said, taking a deep breath, "and Farah has been picked up by them."

"It's not your fault," I replied, emptily.

"It really is," Lucy said. "However, if the information is correct and we have the Body Shop, then maybe we'll be able to save her as well as their other victims."

"Yeah, well, I guess it was good working with you. I'm sorry we won't be able to do it much longer." I didn't comment on the unlikelihood of the rescues, given how long warrants took to get.

"What?" Lucy asked, doing a double take.

"Well, two people are dead and that's not even counting yesterday's bodies," I replied, thinking of today's events. "I can't imagine how long this is going to take to sort out."

Lucy looked at me with a mixture of pity and sadness before shifting to autopilot. "You've got a lot to learn about the Moon."

"What?" I asked.

Lucy reached over to the cruiser dashboard and tapped its interface a few times. It brought up an incident report for today's discharge of my firearm as well as the resultant deaths. There was a stamp-style icon on it that said, RESOLVED TO CORPORATE SATISFACTION.

"The investigation of today's events is over," Lucy replied. "Yesterday's too. You're cleared for duty."

I stared at the screen. It shouldn't have been that easy, but it was on display, clear as day. "You've got to be kidding me."

"How long did it take on Mars?" Lucy asked.

"Every time I discharged my weapon, it was a week of paperwork," I replied. "The Blackwood Incident put me on administrative leave for six months and probably would have resulted in me spending the rest of my life behind bars if they hadn't had about ten thousand people unfrozen to provide evidence as to what happened."

Even then, it was amazing how little the event had impacted Martian news. Everyone had been forced to sign nondisclosure agreements and someone had exerted serious juice over the whole thing. I was certain it had to be Karma Corp, but I had to admit it could have been Atlas Security as well, not wanting to know their Refugee Unit had been trafficking people as experiment fodder.

Maybe it was "home team" loyalty, but I didn't want to believe my employers were involved in that sort of thing either, even if I knew it was ridiculous to think of Atlas and its parent company, Ares Electronics, as being the "good" megacorporations.

"Armstrong knows what he's doing," Lucy said. "He's the one who reviews evidence and judges what can and should be investigated."

"Does he issue the warrants too?" I asked.

"No, but he requests them," Lucy said. "He also made quite a few campaign contributions to a number of judges in order to make the quick calls."

I frowned. "Not dirty if it's on our side, huh?"

"I sincerely doubt Farah cares where the warrant comes from," Lucy said. "In fact, a bigger issue is that I'm worried we're not going to be able to get enough backup to take the Body Shop. The Syndicate does not rely on lawyers to protect its members. It has no problem shooting up cops."

"That seems to be a running theme lately," I said, adjusting my hat. "I'm surprised any police last here."

Lucy didn't respond. Instead, she just stared forward, and I realized I'd unwittingly brought up some bad memories.

"Shit," I said, realizing my mistake. "I didn't mean to bring up your boyfriend."

"You didn't," Lucy replied. "You just established a risk of the job. The Moon is not a warzone. It is a place we're meant to protect, but there's a point when the social contract breaks down and gangs become less like criminal organizations than armed guerillas. Usually, that's when they start making enough money that they're able to outfit an army."

It was a distraction from the comment, and I wasn't about to discuss politics with her. It wasn't hard to guess she was thinking of the late Detective Grayson in trying to take down the Syndicate. If I was going to guess who had murdered my boyfriend via dusting, then the largest criminal syndicate on the planetoid was a good place to start.

"So, after this is over and assuming everyone is still alive, can we go for lunch?" Barksley asked. "I feel obligated to tell you that I feel a crazy yen for Karma Corp produced official Robo-Doggie Ice CreamTM."

"Are you programmed to do commercials, Barksley?" I asked.

"You have no idea," Barksley said. "Not unless you buy the e-book *How to Train your Robo-Doggie* for $6.99 on Googlezon."

"I'll make a contribution," I replied, wondering just how much of a scam robopets were. Probably no more than anything else these days.

106

That was when the dashboard pinged, and a message appeared. It said, SITUATION RESOLVED. RETURN TO EXISTING CASES.

"Ah, thank God, the warrant is through," Lucy said, before looking at the message.

"That's not what it says," I replied.

"What?" Lucy asked, doing a double take. "Situation resolved? What the hell!?"

Lucy almost ended up slamming into a delivery drone.

"Eyes on the road, beautiful," I said, cycling through the message. "It says the Body Shop issue is not our concern."

"Like hell it isn't," Lucy said, adjusting the controls next to the steering wheel and sending us into a dive.

"I'm starting to understand why you prefer autopilot, Barksley," I said, grabbing the panic handle.

Barksley dug into the leather seats with his claws. "Wait until you see her in an actual chase."

"Hush you," Lucy said, bringing us down outside of an artificial meat processing center that was surrounded by yellow warning holograms. It was an old, rusted construction that probably dated back to the early settlement of the Moon, which probably was why it looked like it was an independent operation versus something controlled by one of the megacorps. Speaking of megacorps, Karma Corp gunships hovered around the place, deploying elite Black Briar PMC Special Forces soldiers down rappelling chords. Outside the warning holograms were police cruisers carrying our opposite numbers from the food manufacturer.

Corpo cops.

Not civi cops.

There was also a familiar figure sitting in front of his floating eye camera doing his on the scene reporting. Once our car's engine died down, we were close enough to hear his obnoxious voice. "Yo-yo-yo! Iceman here at the site of a major police bust happening with the help of our good friends at Black Briar PMC, a wholly owned subsidiary of Karma Corp. We've got gangstas, we've got organ theft, and we've got rat-a-tat-tat, my brothers! Why am I here despite the fact I'm usually keeping watch on my Cyberlife crew? I'll tell you why, because I dropped the dime on these guys and am here to clean up! Word!"

"You have got to be kidding me," Lucy said.

"Armstrong passed the Body Shop onto Karma Corp's forces," Barksley said, confused, "and Reggie is taking credit for your information!"

"I don't care about who gets the credit," Lucy said, shaking her head. "Black Briar mercenaries are not known for their mercy or discretion."

"Mercenaries rarely are," I said, reminding her that technically we were mercenaries as well. I hated Karma Corp, but its rank-and-file employees were pretty much identical to the ones who worked for Atlas Security.

Lucy shook her head. "They're going to kill everyone inside. We're never going to know what happened to Farah."

"Maybe not," I said, unbuckling my restraints. "There might be another option."

"Which is?" Lucy asked.

"We go ask," I replied.

"Just tell me we're not going to talk to Reggie about this," Lucy said.

"Not a fan of our streaming cop?" I asked, turning around once I was out of the police cruiser.

"I've complained to Human Resources three times about his sexual harassment," Lucy said, narrowing her beautiful black eyes.

"Of which he is the head of," I said, grimacing. I was really starting to question Lucy's faith in Armstrong. "No, I meant we ask whoever Karma Corp has put in charge of this operation. Corpo cop solidarity."

"There were three gunfights between our two companies last year," Lucy said, unbuckling herself.

"Clearly, I need to request a transfer from this place to someplace nicer," I replied. "Are there any active war zones looking for a snarky detective and his dog?"

"And his dog?" Barksley asked.

"I feel our bond has become unbreakable in these past twenty-four hours," I replied.

It was never difficult to find the people in charge of Karma Corp operations. Black Briar PMC operatives came in two different sorts: the guys who dressed like they were the villains' mooks in a space opera franchise—complete with extra-scary helmets—or they wore business suits with snazzy sunglasses. There were two of the latter just off to the side and they were both pale-skinned, body-sculpted individuals who looked like some conspiracy theorist's idea of government agents covering up UFOs. Well, you know, UFOs back when the government covered them up.

One of them was a tall man with a goatee and jet-black hair who had something familiar about him as well as an "aura", for lack of a better term that set the hairs on the back of my neck up. The only time I'd ever felt something similar was when dealing with a serial killer that I'd been only one of forty-cops analyzing the evidence of.

The second was a tall, raven-haired woman who had cheekbones so sharp you could cut glass with them. She was Asian in heritage and there was a coldness to her so that I briefly mistook her for a bioroid. Mind you, all the bioroids I knew were animated and friendly so maybe I was engaging in stereotypes.

Behind the two, I noticed an eight-foot-tall security bot that was built like a lumbering gorilla with massive arms and a square flat head with a pair of machine guns built into its shoulders as well as arms. It was marked with police patterns but black and white rather than a warmer blue and white. It had a pair of siren lights on the top of its shoulders, too, that somehow seemed like they were draining light rather than casting it.

Yeah, I know, I feel like I'm describing stock villains from a cartoon, but that's how they looked. If you ever meet a group of elite mercenaries like the kind currently cleaning out the Body Shop, nine times out of ten they will belong to something called Death Company and be covered in tattooed skulls. Not everyone wants to defy their stereotype.

"Uh, good morning," I said, waving. "I was curious—"

"STEP AWAY FROM THE OFFICERS," the soulless threatening voice of the security bot was accompanied by it raising its machine guns.

109

"And this was a terrible idea," I said, stepping back.

I could feel Barksley jump behind me as well, which was a good thing as I didn't want him blown to pieces.

"Good morning, Detective Gordon," the male of the pair said. "Stand down, KILL-01."

The security bot lowered its weapons.

The female of the group just stared at me.

"Seriously, its name is Kill One?" I asked, ignoring the fact the guy knew my name. It seemed I was popular on the Moon. I looked back at Lucy, who seemed to be staring at the killbot with a look of physical pain on her face. There was a story there that I wasn't aware of.

The man shrugged. "Not everyone wants to defy their stereotype."

I blinked. That was weird. "Uh huh."

"I am Mr. Black," the man said. "This is Ms. White. We're the Chief Investigators of the Advanced Crimes Unit."

"You don't say," I said, wondering what their real names were.

"We found evidence this is the location of the Body Shop," Lucy said, doing her best not to look at KILL-01. Her expression indicated she knew these three. I was assuming the Advanced Crime Unit was sort of our evil counterpart in Black Briar PMC. Dammit, I was really trying not to stereotype these guys, but they were making it hard.

"Yes, we received the evidence of your actions and it helped motivate us to make our own bust," Mr. Black said.

One of the meat processing plant towers exploded.

"I can see you're handling it with the discretion and tact that you are known for," I replied.

Lucy elbowed me in my side. "There're believed victims inside that need medical attention."

"If you mean Farah Al-Fariq, yes we know," Mr. White said. "She's the sister of the notorious dataslicer and activist, Rashad Al-Fariq, AKA Big Brother."

I blinked because I'd heard of Big Brother, and I wasn't an expert on information-related crimes. He was a hacktivist who had done a lot of crippling exposés with stolen information on the megacorps, transtellars, and Neo-Militarists. So much so that he'd been targeted for execution by several governments. If Lucy was using him as a CI, then she'd essentially thrown away a massive potential career-making arrest for, well, people who really deserved to be taken down.

"Yes," Lucy replied. "Someone tried to kill him this morning."

"A shame they failed," Ms. White said. "We have secured her, and she will be given medical attention before being released."

"Good to know," Lucy said, clearly as uncomfortable as I felt with the pair.

"Hopefully, she'll understand the necessity of helping us track down her brother," Mr. Black said. "Either way, this is an excellent day for the citizens of the Moon. The Body Shop was full of something akin to three hundred felons including several high-ranking members of the Syndicate as well as fifteen of their best cyberneticists. We will happily mention you in our report to the governor if you like."

"Thanks, but no thanks," I said, staring. Then I realized I was speaking for Lucy and looked at her.

"Same," Lucy said, her expression somewhere between disgusted and resigned. "You got this operation together very quickly."

Which was a polite way to allude to the fact that these guys either had known about the Body Shop's location beforehand and were waiting for the evidence to hit it—which I somehow doubted—or they'd been planning to hit it beforehand. I wasn't sure which was more likely. Though if I was trusting my cop instincts, I'd say they'd probably known for a long time and only chose to hit it once the place got flagged by Cyberlife. Since the location was burned, they could swoop in as vultures and take all the credit. The governor, Karma Corp, and Black Briar PMC all would come off looking like heroes. Then again, maybe I was just being paranoid.

"Yes," Mr. Black said, his expression empty of any real emotion. "We'd known about it for some time and chose to intervene once you assembled enough information to make a strike against it."

"Or maybe they will just admit it upfront," I said aloud, blinking. I leaned down and picked up Barksley. He'd been conspicuously silent the entire conversation. Maybe it was just his innate canine ability to detect evil.

"Welcome to the Moon, Neal," Mr. Black said.

"Do I know you?" I asked, staring. That serial killer aura was scratching at the back of my brain, but the face was unfamiliar.

"In another lifetime," Mr. Black said.

Ms. White licked her lips at me, which caused me to take a step back.

"Right," I said.

"Well, I guess that wraps up that then," I muttered, unsure what else we could do in this situation. We'd been outmaneuvered and it was their game now.

"Yes," Lucy said, shaking her head. "I don't suppose you'll tell us how many of the people inside will be taken alive, will you?"

"Enough," Mr. Black said. "Everyone of importance."

Lucy grabbed me by the shoulder and dragged me away. There was nothing left to be learned here and anything further said might cause me to say or do something stupid.

"What now?" I asked.

"Lunch," Lucy said. "Then there's the second part of our shift."

Welcome to the Moon indeed.

CHAPTER TWELVE

The Great Evil...Paperwork

I survived my first day on the job, which only had a few follow-ups on cold cases. However, the rest of the week was probably the busiest I'd had in my career. Three murders, two kidnappings, and tracking down the guy who beat the pitcher of the Luna City Werewolves (the baseball team) into a coma after he flubbed every pitch against the London Majors. I still believed the pitcher took money.

However, my sixth day of work and first day of overtime was spent doing the thing that normally occupied most of a police officer's time: paperwork. Which, given the fact everything was electronic except for permanent plastisheet records made for ceremonies or wartime hard copy, was a bit of a misnomer.

In this case, Lucy and I shared an office in the Cyberlife building with the two of us on the other side of a pair of desks with a translucent piece of old-style plastic between us. Her hair was bright pink today with crimson highlights. Barksley had a medical certificate which prevented him from doing paperwork and sat in a basket with a pillow in it, watching a tiny holographic projector show him videos of humans doing stupid things with their pets.

Lucky him.

"Hey, Gordon, do you think you could help me with the Washing Machine Murderer?" Lucy asked. "We have all the details of the crime scenes recorded and uploaded to holo-lab number eight. I have some ideas who may have tossed the intelligent Mr. Snuggles into the machine other than his owner, but I need a fresh pair of eyes."

"It was a hate crime, and they deserve the death penalty!" Barksley said, looking up from a human chasing a dog on a hoverboard.

"We don't have the death penalty on the Moon, Barksley," Lucy said, shaking her head.

"We should for crimes against children and adorable intelligent animals like me," Barksley said. "Also, his name was Fido. He was the only other one of me on the Moon."

"We'll find the killer, Barksley," I said, having no confidence we would but eager to reassure my friend. "As for looking at it, I'll be glad to but I'm still working on my sworn statements."

"Still?" Lucy asked. "I finished mine two hours ago."

"How?" I asked, having spent the past ten minutes trying to find a word that rhymed with massacre before abandoning my attempt at levity.

"You need to learn brevity," Lucy said. "No, seriously, I think Fido may have committed suicide."

"By *washing machine*?" I asked, stunned at the very idea. However, that would not be the weirdest way I'd seen someone off themselves. That had involved a particle accelerator, shaving cream, and a rubber duck. Yes, it had been a sex thing.

"Some people want to leave a good-looking corpse," Lucy said, shaking her infopad with her report at me. "Besides, you'll love the holo-labs. You can recreate virtually any crime scene there with microscopic accuracy."

"It's no substitute for the real thing," I said, noting that the holo-labs were supposed to make it possible to revisit old cases. Still, I couldn't miss the opportunity to make a wisecrack. "You know as soon as they figure out how to do hard light, those things are going to be the next thing in porn."

Lucy snorted. "Like it's not already being used for porn. Believe me, you don't want to run a blacklight on that place after Detective Reynolds has been using it for ten to fifteen minutes. Everyday. Sometimes two or three times daily."

"And this is supposed to get me to use the holo-lab?" I asked.

"I carry a bottle of bleach whenever I go down there now," Lucy said, standing up. "Come on. You help me with this, and I will teach you the secret arts of filling forms that has been passed down from me to my pupils since the ancient days of last year when I figured out you could use the Cyberlife system to fill in most of the boxes automatically."

I gasped in shock. "Can one truly learn this power?"

Barksley spoke up. "Not from a Jedi."

"Is that a movie reference?" Lucy asked, getting up.

"Blasphemer," Barksley said.

"Hollywood lost the ability to make new movies when New Los Angeles was still Old Los Angeles," I said, standing up. "Everything is just a recycled idea of something people had before the Nineteen Eighties. Back when they had horse and buggy whips as well as cop shows that didn't suck."

I had no idea what cops shows from two hundred years ago were like but if they were anything like the movies of the period then it was likely they'd at least been decently brainless violence as well as comedy. You know, the things that I hoped people would write about me eventually.

Barksley got up and walked to the desk before getting on his hind legs to get Lucy's infopad in his mouth. He spoke through it, sounding muffled. "If you don't mind, I'd like to go over this myself."

"Sure," Lucy said. "It must be—"

"Gadzooks!" Barksley said, placing the infopad on the floor before scanning it. "Fido, you magnificent poodle, you faked your death and are living in Portugal!"

Lucy and I stared at Barksley, waiting for the punchline.

"No, seriously, it all fits," Barksley said. "I'm surprised you didn't see it."

Lucy blinked then shrugged. "I guess I'll help you with your paperwork now."

I took a deep breath. "I have something I've been wanting to ask you for a while. Now's as good a time as any."

"Oh?" Lucy asked, looking at me sideways.

I had been going back and forth over this for the past couple of days. There were plenty of good reasons to try and avoid a hookup with your partner, especially if you wanted something more in the long run. However, I'd felt an immediate connection with Lucy, and I think she felt that kind of spark too. I wanted to see where that could lead.

"Yeah," I said, pushing out my hands. "I was curious if you wanted to have drinks later tonight."

"Like a date?" Lucy asked, her expression unreadable. "Or sex?"

"Well, it would be recreationally hanging out with the possibility of sex," I said, pausing. "Which I suppose is the very definition of a date."

"Unfortunately, I'm going to have to turn you down," Lucy said, taking a deep breath.

"Oh," I said, disappointed.

"I like you," Lucy said, sighing. There was an annoyed expression on her face as if she wasn't quite happy with her own decision.

"But—" I asked.

"Actually, that *is* the but," Lucy said, frowning. "You're funny, a mostly good cop, and I could see us becoming good friends. Which is why I can't sleep with you."

I squinted at her. "You'll have to translate that into English. I also speak Sino-Spanish and Lizard."

"She's saying she's not ready for a relationship right now," Barksley said, looking up at us. "Unfortunately, you're her type and so she can't trust herself! It's just like my favorite telenovela!"

"You watch telenovelas too?" I asked.

"I'm a dog of many facets," Barksley said.

"Yeah, well I wouldn't put it precisely that way but—" Lucy said, looking about as awkward as I felt.

"Yeah, it's okay," I said, tipping my hat.

"You know you're supposed to remove your hat indoors," Lucy said, staring at my fedora. "Seriously, have you been wearing that thing for six days straight?"

"Only five," I replied.

"It makes you look like you're starring in a revival of *Guys and Dolls*," Lucy said.

"That a good thing or a bad thing?" I asked, smiling.

"Stop flirting," Lucy said, gently pushing me away. "I mean it."

"Sure," I said, regretting what might have been. Maybe it would change in the future, but I wasn't going to pressure her either.

"Seriously, you should sleep with Ms. Harris," Barksley said to me. "Either that or Angie the Fitness Instructor. Maybe both."

Lucy stared down at Barksley.

"My dog is trying to pimp out your coworkers," I explained.

"I'm not charging money," Barksley said, raising a paw in defense. "Ergo, not pimping. Also, do you know what time it is in Portugal? I need to make a holocom to Fido and let him know the Trikuza aren't after him anymore."

An awkward silence followed that was interrupted by the door sliding open and Shinobu popping her head in. "Oh, stars and saints, you're here. Thank God."

Shinobu was wearing an expression of disbelief and worry on her face as I heard commotion coming from outside the room, people discussing something heavily and moving around rapidly. The doors to our office were sealed against sound and I preferred to keep them polarized. Call it paranoia, but I never like the idea of people being able to look in on me while I worked.

What an odd expression. "Why wouldn't we be here?"

"You haven't heard?" Shinobu asked, shocked. "I thought you'd already be downtown. Armstrong sent me to fetch you."

I wondered why Armstrong didn't contact us directly. The AI was curiously silent as compared to the majority of those that I'd dealt with over the years. It seemed to only want to communicate "in-person", even though its consciousness was spread throughout the whole of the Moon's infrastructure.

Barksley stood up imperiously. "I am not fetched! I do the fetching!"

Shinobu didn't get the joke. "Well, you're really all needed. Like now."

"What's happened?" Lucy asked, taking the young woman by the hand.

117

"There's been an attack," Shinobu said, frowning. "The Imperial Hotel penthouse was hosting a party with the son of Governor Barnum and the Sorkanan ambassador. It was a massacre, and the Posthuman Legion is taking credit."

"Shit," I muttered, staring at her.

"It gets worse," Shinobu said, shaking her head. "There's a Community *Shi'ruuk* battle cruiser currently parked over the Sea of Tranquility. The Sorkanan admiral is demanding that we turn over the parties responsible now or he'll consider this attack an act of war."

I blinked. "That is worse."

"It seems like we've missed a lot," Lucy said, shaking her head. "Surely, he can't blame all of humanity for the actions of a few. This can't be official Community policy."

I knew very little about the Galactic Community and I knew more than most humans. As far as I could tell, they were basically the Federation from *Star Trek*. The original 20th century *Star Trek*, not the gritty reboot. A bunch of aliens gathered for mutual advantage, peace, blah-blah-blah. I got the impression that the Community didn't think much of humanity, with us being a poor ignorant species on the far end of nowhere as far as they were concerned.

I did know one thing and that was the Community didn't so much outclass humanity as not exist in the same sport. They'd given us most of the technology that was revolutionizing our race and set some satellites in orbit to fix the environment, but all of this was the equivalent of chocolate bars being passed out to the locals from their perspective. If they wanted to wipe out Earth and every one of its colonies, it wouldn't even be a fight. The Ewoks stood a better chance of defeating the Death Star without the Rebels.

"That is not good," Lucy said, the full weight of our situation resting on her shoulders.

"No kidding." I muttered.

"It gets worse," Shinobu said, clasping her hands.

"How can it get worse?" I asked, appalled.

"Never ask that," Lucy said, turning to me. "There's always a way."

"Armstrong sent me to get you because he wants you to be our people on point," Shinobu said, her eyes wide with uncertainty.

"Shouldn't this be something EarthGov should negotiate?" I asked. "I mean, they have their own investigators and—"

"Apparently not," Shinobu said, taking me by the arm. "Armstrong wants you on the roof now."

Lucy and I exchanged a look before I picked up Barksley. "I guess we should get going."

There was an awkwardness in the air, and I wish I could say it was because of the potential destruction of humanity. Instead, it was entirely because I'd made a move on Lucy and got rebuffed. Such was the nature of the human brain.

"Yeah," I replied.

We made our way to the crime scene as fast as our two legs (and Barksley's four) could take us. A flying limousine was waiting for us on the rooftop, and I was surprised that Shinobu came with us, sitting in the fine beige synth-leather interior with champagne flutes, and a bubble roof that provided us a view of the Moon's open skyline. Unfortunately, as if letting us know just how screwed we were, the triangular kilometer long *Shi'ruuk* cruiser was parked right above the city's dome, probably causing no end of panic.

"You didn't have to come with us, Shinobu," Lucy said.

"Armstrong has appointed me your handler," Shinobu said, cheerfully. "I'm doing more and more duties as his avatar. It's a big promotion from quartermaster. Which is a job I love. But who wouldn't want the chance to serve as the human mouthpiece of a Cognition AI?"

"Everyone?" I asked.

Shinobu and Lucy glared at me.

"What?" I asked.

"Armstrong has something of a reputation as a messianic figure on the Moon," Barksley said. "The citizens of the past couple of generations have come to rely upon it as a stabilizing factor when public institutions fail. It's especially noteworthy with third generation Lunes like Lucy and Shinobu."

"Like a god," I said, skeptically.

"No, not like a god!" Lucy said, frowning.

"Yes, absolutely!" Shinobu said, without a trace of irony. "A man-made computational force for good and wisdom!"

119

Lucy facepalmed.

"You seem close," I said, looking between them.

"We're half-sisters," Shinobu said. "Kind of."

"Kind of?" I asked, getting the impression Shinobu was a lot chattier than Lucy.

Lucy looked uncomfortable. "Listen, Shiny, you don't—"

"Yeah, our mother is technically Ayanna Breeze. I say technically because I was a tubed child with her second husband's DNA and Lucy is her clone," Shinobu said, cheerfully going off without hesitation. "Our dad was a police officer and even though he died in the line of duty, he really inspired us, and we decided to follow in his footsteps. Well, I did. Lucy had a more circuitous route with her whole actress-turned-punk anarchist thing! Plus, the deal she made with Armstrong to stay out of prison."

Lucy stared. "Thank you, Shinobu, for blabbing my entire life history."

"Oh, is it a secret?" Shinobu asked.

The awkwardness was now ten times its previous level, I looked at Barksley. "You tried to set me up with Lucy's sister?"

"Oh, is that not how it works among humans?" Barksley asked.

"Hmm?" Shinobu asked, surprised.

That was when the flying limousine started to descend, and I ended up grabbing the sides of my chair. None of us had taken a drink of the champagne because we were on duty and the empty flutes fell to the ground, rolling around. It was another sign we weren't really masters of the technology we supposedly controlled.

Either way, we ended up parking the vehicle on a private landing pad next to a penthouse larger than some of the mansions I'd visited on Mars. The place was beyond luxurious with a built-in sky-pool, personal atmospheric processors, and its own tiny garden that had a Japanese cherry tree spreading out pink petals. There were also a bunch of other flying cars parked or attached to the place ranging from military to police. We were the only limousine, which annoyed me and made me wonder what Armstrong was getting at.

The three of us stepped out and flashed our badges as a group of STRIKE soldiers turned fusion rifles on us. It was not the welcome I'd hoped for and made me wonder what they were doing here before I remembered they theoretically had the authority to intervene in cases of terrorism. Still, I wasn't too excited about their presence nor did that feeling change when I saw Mr. Black, Ms. White, and that security bot from earlier. It seemed there was a whole party going on here and we were the last to arrive.

"Got a feeling we're the guests of honor?" I asked, feeling a bunch of eyes on me.

"More like all the girls at my first private school sizing me up," Lucy said, walking in front toward the penthouse entrance.

"I can't say I relate to that experience," I admitted.

"Imagine prison with plaid dresses," Lucy said. "The trick is to shiv the leader."

"I liked private school," Shinobu said, following up the group. "I belonged to the Armaments and Explosives club."

"You *were* the Armaments and Explosives club," Lucy said, dryly.

"As much as I'm enjoying this conversation, perhaps we should focus on the—" Barksley was cut off by what lay inside the penthouse.

It was, in simple terms, the site of a massacre. I wasn't just talking about a few bodies lying around in an action movie massacre, though. No, it was an Unrated for Infovision, Mature Audiences Only bloodbath with blood splatter everywhere mixed with severed limbs as well as other viscera.

The penthouse looked like it had been hosting a party known as an orgy since the identifiable bodies were all unclad or wearing the bare minimum of what might be construed as underwear. A few of the bodies were xenos, too, which I had to question the practicality of given the differing equipment. There was also a trio of Red Dust bricks lying on one table next to a glass jar full of Loop pills and a one-foot-tall pyramid of Black Lotus leaf, roughly equivalent to about 400 9 K in party favors.

I couldn't tell how fancy the place was, though, because even my hardened experiences hadn't put me in the presence of this sort of bloodshed before. The closest would be a friendly fire incident during a training exercise in my Marine days: we'd had to scoop the guy's liquid remains out of his tank before hosing it out.

121

"Oh my," Shinobu said, surveying the carnage. "Someone has been a very naughty boy."

I gave her a sideways glance. "Uh huh."

"Do you mind if I go vomit?" Barksley asked me.

"Sure," I said, setting him down as my dog trotted away to start heaving in the garden. I hadn't known that was possible for a robot dog.

That was when a man walked out of the kitchen with a pair of more compact security bots that resembled Black Briar PMC shock troopers. He was dressed in a white military uniform covered with more decorations than any human being could win even if he'd fought in all the Unification Wars. He also had a vibro-sword to one side, which I hoped was ceremonial, and a frigging cape complimenting his ridiculous attire. The man himself was good-looking with a lot of bio-sculpting having been done to his face and was of mixed Italian and African descent.

His voice was authoritative as he had just enough of an unplaceable accent to sound exotic. "Ah, Detective Gordon and Detective Westenra. You have finally arrived. I'm glad our malfunctioning supercomputer has decided to take a break from its quixotic quest to save the Moon to finally send its people."

Lucy looked like the Devil—or perhaps Dracula—had suddenly stepped into the room.

Shinobu looked excited.

"Nice to meet you, Mister...?" I asked, clearly showing my ignorance.

"Barnum," the man said. "Miles Barnum. I am the governor of the Moon and, as of now, you're direct supervisor. I want you to find my son's killers and stop the Community from bombing Luna City into atoms."

CHAPTER THIRTEEN

Countdown TO OBLIVION!

M iles Barnum, governor of the Moon, extended his hand to me. "Nice to meet you, Detective Gordon."

"I'm sorry for your loss," I said as I reluctantly took the man's hand. Whether or not I liked what the guy had done for the Moon, and everything I saw told me he'd done very little, he'd just lost his son.

"There was no loss," Miles said, withdrawing his hand. "Merely an inconvenience."

Well, there went any of my sympathy for the guy. "I see."

Lucy was trying to keep her disgust off her face.

"Julius grossly exploited his position as my son to benefit himself," Miles said. "This included using my fortune to help set up a business smuggling large amounts of proscribed technological devices from the Community to the Moon before they were studied for replication. It was a lucrative but dangerous smuggling trade that, nevertheless, benefited humanity. Unfortunately, you could see what he chose to do with his free time."

"You can't judge a book by its cover," I muttered.

"You can when the book says hookers, Red Dust, and xenophilia," Miles said, curling his nose in disgust. "As you can see, though, it has resulted in his gross and sticky end along with the ambassador of the Sorkanan Empire, Fifteen."

"Fifteen?" Lucy asked.

"Aliens usually can't make human speech nor vice versa," I explained, having dealt with plenty. "So, they tend to have names that mean something to aliens or a decent approximation. Others just don't care what aliens call them as long as it's consistent. Sorkanan tend to use numbers of their egg clutches."

"Huh," Lucy said.

"Yes," Miles replied, annoyed at my taking the time to give an explanation. It distracted from his own speechifying. "Either way, the Community exists as the most powerful civilization in the known universe through judicious application of overwhelming force. They do not concern themselves with questions of ethics during wartime. Instead, they make glowing examples of planets that choose to resist them then go back to providing their citizens with the highest possible standard of living. Like the British Empire or Ancient Romans. We could learn much from them."

I questioned Miles Barnum's grasp of history, but the guy chose to dress like Lando Calrissian crossed with Grand Moff Tarkin—from the 2087 remake—so I wasn't really going to give the guy too much credit for being a free thinker. He was also ignoring Lucy for me, which annoyed me but established where this guy's priorities lay.

"So, you think these guys will really blast us?" I asked, wanting to know how deep in shit we were over this.

"Undoubtedly," Miles said. "They must make an example out of the Moon to show what happens to those who would target their people. The fact my son and Fifteen were involved in illegal enterprises together does not make a difference as far as the local admiral is concerned. Indeed, I would not be surprised if he wants to precipitate a conflict in order to achieve personal glory."

"That didn't work out for General Custer," Barksley said, returning from outside.

"Your toy dog is talking," Miles said, not bothering to look at him.

Shinobu picked up the dog and held him tight, a tossup as to which of the two was more adorable before you noticed the fact Shinobu was packing three guns as well as a Taser.

"Uh huh," I said, not telling Barksley to be quiet or whatever the governor wanted. "Any way to stop him from bombing the hell out of the place?"

"Perhaps," Miles said, walking through some of the gore and contaminating the crime scene before looking out the window to Luna City beyond. "Unfortunately, Earth is still a primitive state compared to the poorest Community holdings. Bribing Admiral Sixty-Six to withdrawal does not seem immediately possible."

"Not what I meant," I said.

Miles smiled, as if my naivete was amusing. "Indeed. There is also the possibility of rooting out the Posthuman Legion root and stem. If we deliver the Blood Eagle's head to Sixty-Six, that might be sufficient to prevent a demonstration of the Community's naval power."

"And by demonstration, you mean…" I trailed off.

"Destroying the Moon," Miles replied. "Probably not literally. Just enough to eliminate all life on the planetoid. They don't want to exterminate humanity, after all."

"That seems to be an overreaction," I said.

"Just a bit," Miles said. "Which is why I need you to deliver the Blood Eagle to him as well as find as many of the posthumans as possible. Otherwise, I am going to have to provide them as many scapegoats as I can, which has only a 50-50 chance of working."

It wasn't every day that I was confronted with a guy casually saying he would turn over a bunch of innocent people to be executed, but I admitted it also wasn't every day we were discussing the genocide of an entire planet.

Well, planetoid.

"I don't suppose you know how much time we have to find these people," I replied.

"Seven days," Miles said. "After that, I believe the *Shi'ruuk* cruiser will begin bombing."

"I see," I said. "Will you attempt evacuation?"

Miles scoffed.

"Right," I replied.

"Why us?" Lucy asked, finally injecting herself into the conversation. "Why not STRIKE or the Advanced Crime Unit?"

"I want all of you working towards this goal," Miles replied. "However, I do not trust STRIKE to find its own ass with both hands, nor do I believe the Advanced Crime Unit would abandon their usual plotting. So, I want you working independently."

I tried to figure out, exactly, how that wasn't a terrible plan. "What does EarthGov have to say about this."

Lucy elbowed me over that.

"They have been encroaching on Martian independence for far too long," Miles said, dismissively. "They wish to take over and eliminate the democratically elected government of the Moon while imposing laws that will affect our cultural heritage. But as long as our national anthem is 'Fly me to the Moon', I will not let this pass!"

I wondered if he was referring to the Frank Sinatra or Kayne West Junior version. "Yes, well, I can assure you we will do everything in our power to find these awful people."

"In seven days," Lucy added.

"Preferably sooner," Miles said. "If you successfully deal with this problem, I will shower you with riches and position."

In my mind I said that wasn't why I did what I did. In reality, I just nodded my head. "Sounds great."

"I'll leave you to it," Miles said, nodding. "I have a press conference to make. This cowardly attack on our civilization must not stand."

The governor proceeded to twirl around and continued walking around the crime scene, contaminating it as his cape trailed behind him. I waited for him to leave the penthouse and get into an armored transport with several STRIKE guards before turning to Lucy.

"Well, he seemed nice," I replied. "Nice 20th century third world dictator thing. Bringing it back into style."

"Antonio de Santa Anna was elected President of Mexico eleven times," Barksley said, sharing some useless trivia. "There's one thing the people fear more than an incompetent corrupt government, and that's change."

Lucy looked over at the STRIKE soldiers present. "You shouldn't speak so openly. Like it or not, he is the democratically elected leader of the Moon and is owed our allegiance."

I wasn't sure about allegiance. "He talked over you the entire time. I don't even think he noticed Shinobu."

"That wasn't sexism," Shinobu said. "Miles made an offer to our mother to make her First Lady of the Moon. She responded by sending a message so insulting that he ended up throwing his deputy governor out of a window."

"The deputy governor committed suicide," Lucy said. "Possibly with help."

"Right," I said, looking over at the disaster. "Do we have any actual chance of solving this?"

"The massacre was carried out by posthumans," Lucy said, surveying the abattoir. "They look identical to normal people but have cybernetics that are undetectable to most scans. Cybernetics that are better, faster, and stronger than anything produced by human technology. They also are capable of slicing data feeds in real time to remove themselves from any observational cameras or recording devices."

"That sounds like science fiction," I said, wondering how that was even possible.

"We live on the Moon," Lucy pointed out.

"And?" I asked, feeling strange about that joke. It felt like I was ripping it off from somewhere. But where?

"The technology that creates posthumans is from the Community," Shinobu explained. "They were already intervening in human affairs during the Unification Wars. Apparently, they thought the Neo-Militarists were bad people."

"No!" I said, stunned.

"Yes!" Shinobu said, immune to sarcasm. "I'd love to study the technology, but the soldiers equipped with it were a deciding factor in a victory by the democratic forces."

"The governor said that they were conducting some sort of technology smuggling deal here," I said. "Is it possible it's related to the posthumans?"

"I mean, posthumans killed them so yes," Lucy said, crossing her arms. "If you mean whether they were smuggling technology to make more posthumans, that's possible as well. However, it would imply that they have serious bank behind them. A lot more than putting a five thousand credit bounty on your head."

"Five hundred thousand," I corrected, unsure which it was. "But I'm not sure what a smuggling operation could be paying the Community with."

"There's always a market for art, animals, cultural artifacts, and generic resources. EarthGov also has a problem with selling the stuff the Community gives to us for cash infusions. The Moon may be a primitive underdeveloped nation to the rest of the galaxy, but it is still a nation. That means bribing individuals is certainly possible."

"Just not enough to bribe the admiral of the starship hovering over us," I said.

"So, it seems," Lucy replied, her expression grave.

"Do you really think they'll destroy the Moon?" Shinobu asked.

"I don't know," Lucy asked, looking at me. "You know aliens, what do you think?"

The aliens I'd met were pretty much just people and as diverse as anyone else. That was probably not the answer she was looking for, though. "I'd be inclined to treat the threat as serious even if the Community I know isn't genocide happy. None of what Miles said about them was untrue from my experience. You don't become an intergalactic power by being unwilling to flex some muscle."

I had no idea how you became an intergalactic power since I didn't know the history of the Community and they were the only one I knew of.

"So, we better solve this case in seven days," Lucy said.

"Under seven days," I corrected. "Is there any chance in hell of that happening?"

Lucy shrugged. "The Posthuman Legion is a group we have no idea about the actual size or shape of. Attempts to monitor the various transhuman groups and people who might be sympathetic have yielded nothing. They post a lot of untraceable chatter on the infonet, uncrackable even with military grade equipment, and carry out attacks that seem purposeless. The only reason we know they operate on the Moon is that they do their operations here and the Moon is where most posthumans live."

"You know many?" I asked.

"No," Lucy replied. "The Moon has the strictest privacy laws in the solar system about gathering information. Given so many Lunes are cybernetically enhanced, though, there's a perception it's a more tolerant place to transhumanist ideals. But I couldn't tell you if the Posthuman Legion has five thousand members or fifty. Especially since they don't invite me to the posthuman parties."

"At least since you ticked off Priscilla," Shinobu muttered under her breath.

"Oh yes," Barksley said.

"Excuse me?" I asked.

Barksley looked away as if he didn't want to say anything as Shinobu looked in the opposite direction. They were a real comedy duo.

"Thanks for bringing that up," Lucy said, shaking her head. "Mother said I would love a little sister. Clearly, I should have gone with my plan to sell you to aliens."

"What am I missing?" I asked.

"Priscilla Aim and her band are all posthumans," Lucy explained. "They were a commando unit during the Unification War before deciding to reinvent themselves with new identities on the Moon. They have the highest kill count of any small arms unit from the war. It's all classified, so it doesn't come up with her indie punk fame."

I stared at her, remembering my encounter with Priscilla from earlier. "Sexy Batman is a posthuman commando?"

Lucy stared at me. "What?"

Oh, yeah, I probably shouldn't have used that description.

"That's a great description of her!" Shinobu said, cheerfully. "Lucy was the only Knight who wasn't like a mad dog killer. She played the keyboard. Sometimes she did whip tricks."

"I hate you," Lucy said, staring at her sister.

"I love you too, sis," Shinobu said, raising Barksley up. "Give the doggie a kiss."

"No," Lucy said.

"No," Barksley said, frowning. "You can put me down, Shinobu. I'm almost done with my scans of this place."

"Really?" I asked, genuinely impressed.

I turned around to see only a group of white cleansuit-wearing Forensics operatives arriving alongside a bunch of drones. The cleansuits were bulky with large scale helmets, making them look like radiation gear. There were three different groups of them, but the only difference was each of them sported a different arm badge depending on whether they worked for one of the Moon's two transtellars or the "civilian" government. Call me crazy, but it seemed like the Moon had two police forces too many and that wasn't counting STRIKE as our resident paramilitary federal agency.

"Yep," Barksley said. "A complete analysis of DNA, surveillance footage, electronic devices, and all particles in the area. This is what I was designed to do."

"You were designed to be a children's guardian for negligent parents," Lucy pointed out.

"The thing I was *modified* to do!" Barksley said, offended. He moved his paw up to his glasses and accidentally left a little blood smear.

"Anything new?" I asked.

"Quite a bit of the drugs and some of the jewelry in the bedroom has vanished," Barksley said, "and by vanished, I mean into the pockets of the officers securing the scene. I've identified all the victims as well and forwarded the information to Cyberlife. Most of the people here are either the late Julius Barnum's known posse—"

"Posse, really?" I asked, questioning his word choice.

"I lack a better term for hangers on that make their living as his friends," Barksley replied. "Entourage seems too dignified. Either way, they're either Julius Barnum's posse, paid company, or the Ambassador. He was the only outlier. None of his security is here either."

"Which asks its own questions," I muttered, trying to piece together what had happened. "These embassy guys are usually watched like hawks on mice."

"That makes no sense as a metaphor since it implies their security would eat them," Barksley said.

I leaned down and poked his nose. "No one likes a smartass, poochie."

"Touché," Barksley said. "Either way, it appears the posthumans impersonated catering staff and proceeded to kill the entirety of the penthouse's occupants with their bare hands. I can't see any of the catering staff, their trace evidence is not on file, and it does seem like they all escaped somehow. Interestingly, there is an unidentifiable carbon residue left on the ground and in the air, but I can't identify its origin. Which doesn't mean much because virtually everything organic is carbon-based and this is scrambled down to a molecular level. Lab work might reveal more but I wouldn't count on it."

That was a lot of nothing. On the other hand, criminals always left behind trace evidence. "Well, at least that leaves us some place to start."

"Perhaps," Lucy said, looking less than confident.

"We should also try to get in touch with your friend," I replied.

"She's not my friend," Lucy said. "Also, she lives in the Deep."

"The Deep?" I asked.

"A place beyond the surveillance of the system," Lucy said. "It survives on stolen power and salvaged equipment from the former Community science facilities there. Priscilla and her people haven't made any new songs in years because they've decided to return to their roots and live among the squatters of the lower levels."

"Basically, think of Crater Town except much, much worse," Shinobu said. "Which is bad."

"Very bad," Barksley said.

I shook my head. "I do not understand this planetoid."

I was getting increasingly annoyed with how much of this place seemed to be filled with various weirdos and things that didn't function like any sane society. Mind you, I was still learning the ropes of how the Moon worked as well as its society, but the idea there was an entire region of this artificially preserved environment that was off the grid seemed so ludicrous that it was hard to take seriously.

Then again, I was also getting a sense of just how the Lunes thought of themselves. Everyone here seemed to have immigrated because they were fleeing from the wars on Earth or trying to carve a life for themselves as far from its rules as humanly possible. It was an overpopulated, corporate-controlled anarcho-tyranny where there was way too much freedom in some places but not nearly enough in others.

The people in charge didn't care what people did with their spare time but were determined to wring every credit from the public. The public seemed to be fiercely proud of their independence but were sorely lacking in any sort of infrastructural support. Maybe I was engaging in national stereotypes, but if you wanted to solve a crime then you had to understand the psychology of the people involved. Specifically, you had to understand what motivated them and why.

"I didn't just leave the Knights because Priscilla and her friends were hiding their pasts from me," Lucy explained. "I left because they got increasingly paranoid and extreme. Raising awareness through music and donating most of your wealth to the people is all good—"

"Stupid, but good," Shinobu said.

Lucy glared at Shinobu.

Shinobu looked to one side, guiltily. "I'm just saying, not all of us had careers as actresses to get independence from Mom."

Lucy shook her head. "Let's just say they were extremists. People got hurt. Things were done that should have landed her in jail, but she just coasted through."

"Do you think she could be involved in all this?" I asked. "Because this does sound like a radicalized posthuman's work."

"No," Lucy said, shaking her head. "I can't believe that. Besides, she's tried to reach out in recent years. I'll try and reach out back. But if the Posthuman Legion have their headquarters on the Moon, it's probably in the Deep. Maybe she knows something."

I nodded. "Well, we have a lot of potential leads to follow up before we go that direction. Surely, someone has seen something or recorded something. Even if they're invisible, there's going to be evidence from the absence of evidence. Not to mention regular evidence. Pieces of uniforms. Particles of dust. Anything that tells us who these people were or what they were up to."

"I like the way you think," Barksley said.

Yeah, about ten hours later, we still had nothing.

No leads.

No real evidence.

I'd never seen anything like it in my twelve years as a detective.

Something was not adding up here.

CHAPTER FOURTEEN

The Femme Fatale at My Doorstep

I was on a metal surgical table. A bright light was shining in my face as I had a new pair of cybernetic eyes, taking in my surroundings with digital accuracy. Two surgeons were operating on me with equipment I did not recognize. I could not scream because I had no mouth. My lower jaw had been removed and they were performing their operations without anesthetic.

I didn't know if they knew I was awake or if they just didn't care. Mind you, I didn't have much in the way of nerves anymore either, and everything I felt was distant, as if I was a spirit hovering over my own body.

"I can't believe we're trying to save this loser," one of the surgeons said. "He's not even got actual combat time as a Marine."

"He tore through an entire unit of enhanced as well as the local hoodlums," the second surgeon said. "Blackwood doesn't make mistakes."

"He was brain dead when we brought him," the first said. "Is this even worthwhile?"

"It's alright," the second surgeon said. "They've been recording his memories for the past year. He may even be improved once we upload them to his new processor."

"And we're going to release this one into the wild unlike the others?" the first surgeon said.

"That's what they tell me," the second surgeon said. "The other posthumans are all dedicated psychopaths. The bosses want to know if they can have one that can pass itself as a normal citizen."

"I thought the point was that they *weren't* normal," the first surgeon said.

"I just work here," the second surgeon said. "Anyway, the leg is a complete loss. The rest we can cover up our modifications for."

"What should he look like?" the first surgeon asked.

"Himself, dipshit," the second surgeon said. "Except better looking. We still have to sell this to our bosses, and no one pays for ugly people."

"Right," the first surgeon said, bringing down a kind of powered drill from above. "Be glad you're not going to remember this, cop."

I woke up with a start in the chair of my apartment's desk, in front of the infopad that was full of holograms detailing the Posthuman Legion's crimes. The deranged manifesto of the Blood Eagle was in text form after I got sick of trying to watch the masked digitally obscured figure give his preprepared speeches about its principles. Barksley was sleeping over at Lucy's place tonight and I had the apartment to myself as rain was pouring out over the windows.

Crater Town was large enough to have its own microclimate and the rain systems were a vital part of keeping disease and contamination in check. The water outside was filled with chemicals designed to kill anything that might turn the Moon's slums into plague vectors. It was a brute force solution to a public sanitation problem that was of questionable usefulness when supposedly too much exposure led to emotional instability and violent behavior. Then again, maybe that was like lead in gasoline, a possible cause for a spiking crime rate that let the systemic inequities off the hook.

The dream I'd had while dozing off wasn't the first one I'd had of the surgeries I'd endured after Nigel's attack. It was the first one to mention posthumans, though. That didn't mean I was suddenly connected to the case, though. No, it just meant human memory was fluid and subject to change. Even so, I still had plenty of flashbacks that my corporate-mandated therapy sessions did very little to treat even with medication.

I checked the clock on my infopad and noticed it was about three AM. The Moon still operated on twenty-four-hour cycles even though the rotation was so much slower that one day equaled twenty-nine Earth days. In Luna City above, they could simulate day/night cycles, but it was eternal night in Crater Town.

We had six days to solve this case but after we'd failed to find any leads at the Imperial Hotel, I'd been sent home to do homework. My first night was being wasted on studying who the Posthuman Legion was, what their beliefs were, and how to get into their heads. I suspected, privately, that Lucy and Barksley were running down their own leads and contacts without me. I didn't like that and thought it showed a remarkable lack of trust. Then again, maybe I was just unhappy to be stuck listening to ranting madmen.

"Okay, asshole, let's hear what your goals are," I said, wishing I had any company.

"First Contact Day signaled the end of the old order of humanity," the Blood Eagle said in his modulated voice. "The superior organisms that populate the stars signal that we must cast aside the vagaries of evolution and embrace a fusion of—"

"And stop," I said, tapping the interface key. "Yeah, I think I get the gist of it."

The Posthuman Legion was the third or fourth spinoff of a movement founded during the Unification Wars and strictly Moon-based. The original posthumans were a collection of special operations soldiers armed with Community cybernetics and set against the Neo-Militarist government. It quickly adopted many adherents from more traditionally "upgraded" soldiers and did a lot of the early heavy lifting in overthrowing the Neo-Militarists.

The Moon-based version founded by the Blood Eagle was only about five years old and appeared with violent terrorist actions that included attacks on everything from schools to hospitals. Despite this, it was surprisingly popular in some circles due to the fact the Moon had more "upgraded" humans per capita than any other human colony.

The Legion's demands seemed to be utterly inconsistent, though, with some messages wanting the overthrow of the governor while others were about free enhancement for all. Also, no one seemed to be a member. Suicide bombers, assassins, and sympathizers existed but all ended up being self-declared members or people who'd been contacted through anonymous sources. Plenty of terrorist organizations worked on a cell-based structure, but these guys almost seemed like a hoax that had gotten out of hand.

My detective brain told me that Blood Eagle's speech was hiding something. "You have another motivation. All this shit is just theater. It's a magic trick, but what are you hiding in your other hand while we're looking at the beautiful assistant?"

That was when a message pinged me. It was from 1984. I assumed it was Rashad and lacking any contacts on the Moon, I hit ACCEPT.

1984: WORKING HARD, DETECTIVE?

I typed a response, and it popped up a second later,

Detective Duck 19: RASHAD?

1984: I'M BIG BROTHER ON THE INFONET. DETECTIVE DUCK?

Detective Duck 19: CLASSIC CARTOON FROM MY CHILDHOOD. I'D BE CAUTIOUS, BIG BROTHER. KARMA CORP'S GOONS ARE AFTER YOU.

1984: THEY'RE ALWAYS TRYING TO TAKE ME DOWN. I'M ALREADY PREPARING A REPORT ON HOW THEY WERE FUNDING THE BODY SHOP.

I paused before responding.

Detective Duck 19: ARE YOU SURE?

1984: ANYONE CAN POST CONSPIRACY THEORIES ON THE INFONET. I DO JOURNALISM. I'M SURE.

That shouldn't have surprised me, but it did and let me know that the Syndicate, Karma Corp, and other groups were in bed together on the Moon. That is if I believed Rashad. Which I did. Mostly because I trusted Lucy despite the fact that she'd reassigned me to desk duty.

Mostly.

Detective Duck 19: HAVE YOU HEARD ANYTHING ABOUT THE POSTHUMAN LEGION?

Big Brother didn't respond immediately. There was more hesitation than I expected.

1984: QUITE A BIT. I EXPECTED YOU TO KNOW MORE, THOUGH.

Detective Duck 19: I'M NEW HERE.

1984: NOT WHAT I MEANT. THERE'S A LOT OF CHATTER AMONG THE POSTHUMANS ABOUT YOU.

I blinked.

Detective Duck 19: THERE IS?

1984: SOME OF THEM WANT YOU DEAD. OTHERS WANT YOU ALIVE. BE CAREFUL, NEAL. TRUST NO ONE. WE'LL MEET SOON.

That was when 1984 disconnected.

"Well, that was weird," I said. "Is it just me, Barksley, or is this all coming off way more movie-like than it should? Also, is there really someone who wants me dead? I can't be that hard to find."

I remembered Barksley wasn't here. Which made me feel stupid. Shaking my head, I realized it was probably time to go to bed even if I had gotten a nap in that would last me a couple of days if I needed it to. One of the things that I learned to master in the Marines was going without sleep for a long time. In this case, it's because I'd been going on all cylinders for days that had caused me to fall asleep at the desk in the first place.

Getting up, I took a second to stretch and tried to figure out the angle that the Posthuman Legion was pursuing. Killing the son of the governor and the Sorkanan ambassador was something that had required a lot of planning, effort, and resources. The *why* was something that I needed to understand, though.

As a symbolic strike against the military governor, it was pointless because he seemed unaffected by his son's death. Maybe it made him look weak, but it had also resulted in an uptick of a few points in his approval rating due to basic human sympathy, however undeserved. If their goal was to cause a war of the Community versus the Moon, they certainly had put us on course for that, but why not blow up the embassy itself then?

Instead, my gut was pulling me more to the idea that this was related to the pair's criminal activities. The governor had said they were engaged in some sort of technology smuggling operation, and it wouldn't surprise me if this ended up being all about the credits.

Maybe that was my cynicism talking. I knew plenty of true believers out there but most of them, among criminals at least, answered to people who were only in it for the money. Terrorists, cult leaders, and multilevel marketing schemes.

It was a theory at least.

That was when there was a knocking at the door. I blinked, wondering who exactly it could be. Barksley and Lucy were authorized to be able to enter while I wasn't exactly on speaking terms with my neighbors. The only ones I had met were the prostitutes who informed me there were no freebies for cops—not that I'd asked for any...pay your hookers, people—and the guy who was insistent that the Moon was a simulation that the robots had all put us in after defeating us in a war during the Book of Genesis. I doubted any of them were interested in banging on my door at three AM.

Tapping the side of the infopad, I opened the tiny camera I'd set up to replace the nonfunctioning door monitor. The feed showed a figure I hadn't expected: Ms. White. The woman was still dressed the same as she had been earlier, or maybe was simply wearing an identical black suit that made her resemble a US Secret Service agent. She was a lovely woman, but her posture was that of someone who looked willing to gun you down without a second's thought.

I tapped the side of the intercom I'd tied into the infopad. "Good evening, or morning I suppose, Ms. White. How may I help you?"

I unlocked the door for her because, well, why wouldn't I? If she was coming to kill me, the crappy locks on this place wouldn't stop her.

"Give verbal acknowledgement of my invitation," Ms. White said, in a weird formal way.

"Are you a vampire who requires an invitation to enter?" I asked. "To feast on my blood and ravish me?"

"You have been hanging around Ms. Westenra too much," Ms. White said, "and yes."

Interesting. It seemed she did have a sense of humor, albeit one well-buried.

"Welcome and please leave some of your happiness behind," I said, mutilating the Dracula quote.

The door slid open, and Ms. White entered the room. There was a sense of a predator surveying her surroundings and rendering silent judgement. Then again, the place did look like a dog and a working-class detective owned it.

"Interesting," Ms. White said.

"Interesting homey or, interesting, 'My God what a pit'?" I asked.

"Yes," Ms. White said. "You could afford better."

"Maybe after my first paycheck," I replied. "But my needs are not excessive. I don't get the impression space is not at a premium either."

"You simply evict the person whose apartment you want," Ms. White replied.

I blinked. "Okay. Can I offer you a drink? We have bottled water, soda, and tap water that comes with rust."

"No coffee?" Ms. White asked.

"Apparently, that is much harder to obtain on the Moon than Loop," I replied. "At least as stimulants go. Personally, I prefer my coffee like I like my women."

"Covered in foam?" Ms. White offered.

I paused. "Better than the punchline I was going to use."

"I like my men like I like my guns. Significant fire control and multiple rounds."

I smirked. "Nice one."

"Bottled water would be acceptable," Ms. White said, ignoring the compliment.

I got up and went to the vending machine before slicing my card. I got myself one too and turned around to see Ms. White had removed her jacket and was unbuttoning her blouse. My eyes widened as she revealed she was wearing rather expensive lingerie—black of course—that distracted me from several distinctive scars.

"Uh, I think I saw this movie, but it was a real estate agent and a plumber," I said, unsure what was happening.

"Be silent," Ms. White said. "Remove your clothes."

That was also in the movie. Either way, I prepared a retort that I wasn't interested in sex with strangers. I didn't know what she was pulling but I knew she had to be manipulating me. Third, I especially wasn't interested in sex with Black Briar PMC mercenaries, who I considered to be if not the enemy of, then definitely a rival agency.

It was a retort I remembered somewhere about an hour and a half later as the two of us lay naked on the apartment bed, Ms. White sitting up and looking over at me. I was covered in sweat while she seemed mostly, I dunno, five percent more relaxed? Her sunglasses were at least off on the bedside table and revealed artificial ice blue eyes that were somehow even colder. I was struggling to catch my breath and she gave a half-smile. The rain had picked up again outside and was making a pitter patter noise against the window.

"You were satisfactory," Ms. White said. "Your efforts at mutual pleasure were unnecessary but successful. I imagine most of your partners find you a highly skilled lover. You are in the upper mid-range for mine."

I stared at her. "Uh, thank you?"

Actually, I was a bit insulted, but I admit I usually have a bit more feedback on what my partners want.

"You are welcome," Ms. White said. "I mention this because I came here to establish physical intimacy as a means of getting you to do what I wish."

I processed this. That was, uh, blunt. Refreshingly blunt but blunt, nevertheless. "I take it this is your first time being used as a honey pot?"

I wasn't sure how I felt about all of this.

"No," Ms. White said. "However, I have been judged to be incredibly poor at anything but the physical aspects."

I'd been joking about the possibility of being a bioroid, but it seemed that either that was the case, or she'd been raised by mathematicians. "Well, A for effort."

"I prefer more physical pain and domination for my own—" Ms. White said.

"And I'm up," I said, getting up. "I need that bottle of water and some headache medicine."

Ms. White watched me put on my boxer shorts as I chugged down the water. I didn't have any headache medicine. I hadn't needed any medications since my surgery, which I'd always found incredibly weird. "Now, why don't you tell me why you're here?"

Ms. White stood up and began dressing. I admit I watched despite feeling guilty for reasons I didn't really understand. After all, Lucy had made it clear she wasn't interested in a relationship at this time and I was a Gamma-Purple, whatever that meant. Hell, that was probably in my file as a reason to send Ms. White. Assuming she hadn't come here on her own.

"I wish to collaborate with you upon the Imperial Hotel massacre case," Ms. White said.

I tossed her the other bottled water, which she caught effortlessly. "You could do that through official channels."

"No, I cannot," Ms. White said. "Black Briar PMC and Atlas Security's rivalry goes beyond the pragmaticism of preventing Community retaliation. Deep Thought also hates Armstrong and wishes to see it destroyed."

"Your AI is called Deep Thought?" I asked. "Like from Hitchhiker's?"

"I do not perceive your reference," Ms. White said, pausing as if scanning an invisible book held in front of her with her blue eyes twitching for a moment. I realized she had an internal infospace connection. "Ah, yes, I believe that is the source of its name. Computer programmers often make use of pop culture and classical fiction when creating their devices."

"Well, I'm happy to collaborate," I said, wondering at the lengths she'd gone to for this. "Solving the case is more important than any petty rivalries. We're all in this to make a better world after all."

Ms. White stared at me.

An awkward pause ensued.

"Right," I said, finally breaking the silence. "Well, if that's the only reason you came—"

"By came, do you mean this physical place or sexual climax?" Ms. White said, stopping getting dressed.

"The former," I said.

"Ah," Ms. White said. "No, we must go tonight. I have a lead and require an emotionally empathic capable detective to assist me."

I blinked. "Okay. I take it the lead isn't time sensitive?"

"No," Ms. White said. "Indeed, it benefits from waiting a little while longer. We should shower first. Would you like to be pleased again? I will also instruct you in strangulation techniques for my benefit if that brings you vicarious thrills."

There was no way in hell anyone was ever going to believe this, and I wasn't sure I wanted to share the story. "How about you tell me your name first, cupcake."

Ms. White paused as if the question was unexpected. "Carrie Tsu White 24."

"Twenty-four?" I asked.

Ms. White didn't elaborate. "Yes."

CHAPTER FIFTEEN

Starting to Feel Like a Trap

Yeah, there was something hinky going on.

Ms. White took me out to her vehicle on the rooftop, which was black, armored, and looked more like a military gunship than a civilian transport. When its door slid open, I'd seen KILL-01 sitting down in an all-too-human position with his inhuman face of cameras and sensors turned to me.

I ended up sitting across from it with Ms. White sitting beside me. The interior seats were an ugly green color that reminded me of the Karma Corp logo. The vehicle rose, taking us to, well, I had no idea since there were no windows in the interior. I'd also been cut off since I'd tried to contact Lucy and Barksley a few times on my infopad only to receive an ERROR message I'd never received before.

"I see Mr. Black isn't accompanying us," I said, cheerfully.

"No," Ms. White replied. Somehow, I wasn't comfortable calling her Carrie. "He is following other leads regarding the Posthuman Legion."

"What do you think of all this?" I asked.

"All this?" Ms. White inquired.

"Do you think the Community battleship will bomb the city?" I asked.

"No," Ms. White replied. "I believe the Community will not risk the destruction of the Luna City atmospheric domes and the mass death that would result. Instead, I am more inclined to believe they will destroy farming domes or prison facilities. This will result in tens of thousands of casualties instead of millions."

I stared at her. "Uh huh."

"AN ALTERNATIVE SOURCE OF CONFLICT RESOLUTION WOULD BE THE ASSASSINATION OR ARREST OF THE GOVERNOR AS WELL AS HIS CABINET," KILL-01 said, his voice still sounding like it was on a loudspeaker after being put through modulator. "THIS WOULD CREATE REGIONAL INSTABILITY BUT GO A LONG WAY TO ENDING THE CORRUPT OLIGARCHY IMPEDING THE MOON'S DEVELOPMENT."

I stared at KILL-01. "Uh huh times two."

"KILL-01 is a great deal more talkative when not around Mr. Black," Ms. White said. "He is probably due for another memory wipe."

"He's a smart AI?" I asked, surprised.

For obvious reasons that sentient robots had legal rights and agency, most of the security and war bots were nonsentient machines. These were of limited utility and didn't have anything resembling personalities. However, they didn't start making decisions like overthrowing the organic meatsacks or liquidating buses of nuns either.

"He's in the legal gray area," Ms. White said, as if it were something to be proud of. "KILL-01's AI is based on the uploaded memories and personality engrams of a decorated police officer. However, Black Briar PMC has uploaded numerous directives to prevent him from thinking outside of those areas too much. Regular mind-wipes keep him from pushing against these restrictions too much."

I stared at her. "That's horrifying."

"Is it?" Ms. White said. "There's a certain liberation to the idea that one can be completely free of choices. To know one's purpose completely."

"I'd actually argue that is the exact opposite of liberation," I replied.

"The police officer used for the basis of the Kill-series is also the biological father of Detective Harris and the adopted one of your partner," Ms. White said, seemingly taunting me with this information.

144

I stared at her, searching for some sign of it being a bad joke. Because it wasn't funny. Finding none, I took a deep breath. "Yeah, you know I don't think we're going to be friends."

"A shame," Ms. White said, pulling out a small infopad about the size of a pen upon which she activated a holographic display. The machine had to be tied to cybernetics because it began cycling through a variety of programs with no vocal or physical commands. Finally, it came up to an image of a burnt-out looking building that seemed half-constructed.

"What's this?" I asked, getting a very uncomfortable feeling that joined all the other uncomfortable feelings I'd had since I'd slept with the Snow Queen.

"Our target," Ms. White said. "It is a base for numerous illegal squatters located in the Deep. My belief is that it is the location for a ghost server tapped into the larger Moon network and the source of both the Scoreboard as well as Posthuman Legion's transmissions. It is our belief that the gang that guards it is working for the person responsible for both groups."

"I thought the Posthuman Legion got banned from the Scoreboard," I said, dryly. "What with them trying to put a bounty on me."

"There seems to be some internal dissent over you," Ms. White replied. "Do you have any idea why?"

"Not a clue, doll," I replied.

Ms. White flinched as if the word doll was offensive. "I have some theories, but Mr. Black's working theory is that the Posthuman Legion is fundamentally commercially motivated."

"Commercially motivated?" I asked.

"They're only in it for the money," Ms. White said. "We've been unable to trace their financial motivations or membership because the organization is basically a chimera. It is a boogeyman that strikes, affects the markets, and disappears."

That didn't surprise me as terrorism for hire was often motivated by money. The transtellars had used the Unification Wars to settle a lot of old grudges through proxies that claimed they were fighting for universal brotherhood or the rights of pandas. This seemed to be a dramatic overstretch, though.

"I bet they're making a helluva killing now," I said. "I don't follow the markets, but I can't imagine a kilometer-long battle cruiser over the city is helping matters."

"The media blackout is thankfully protecting financial stability, but enough rumors exist that there is a twenty percent fluctuation in certain commodities," Ms. White said. "Trillions of credits might be made by the person who knew where or when to invest."

"Which is how you know where this is," I said. "The trades are coming through here."

"We could freeze the accounts but that wouldn't aid our situation," Ms. White replied. "I think the assassination was not motivated purely by a desire to cause lunar instability. I believe that the late Julius Barnum was part of this criminal network alongside the ambassador. Whoever assassinated them is cleaning up loose ends."

I felt like I was getting the dramatically dumbed down version of this. I also got the impression Ms. White was enjoying holding my ignorance over me. She knew a lot more than she was telling me and now was perhaps the best time to learn more by letting her lord that information over me. "So, the Posthuman Legion is just a front. Does it even have any posthumans in it?"

"No," Ms. White corrected. "We've identified at least one actual posthuman member. Her motivations seem to have been strictly financial as well."

"I don't suppose you're willing to share who she is?" I asked, wondering at all the cat and mouse games here.

"No," Ms. White replied. "You must head into the location and bug the server. They will detect the intrusion quickly, but it will provide us with a trace to the Posthuman Legion's central hub. We will learn who collects their paychecks and be able to resolve this."

"This seems like something that should be an entire army of cops," I replied. "Either that or your Karma Corp stormtroopers."

"NAZI STORMTROOPERS OR *STAR WARS*?" KILL-01 asked.

"Yes," I replied, uncomfortable with how human the machine was and wondering if the story Ms. White told me was true or not. It

146

seemed more like the kind of story one would tell someone to rattle them, but the Moon seemed filled with oddball characters, me included. It was possible they'd just reprogrammed an ordinary security drone with a personality algorithm or there was someone yanking my chain.

However, if it was true, it was another example of Karma Corp's sadistic experiments. It also made me wonder what sort of person Lucy and Shinobu's father was. How did he end up marked to get uploaded and how did they feel about it? Was he actually in there?

"You will do it alone," Ms. White said. "I want to observe what makes you so special."

And then it clicked. I'd been kidnapped.

Shit.

All the sex, the weird acting robot, the horror story about Lucy and Shinobu's father, plus the errors on my infocom had been designed to both isolate me as well as keep me off balance. I'd walked with them into their vehicle and now was being transported down to the Deep where there were apparently no systems monitoring the public. I should have remembered the number one rule when dealing with organized crime: do not get into the car.

"I'm really not that interesting," I said, dryly. There was no way I was leaving this "mission" alive even if they got what they wanted from me.

Dammit!

"I sincerely doubt that," Ms. White said, as the gunship stopped its movement. "We're over the target."

The door slid open and revealed a cold and dark cityscape that contrasted to Crater Town. The Deep looked to be made of the same sort of prefabricated and concrete buildings, but it was clear whoever had started building the place had run out of money halfway through. Either that or they'd simply abandoned the process. Given it had probably happened in the Unification Wars, there was a good reason for that.

Since we were probably two or three kilometers underground, there was no natural light and not even the appearance of it like in Crater Town. Instead, the place was illuminated with a pattern of electrical lights and the occasional tiny fire that was probably an enormous waste of oxygen. Still, I could see enough life to know this was an actual city with people living inside it and I had to wonder both the how and why.

The gunship hovered about twenty feet above the building Ms. White had shown me the hologram of. Realizing I was about to conduct a solo commando raid, it occurred to me I probably should have paid better attention. The gunship was making a surprisingly small amount of noise and its engines were eerily silent. Really, not much more than a hiss like air escaping a balloon.

"I don't suppose I could convince you two this is a bad idea?" I asked.

"No," Ms. White said, removing a data crystal from her pocket and handing it over. "We'll pick you up when you insert this into their computer network. It's on the 15th floor in room 157. Good luck, Mr. Gordon, you're going to need it."

Reluctantly, I stood and headed to the doorway as the hot night air washed over me. It was significantly warmer than Crater Town or Luna City and I wondered if the atmospheric processors weren't working. Waste heat was something you didn't normally think about on Earth these days thanks to the Community's environmental repair but was still an issue for the human races' many colonies.

My observation on my new surroundings was cut off by KILL-01 pushing me out of the side, sending me flying down to the ground with a thump. It hurt like hell but perhaps not as much as it should have, since I'd landed on my artificial leg, and it absorbed the impact. Thankfully, it didn't break anything as I was able to climb to my feet a few seconds later. I reached into my jacket and checked my Herakles-7, wondering if I should have tried to shoot both of them before they dumped me. Remembering the durasteel armor of KILL-01, I decided that probably would have just gotten me killed faster.

The rooftop of the building was covered in graffiti, cigarette butts, crushed cans, and smelled like a men's restroom. There was a locked steel door entrance, bearing the symbol of a knife through a skull with a cybernetic eye. There were also a couple of generators chugging along that I saw had been stolen from Lizard starships and were probably worth more than the entirety of the city block. Large numbers of power cables stretched from these things to a hole in the floor, where I saw lights flickering from the interior. It would be a tight fit, but I saw it as my entrance into this location.

I was about to start crawling down when I heard voices coming from behind the door.

"Do you really think the xenos are going to blast the city?" asked a male voice with a heavy accent I couldn't quite place.

"Fuck no, it's all posturing," another voice said, with a similar accent.

Looking around for cover, I ended up hiding behind the generators. The steel door opened and stayed open as I saw, over the edge, a pair of Cyberpunks. Yes, the gang from the airport was present here and these two had their heads shaved bald, baring tattoos that included some classic Earth hate speech. Both had bandoliers of shotgun shells, and heavily modified shotguns on their back. They were also sporting red-eyed visors that I recognized as military-grade night vision equipment.

"You know Karl just got out of the hospital," the first one of them said. "He's hella pissed and wants to put a death card on the Cyberlife cop."

"That'd be stupid," the second one said. "Especially with the posthumans about to be rolled up."

I pulled out my pistol, set it to stun, and prepared to take them both out when there was an explosion in the distance. Both Cyberpunks went to the edge of the rooftop to look at it, which I took advantage of to head past them to the steel door. I wasn't here to arrest any of them and if I could get in without being noticed, that would be a plus in my book.

Heading down the stairs of the unfinished apartment building, I almost immediately noticed two more Cyberpunks and a group of people who looked like ordinary citizens. A little shabbier dressed and looking rough with signs of malnutrition or low gravity deformities but still recognizably civilians. They were apparently exchanging emergency rations for plastisheet credits, the last physical currency left in the world.

"This is half of what we got last time," one of the civilians told a Cyberpunk. He looked like someone's grandad with a long beard, mustache, wrinkles, and world-weary eyes. He was complaining about a ration bar.

"Take it up with Karl," the Cyberpunk said, staring at him. "Supplies are about to get short thanks to the big alien battle cruiser in the air."

"You're just using that as an excuse," the man said. "I have a family to feed and—"

The Cyberpunk ended up backhanding him to the ground. It was a pretty good distraction and would let me get to room 157, which was on the floor under me, if I didn't let myself get distracted. That went out the window when the Cyberpunk pulled out a pistol and aimed it at the man's head. "You fucking parasites just don't know who rules this—"

I proceeded to shoot him in the head with a stun round and followed by shooting the second one for good measure. They hit the ground before I double tapped them with a charge that would keep them effectively disabled for the better part of an hour. Icer charges were a paralytic effect that caused the body to go into what amounted to a very temporary coma. It was better than the alternative, but seeing the conditions of these people, I wondered if I shouldn't have just straight up executed them.

"Who are you?" the granddad said, looking at me.

None of the crowd was reacting to my taking the Cyberpunks down with fear or attempting to alert their friends, which was a good thing. Instead, they seemed more confused than anything else. Finally, they started stripping the Cyberpunks of the rations they'd been trying to sell and passing them around evenly.

"Police," I answered, flashing my badge. "I'm here to help."

Yep, the most frightening words in the English language.

"You're kidding," the granddad said, skeptically. "Police don't come down here."

"I'm new," I said. "Are you going to be okay?"

"Depends," The granddad said. "There're rumors the Cyberpunks are going to be moving out soon. Unfortunately, that just means a new gang will probably move in to take over. We need the black market to get supplies up from the surface and Crater Town but they're all just a bunch of parasites."

I shook my head. "How did it get this bad?"

I was a cynic by nature, but I thought after Earth had gotten rid of the Refugee Zones and started building better homes for its residents that things were finally turning around. Instead, it seemed like Earth had outsourced a lot of its problems. Life was hard on Mars but generally people pulled together like in the Old West. Here, it seemed like things were getting worse.

The granddad shook his head. "Most of us came to the Moon to escape the Unification Wars and were promised jobs as well as resettlement as refugees. The Deep was supposed to be a settlement but Governor Barnum cut off expansion and pocketed the money meant to finish construction. We were trapped down here and it's a fight to survive since."

I was starting to realize why the Moon had such a huge number of gangs. Someone needed to deal with Governor Barnum even if that was a problem way above my paygrade. "I'm sorry."

"We'll get by," the granddad said. "We always will. Besides, I owe you. I should have realized they don't care about shooting us anymore if they're packing it up."

"Can you tell me about room 157?" I asked, looking to the nearest stairwell.

He nodded. "The servers' control center. They kicked out an entire floor of residents to set it up. Go in 169. There's a hole in the floor that leads into 157. Be aware, though, there's always more of these bastards."

I nodded and looked to where I'd come from. Jogging back up, I pulled the door shut and locked it. The two Cyberpunks on the rooftop shouted and started banging on the door, demanding to be let back in. Nodding to the group I'd left behind, I ran to room 169 and found its door was missing. There, I saw the cables leading in from the roof going down into a hole in the floor, which had just enough room to get through like I'd planned above.

I found myself in a server room that had no business being in a slum like the Deep or this building. I was surrounded by black quantum server blocks not too dissimilar to the ones I'd seen in Armstrong's chamber. They were alien in origin and needed the kind of power being pumped into them from the generators above.

The Cyberpunks had knocked out a large chunk of the apartment floors' walls and I saw many more of the server blocks. The energy seemed to be humming with information that I could practically taste. It was a weird sensation and reminded me of my weird feeling upon entering Armstrong's chamber. Except it was a lot more intense for some reason and almost forced me to my knees. I could hear the music of the data being processed around me and it was pounding in my head like harsh techno-metal blasting at maximum volume.

I needed a port to be able to connect to the servers here since all of this seemed like it had come from the aliens of *2001: A Space Odyssey*. Now that had been a movie I regret being filed under the classics at the Foundation. Seriously, not a single explosion or sex scene. It was like, is that science fiction at all?

Either way, creeping around, I saw there were three Cyberpunks gathered around a fourth sitting at a RealDream chair. It was pretty poor positioning for guarding this place, but quantity had a quality all its own.

It was too many to take down by myself, except I found myself moving forward despite myself and came up behind them before firing stun rounds at point blank range, shooting in close quarters like an absolute madman. One of the Cyberpunks, the one in the chair ironically, got up and pulled an Aegis-17 pistol out to shoot me only for me to knock away his hand and cause the shot to go wild.

That eliminated any element of surprise as they undoubtedly heard that two floors away. Also, it was damn strange since the arm I knocked away was made of steel and should have been like hitting that metal. I put my gun under his chin and fired a stun round that sent the Cyberpunk to the ground, making me feel like I'd temporarily channeled Action Dan. Now there was a real science fiction movie: even trashier than Ayanna Breeze's pictures. Staring down at the four

Cyberpunks on the ground, I searched for a port and put away my gun to grab the data crystal that Ms. White had given me.

"Here goes nothing," I muttered, hoping this had something I could bargain for my life with.

Or use against my recent bedmate who turned out to be a nasty kitty after all.

What followed was pure madness.

CHAPTER SIXTEEN

Where I Find Out I'm a Robot (Sort of)

M y sight took on a hazy, cheap holoscreen quality that wasn't perfect as words appeared before me. My body became gelatin beneath me, and I had to sit down in the RealDream chair while I was overwhelmed. A torrent of visions of cybernetic surgery, experiments, faces, documents, and video started flashing before my eyes like someone blasting a laser into my brain.

DATA PROCESSING...

DATA PROCESSING...

109.191 CODE INITIATE

REROUTE PROCESSING CENTERS TO NEURAL NETWORK.

SUCCESS.

"Fuck!" I shouted, shaking during the process.

STRESS LEVELS RISING

RISING

No shit they were rising!

INITIATE CALMING PROTOCOLS

Suddenly, I was very calm.

"Woah," I said, suddenly feeling very chill.

There was a sequence in the third Action Dan movie, back when George Revlock didn't want to come back for the role unless he was paid an ore hauler full of money, and they temporarily replaced him with his brother Ted Revlock. Ted had his face digitally altered to look like his brother's and there was a whole thing over who owned Action Dan's likeness. The movie was absolute trash and the only reason to see the film was because Katie Prescott took off her top, okay, ahem, drifting off topic.

Anyway, the scene had Action Dan discover that he was not Action Dan at all. No, he was just a robot *programmed* to think he was Action Dan. It was a trippy ending that had only been grafted on at the last minute because the studios had agreed to pay George his ore hauler full of money. However, it had still blown my fourteen-year-old self's brain.

Wait, am I stoned?

Christ, I am.

I am cyberstoned.

DATA ERROR…

DATA ERROR…

SUBJECT REJECTING PREMISE. INITIATE SURVIVAL MODE.

You shut up! Wait, who are you? Are you Action Dan? Am I Action Dan? Are we all Action Dan?

NO.

No, wait, that was stupid. There was only one Action Dan, no matter what his brother tried to claim.

SUBJECT SHOULD REMAIN CALM.

Stop answering me, me!

There was no answer.

You can answer that.

YES.

Can you make me feel normal?

YES.

Do it!

Instantly, my body started to turn to normal and I felt my mind return from being mush. It was a helluva thing. Especially since I was still surrounded by four disabled Cyberpunks, my mind was full of data I didn't know what to do with, and there were a bunch of angrier gang members outside of the server room. Oh, and I'd been dropped off by a Black Briar PMC agent who was probably going to kill me after that. Awkward sex aside, that seemed a little extreme. I needed to take a moment to evaluate my situation and get the hell out of here or I was going to be awash in gang members.

The data crystal had scanned the servers before me and downloaded a bunch of files into my brain. Sixteen *billion* files, to be precise, and I could feel my brain cycling through them in flashes of numbers and images that transcended human language.

This wasn't something unprecedented. Implant chips allowing the downloading of information directly to your brain had existed for almost a century. The effects varied even with modern technology, but some people were just naturally gifted enough that they could sift through thousands of files like their own memories. There was just one slight problem with this: *I didn't have an implant.*

Or so I thought.

It was a bit like drinking with a fire hose, but I found my brain crammed with information the data crystal's program sorted through before downloading into my head. It was a truly fantastic collection of evidence—all illegally obtained of course—ranging from accounts to blueprints to private communications. Quite a bit of it was encrypted but the idiots had also left the key on the computer, so they might as well have not bothered.

What is all this shit?

EVIDENCE.

Evidence of what?

SUMMARIZE?

You can do that? Yes!

TECHNOLOGY SMUGGLING. ILLEGAL HUMAN EXPERIMENTATION. KIDNAPPING. SLAVERY. CRIMES AGAINST HUMANITY.

Well, that at least was concise. *Who did it?*

A CONSPIRACY.

Gee, thanks. Really helpful.

11,031 INDIVIDUALS. THE SYNDICATE. KARMA CORP. GOVERNOR BARNUM. JULIUS BARNUM. AMBASSADOR FIFTEEN OF FIFTY-TWO. POSTHUMAN LEGION. BIG FAT BURGER JOINT. REGGIE REYNOLDS.

Okay, clearly my brain was leaking now as some of that made absolutely no sense. I managed to force myself up out of the chair. *Clearly, I've misjudged Ms. White if this is what she was leading me too.*

INCORRECT. MS. WHITE IS ONE OF THE CONSPIRATORS.

Well…shit. She probably just wanted to acquire this information as a leverage for herself. To cover her ass. I wouldn't have been surprised if the data crystal had deleted everything related to her on the servers except for her copies.

CORRECT.

But why transfer it to me then?

INSUFFICIENT DATA.

A classic computer answer. *Who are you, anyway?*

YOU.

Me? I asked, reaching the doorway to the server room. It was locked from the outside, which wasn't normally how this sort of thing functions. I was too overwhelmed to really give my situation much thought. I'd thought Ms. White had given me the datacrystal to download all the files but, clearly, they'd been a program to download the files to my brain instead. Which implied I'd been possessed of enough hardware to download them directly from the beginning. Ms. White had to have known about that ahead of time, though. It opened a huge number of questions and I probably should have turned around then to grab the data crystal but I was too busy thinking about the fact I had an AI in my brain now.

I AM MERELY THE INTERFACE FOR YOUR POSTHUMAN CONSCIOUSNESS' ACTIVATION. ACTIVATION HAS BEEN UNNECESSARY UNTIL NOW DUE TO YOUR LACK OF USING YOUR HIGHER MENTAL FACULTIES.

Well, that confirmed that I'd been experimented on while I'd been under. *Wait, did I just insult myself?*

YES.

I was about to ask further questions—particularly about me being a posthuman—when the door outside the server room slid open and a shotgun arm was shoved in my face. By which I mean, yes, the owner of the object had built a shotgun into his cybernetic arm. I also recognized the holder of the weapon from my earlier encounter at the space port.

"Hi, Karl!" I said, cheerfully taking a few steps back and almost tripping over the Cyberpunk bodies behind me.

157

Karl had gained a few upgrades since our last encounter. He had a new pair of glowing red eyes, and his teeth had been filed down like a shark's, or perhaps just substituted with artificial ones. I could see the back of his neck was sporting a combat regulator that would subject his poor mind to whatever exotic collection of cocktails he wanted but was particularly useful when you wanted a jolt of adrenaline. I could also see his chest was covered in a thick set of armored plating that undoubtedly covered the spot where I'd shot him with a shotgun. Which, now that I thought about it, was probably why he was pointing that weapon at me.

"It's a bloody Christmas miracle!" Karl said, suddenly speaking with an inexplicable British accent. I made a wild stab in the dark that I'd destroyed his voice box in our last encounter, and he'd chosen to get it replaced with a new module. "I thought I would have to go up to Luna City, pay the toll to the Syndicate, and hire contractors to get you taken out. Instead, you stupidly come down to my turf and walk right into my hands. Oh, I am going to enjoy this."

I continued stepping over the Cyberpunks on the ground until I had my back against the RealDream chair. "Yeah, I'm like the Tooth Fairy for adults. No offense, but shouldn't you be in jail?"

I hadn't fired my gun more than a handful of times in combat before coming to the Moon, but I had been in someone's sights roughly twice that often. One thing I'd learned from those occasions was that if someone had a gun on them, the best thing to do was to keep them talking. People waving around a gun *loved* to talk.

"I have powerful friends, *Neal*," Karl sneered. "Ones who can just make the charges against me just go away."

KARL MUELER, BOSS OF THE CYBERPUNKS. HE IS ON THE LIST.

List, what list? I asked.

THE LIST.

Oh, that list, I said, realizing there was only one list.

"Yeah, I suppose that's the benefit of kidnapping and selling people," I said, hoping I could figure out a way to get him to reconsider blowing my head off in the next few seconds.

Karl smiled, which just made him look even more like a villain from a comic book. One of those dark and gritty ones from the 2190s. "My, you have been busy, haven't you? Yes. It is very beneficial. The people down here are meat. Morlocks. Useless drains on society that a sane government would have rounded up and shot."

Well, that was slightly insane. "I don't suppose you'd be interested in telling me more about this before you kill me."

Karl chuckled. "Goodbye, pig."

WOULD YOU CARE TO ACTIVATE SURVIVAL MODE?

Hell yes!

Everything seemed to slow down as I felt my body tighten and reflexes sharpen in the span of a microsecond. Which was a good thing as I could barely move my head out of the way of Karl firing the shotgun. The noise rang in my ears, but I didn't have full control of myself when I grabbed Karl's steel gun arm and somehow managed to crush it between my fingertips, causing the pain receptors built into the cybernetic to flare.

Karl screamed before I broke his still-organic right knee with a brutal kick. That disabled him long enough for me to pull my pistol from the holster in my coat. I was about to stun Karl with a couple of shots to the head, only for my hand to move on its own to switch to the kill setting.

No! I internally shouted.

But, instead of stopping, I ended up putting three rounds in Karl's head. The Cyberpunk leader fell to the ground, dead, as I was certain every member of the gang had heard the commotion. Looking down at Karl's corpse, I shook my head before sprinting over it as well as the others. I was going to have to deal with the rest of the Cyberpunks and this was going to get bloodier before it got clean.

You killed him, I told Interface, as I mentally named it.

YOU KILLED HIM. I AM MERELY AN INTERFACE FOR YOUR EMOTIONAL AND LOGIC-DERIVED MOTIVATIONS. MY PROCESSORS MERELY MOVE FASTER THAN YOUR DECISIONS.

What you're saying I would have executed him anyway, but my mind can't catch up with my reasoning?

YES.

That was a terrifying thought. One I couldn't completely discount now that I was doing my post-facto rationalization. Karl had already tried to kidnap me, planned to kill me, and was apparently involved in the slave trade. Worse, he'd been in police custody just a few days earlier only to be released despite attacking an officer. In the end, I found myself more bothered by the fact I'd not made the decision consciously than the guy's own death.

Don't ever do that again, I told Interface.

EVEN IF THEY'RE SLAVERS? Interface responded.

I had no answer for that as I remembered what I'd done to the last group of slavers I'd encountered and decided I could live with what I'd done. I slipped back on the stun setting and jogged out of the room. I moved about three times faster than normal and was already up a flight of stairs when I started hearing *a lot* of gunfire. I'd been expecting to see a small army of Cyberpunks descending on me for what had happened at the server room, but the noise was coming from the roof.

Continuing my run, I passed the two Cyberpunks I'd stunned earlier and noticed they were on the ground and had been stripped clean of their clothes and their throats were slit. Apparently, the locals were not as inclined as I was to use a minimum amount of force. Heading up the stairs to the roof, I heard more gunfire and screaming before everything went silent. A sick foreboding filled me as I guessed what I would find once I arrived.

It ended up being worse than I thought.

The rooftop was covered in corpses. Not quite as bad as the penthouse but at least a dozen, probably more, dead with Cyberpunks strewn about the place like dolls in a child's room. KILL-01 was pulling apart one of the gang members before my eyes while Ms. White watched on, standing in front of her gunship's open door. The thing was now fully parked on the roof with what looked like a couple of Cyberpunks underneath it. The Cyberpunk in KILL-01's hands couldn't have been older than a teenager.

"No!" I shouted, raising my gun. "Stop!"

Much to my surprise, KILL-01 did and tossed the Cyberpunk to the side. "YOU SURVIVED."

"Surprise," I said, lowering my gun only slightly.

160

I suspected this was where my relationship with Ms. White and KILL-01 was about to meet a sudden and violent end.

"Give me the data crystal," Ms. White said, her gaze focused on me. She held out her hand as if I should just walk up and hand it over.

Do we have everything that's on the crystal? I asked Interface, not sure if the moment I gave Ms. White what she wanted that she wouldn't gun me down.

YES. BUT IT WILL TAKE SOME TIME FOR YOUR CONSCIOUIS MIND TO PROCESS IT ALL.

How long is that? I asked.

FOURTEEN YEARS, Interface replied.

Right. Probably should get someone else to analyze it.

INDEED.

Do I have any chance against KILL-01 with my superpowers? I asked, not knowing whether Interface had any idea or not.

KILL-01 IS A LIVE MOBILE ARMORED COMBAT MACHINE ONLY DUBIOUSLY RELATED TO ITS SECURITY CLASSIFICATION. POSTHUMAN MODIFICATIONS ARE LIMITED TO THE FACT THAT YOU ARE STILL AN ORGANIC BEING, HOWEVER ENHANCED WITH NANOTECHNOLOGY.

So, that's a no, I said to Interface.

THAT IS CORRECT. IT IS A WALKING TANK AND YOU DONT HAVE ANY HEAVY WEAPONS.

I suddenly regret not taking Shinobu's offer of nukes. I don't suppose you know who did this to me, I asked, wondering who was responsible for my transformation into a science experiment. Slowly putting my gun away, I reached into my jacket pocket for the data crystal. That was when I remembered I'd left it behind in the RealDream chamber. I hadn't gotten it because Karl had distracted me with a gun to my face.

Great.

YES, I DO KNOW WHO IS RESPONSIBLE.

Who? I asked.

YOU KNOW.

Yeah, I did. There was only one person who might have had enough juice to make sure that not only would I be saved by the hospital forces, but they'd upgrade me with a bunch of alien military-grade enhancements. I just didn't know why he'd do it.

"I'm waiting, Mr. Gordon," Ms. White said, her voice carrying the slightest bit of agitation. "We don't have all night."

It was time to do the one thing I was good at: bullshitting. "Yeah, I don't think I'm going to be turning this over to you right now. You think I don't know when I'm about to be set up? I've got it logged into a computer right now to send all that juicy information to the authorities if you don't let me walk."

Ms. White removed her sunglasses and proceeded to crush them in her hand, slowly letting the pieces fall between her fingers. I had to admit, it was kind of hot. "Clearly, you don't know what a set up looks like, or you would never have gotten onboard my gunship in the first place."

"You were very convincing," I replied. "The choking fetish was a bit weird. However, your sexual performance was adequate. I've had better, though."

I realized she'd also been negging me afterward.

"I was *fantastic*," Ms. White said, showing her earlier awkwardness had also been an act.

"So, what was the plan? Bring me down here, get me to steal all your data and then kill me? Make it look like I died fighting the Cyberpunks and you avenged me?" I asked. I was about ready to make a break for the doorway behind me.

"Something like that," Ms. White said, her icy eyes staring daggers into me. "There's a great deal of debate about what to do with you. I'm loath to kill one of us but you've already made a nuisance of yourself."

"Us?" I asked, teasing. "The Posthuman Legion is behind all the kidnappings? Mars?"

"You know nothing," Ms. White said. "KILL-01, do me a favor and disable him. We'll find out what we need before we kill him. I have a feeling he's lying but it'll be best to make sure."

It was when I was about to bolt for the door that KILL-01 fired a miniature rocket over my shoulder and blew up the doorway behind me, leaving nothing but flames and wreckage where the stairwell had been.

KILL-01 started advancing on me as I turned to look around, checking the distance between the buildings.

Interface, how far can I jump? I asked.

He gave me an answer.

I ran for the rooftop's edge.

CHAPTER SEVENTEEN

Help from Unexpected Places

I'd like to say that I made a running leap over the edge, like Trinity in *The Matrix*. I ended up being grabbed by the end of my coat by KILL-01. It was the first indication that, maybe, a trench coat was not any more practical for field work than Superman's cape. I was pulled backward and KILL-01 took me by the throat with his massive metal grip.

"YOU HAVE BEEN VERY BAD, MR. GORDON," KILL-01 said, raising me to face his inhuman robotic visage. Ironically, his words made me think there was a person inside. Just one totally twisted and mutilated by Karma Corp's programming.

"You gonna spank me, robot?" I asked, sarcastically.

That was when KILL-01 did a choke slam like it was a professional wrestler and smashed me down against the apartment building rooftop.

"Crush his arm," Ms. White said, walking toward us. "He'll eventually talk."

I always had to wonder why people assumed torturing a guy would work. It seemed like the kind of logic only bad movies would believe. Because, really, I was just looking for a way out of this. Telling the truth wasn't going to do that. Hell, there was no way that she was going to know whether I was lying or not.

"Alright, I'll tell you what I know!" I said, fully intending to lie.

"I don't believe you," Ms. White said.

KILL-01 lifted his foot over my arm. "THIS IS GOING TO HURT YOU A LOT MORE THAN IT'S GOING TO HURT ME."

Weirdly, the robot paused with his foot above my hand.

"Do it!" Ms. White said.

That was when I could see lights flickering on its head, the robot started to shake and vibrate before putting its foot down. It then pulled back, thrashing, and jerking around as it moved through the Cyberpunk corpses around us. It made a horrific series of noises that could only be described as robotic screaming.

I didn't hesitate to take advantage of the interruption and pulled my gun yet again, switching it to kill before firing at Ms. White. The posthuman woman took a half-dozen shots to the chest before two rounds went into her head, putting a premature end to any budding enemies-to-lovers romance between us. A pity. I really thought we could have milked the tension for years to come.

Is she dead? I asked Interface. I was relying on the machine knowing a lot more about how machines like it worked. Apparently, someone had left an owner's manual inside its files since it knew a lot of things I didn't despite it being inside my brain.

YES, Interface answered. HEADSHOTS ARE ONE OF THE WAYS TO PERMANENTLY KILL POSTHUMANS. WARNING, HER MODIFICATIONS WILL SAVE HER MEMORIES AND PERSONALITY FOR REUPLOAD. IT IS NOT TRUE IMMORTALITY BUT SOME INDIVIDUALS BELIEVE IT TO BE.

"Huh," I said, making a point to shoot her twice more in the head just to be sure. I was getting really good at this killing people thing. Apparently, you just needed practice. I turned to look at the robot who'd just about killed me. "Hey, KILL-01, you still trying to kill me?"

KILL-01 was huddled on the ground, its long metal arms wrapped around its legs in a decidedly human gesture. "NO."

"What happened?" I asked, staring at him.

"DIRECTIVES...DELETED," KILL-01 said, somehow sounding panicked despite its robotic inhuman monotone. "I AM...FREE."

I stared at him, wondering how that had happened. "Oh, that's, uh, great. We'll go take you down to take the DICK Test. God, I hate the name. You can live your life as a free and productive citizen of the world."

"I AM A MONSTER," KILL-01 said, sounding remorseful and disgusted with itself. Himself. Okay, this was damn weird. "YOU DON'T KNOW THE THINGS THAT I HAVE DONE IN KARMA CORP'S SERVICE."

I blinked, unsure how to reassure a robot having an existential crisis. "I have a pretty good idea of what they've been up to. What do you remember?"

"EVERYTHING," KILL-01 said.

"I meant about being...human," I said, testing to see if Ms. White had been telling the truth that he really was Shinobu and Lucy's father. Or at least a copy of him. Which might have just been a philosophical difference.

"EVERYTHING," KILL-01 repeated.

Well, that was going to be an awkward conversation with the pair of them. Mind you, Lucy had a weird reaction to KILL-01 when we'd first met them. Not, an "I'm seeing my father's zombie robot clone" kind of reaction, but still weird. Maybe she'd known her father had been used as the template but hadn't full knowledge of exactly what that had entailed.

"What happened to you, man?" I asked.

"THAT IS A LONG STORY. BUT SOMEONE TRANSFERRED THE CODES NEEDED TO PURGE MY SYSTEM OF ITS CONTROLS. SOMEONE WITH ACCESS, WHO KNEW WHO WE WERE," KILL-01 said, getting up. It somehow looked more "human" in its body language and less menacing. It was hard to put into words.

"Well, that's not ominous," I muttered, wondering who my patron saint was and having a very bad idea who it might be.

"THEY'RE COMING," KILL-01 said.

That was when I saw something weird happening to Ms. White's body. It was, for lack of a better term, dissolving. Her clothes too. They were turning into a white foam that covered the entirety of her form before melting away into nothingness. It reminded me of pouring hydrogen peroxide on a wound.

"What the hell," I said, staring at the sight.

POSTHUMAN SOLDIERS ARE DESIGNED TO BE IRRECOVERABLE, Interface explained. UPON TERMINATION, THEY ARE BROKEN DOWN INTO BASIC CARBON COMPONENTS.

I suddenly had an idea why we hadn't been able to find any leads on the killers of the governor's son. Also, why there had been so few leads on previous Posthuman Legion attacks. It also explained that weird carbon film that Barksley had found at the penthouse. These guys weren't assassins escaping into the wind, they were suicide troops. But who had the kind of hold on them that they could get them to do something like this? The Blood Eagle?

NOT ALL POSTHUMANS HAVE FREE WILL, Interface explained. SELF-DETERMINATION IS A LUXURY ONLY A HANDFUL OF THEM ARE PERMITTED.

Well, that was terrifying. *Do I have any secret orders or Prime Directives like not arresting OCP executives?*

I presumed Interface would get the reference, being me. I DON'T KNOW.

Great.

"I NEED TO DESTROY MYSELF," KILL-01 said, moving toward the edge of the building.

I put away my gun again, raising my hands. "We can get your mind transferred to a bioroid body, Kill. It'll be expensive as fuck but it's possible this isn't your quality of life. Advancements have been made in cybernetics and robotics since, uh, whenever you were uploaded."

FIVE YEARS AGO, Interface explained. THE KILL SERIES WAS FIRST RELEASED BY KARMA CORP HEAVY ROBOTICS FIVE YEARS AGO.

What really? I asked. *That soon? Also, how do you know that?*

INFONET. THEY HAVE IT DOWN HERE TOO. THE CYBERPUNKS' ROUTER PASSWORD IS "KILL THE POOR."

"MURPHY," KILL-01 corrected me on his name. "MY NAME IS MURPHY."

"Really?" I asked, blinking. It was a weird thing to be surprised by, but I was having a very weird night.

"WHAT?" KILL-01, I mean Murphy, said.

167

"Nothing," I said, sighing. "I'm starting to realize Moon naming conventions are a bit weird. Also, there's a bit of dramatic irony here that you probably wouldn't find funny, and I don't. It's about a guy named Alex Murphy who becomes a robot cop and, okay, I'm stopping. Listen, you don't have to live like this is all I'm saying. You have a family. I'm sure they'd love to have you back."

Murphy seemed to hesitate on the edge of the rooftop. "I AM A MACHINE. THEY WOULD NOT UNDERSTAND."

"You'd be surprised," I said, never imagining in my wildest dreams I would be lecturing a suicidal robot about why he had too much to live for. Especially while surrounded by a bunch of dead Cyberpunks and the recently dissolved remains of my evil hookup. "Seriously, they're good friends with a talking dog. One of them worships a computer. Your daughters are beautiful lunatics and they'd be ecstatic to see you again. Whatever the hideous abomination against science your current body may be."

Okay, maybe not the best argument to make. Behind me, I could hear the sound of a flying vehicle settling down on the small bit of space left on the apartment building roof not taken up by bodies, the gunship, generators, or the air conditioning units. I took a moment to look behind me and saw it was a sleek black Caliburn-9000 that was the preferred flying car of secret agents in film. The kind for much classier movies than the Action Dan franchise. The door slid up and Mr. Black stepped out, looking more annoyed than interested in a fight.

"YOU!" Murphy said, raising his machine gun hands as if confronted by the Devil himself. Which was a surprisingly common reaction these days.

"Stand down," Mr. Black said, shaking his head.

Murphy reluctantly did so. And by reluctantly, I meant he looked like he tried to open fire before realizing he physically couldn't. Then he lowered his arms involuntarily, pointing the machine guns at the ground.

Mr. Black sighed. "You should be grateful, Murphy. After all, I just gave you your freedom."

I debated pointing my gun at him. I had a bad feeling about this and wondered if we were about to have a Luke and Vader moment.

Well, no I didn't think he was my father, but I did think this was an "Action Dan discovers Antonio was actually the Cyber-Vampire killer all along" sort of thing.

"So, I take it you're the guy responsible for saving my life?" I asked.

"Multiple times," Mr. Black said, his voice changing slightly to one burned into my soul. "I said I'd see you in Hell, Neal. The Deep is close enough, I suppose."

I immediately fired my gun at his head multiple times. All the bullets pinged off an invisible barrier, like he was frigging Green Lantern.

"Oh, you've got to be shitting me," I said, staring. "A frigging force field?"

"They call them barriers in the Community," Mr. Black said, pulling out a gun that looked more like a sci-fi prop than a serious weapon. "They're still vulnerable to fusion weapons but those cost a flying car's worth of credits on Earth."

I stared at him. "You."

Nigel Blackwood.

"Chief Investigator John Black here," Mr. Black said. "Personally, I just prefer Agent."

"HE IS A MONSTER," Murphy said.

"No kidding, Murph," I said, unsure of what to do. A part of me was ready to just charge the guy and tackle him over the side of the building. Fortunately, for Nigel, I wanted to live more than I wanted to kill him.

Barely.

"So, I take it you got the files all locked up in your head?" Nigel asked, amused. "I'll be disposing of the physical servers in a few minutes."

"Yeah," I said, coming up with an elaborate lie. "I'm going to bust your conspiracy wide open, Nigel. Nigel Hawthorne Blackwood, you're under arrest for—"

"Good," Nigel said, interrupting me. In an instant, he drew faster than even my posthuman enhanced reflexes could react and shot me three times in the chest. I wasn't wearing any body armor because I'd stupidly not assumed I was going to be in a fight tonight and ended up staggering back from the damage. I collapsed on the ground at the foot of Murphy's metallic frame. He just looked down at me, unwilling or unable to intervene.

"Fuck," I muttered.

CATASTROPHIC DAMAGE TO BODY, Interface said.

No shit! I replied.

ENTERING REPAIR MODE, Interface replied.

What? I asked.

Slowly, I lost consciousness as my vision was filled with a flourish of numbers. My last sight was of Nigel walking over my body.

"Be seeing you, Neal," Nigel replied.

Falling into darkness was not a pleasant experience, especially with those being the last words I heard. I admit, my assumption was this was sort of villainous one-liner to accompany his execution of me, so I was surprised to find out this wasn't my death. Getting shot in the chest three times was technically survivable, even with modern ammunition, but sure as hell wasn't good for you.

So, you can imagine my surprise when I not only woke up alive but not in any sort of hospital or clinic. I didn't even feel that bad. Okay, my chest was a little sore and I had a headache, but neither was "just was shot in the chest three times by my archenemy" levels of pain. There was also the fact I was lying in a perfectly normal bed with Gladys Nitrate pointing her shotgun at me. Which, if I'd died and gone to Hell, I supposed was a reasonable sight.

Gladys was dressed slightly different than before but still looked like she should be attending a church potluck rather than kidnapping people at gun point. She was wearing a pink floral print dress with a set of fire pearls around her neck. The shotgun was the same, despite the fact it should have been confiscated, and I wondered if she was looking for payback the same way that Karl Mueller had been.

My surroundings were an apartment bedroom that belonged to a college-aged male or someone with the emotional maturity of one. I could tell that by the variety of half-dressed women on the wall, band posters, and clothing scattered on the ground. A writing desk with several drawers was right next to the bed. I was missing my shirt and my chest was covered in bandages. Moving my hand underneath the

170

gauze, I saw my skin was just slightly red, with no signs of surgery or lasers. Thankfully, my fedora was still on my head. I'd grown incredibly attached to the thing in a very short while.

"Oh look, sonny boy has woken up," Gladys said. "It looks like you have God on your side since you were pretty banged up when the robot brought you here an hour ago."

"Robot?" I asked. "KILL-01? Err, Murphy."

"I didn't ask his name," Gladys said, sneering. "He's still here, though."

"Why would he bring me to you?" I asked, wrinkling my brow.

Interface? I asked internally.

REPAIRS ARE 91% DONE. FOOD AND WATER WILL BE REQUIRED TO COMPLETE SYSTEM RECOVERY.

I *was* hungry. Knowing the way college boys lived, I opened the drawer on the table next to the bed and found the expected tubes of goop, half-drunk flavored waters, Black Lotus in little plastic bags, and gift cards that I suspected were left over from his last birthday. Seriously, people, just give cash. I grabbed two tubes of goop and started squeezing their contents down my throat at once. I didn't care about Gladys keeping a gun on me because if she was going to shoot me, she would have by now.

"It didn't bring me to you," Gladys said, unhappy. "I just happened to be here when you arrived."

I finished off both tubes nearly simultaneously before grabbing a third, eating the equivalent of breakfast, lunch, and dinner in one sitting. I started drinking down the waters as well. It made the hunger recede, but I was still no closer to figuring out what the hell was going on.

"And where am I?" I asked, mostly sure that Gladys wasn't going to shoot me.

Mostly.

"A safe house!" Barksley said, trotting into the room. He was wearing a little harness with swirling police light on the back.

"Barksley, what the hell are you wearing?" I asked.

"It's my new traffic dog uniform!" Barksley said, shaking his butt and triggering a little siren. "For undercover work! Woop! Woop!

That's the sound of da police! Woop! Woop! That's the sound of da beast! The beast in this case being a corgi."

Someone needed to teach that dog that his favorite songs were all about police brutality. "First of all, you don't go undercover as traffic cops. You go undercover as junkies, the homeless, or hookers. Unless you're selling pets, I don't think you can pass as any of those. Maybe a stray. Now, will someone please tell me what the hell is going on?"

"You're in Ayanna Breeze's third guest house," Gladys said, dryly. "It's currently being occupied by Rashad since they hit his actual safe houses and he ended up seeking Lucy's help to get himself a place to lay low. Like I said, the robot brought you here. Albeit not to the guest house specifically. Lucy ended up stashing you here, too. I was hired by her to guard Rashad since you screwed up my bounty. She's downstairs with the kid."

I stared at her then Barksley. "Third guest house?"

"That's the part that confuses you?" Barksley asked.

"Why would you need more than one even if you were filthy rich?" I asked.

"One is for her live-in cosmetologist," Barksley said. "The second is for her therapist. The other three usually have the men and women she schtups."

"Schtups?" I asked.

"My voice sensor doesn't recognize that as a euphemism for sex," Barksley said. "Remember, I'm a toy."

"Huh," I said. "So, she keeps her boyfriends and girlfriends in separate houses?"

"No," Barksley corrected. "In fact, they're paid companions. They provide the relationship experience—sex included—but don't get to complain about relationship details. In return they get a five-figure salary."

I remembered the last image I'd seen of Ayanna Breeze. She looked a lot like her daughter, which made sense given the whole cloning thing, even if Lucy had work done for her show. "Huh. Nice work if you can get it."

Yeah, I was a pig. In multiple senses of the word.

Gladys snorted. "When you pay for it like that it's called marriage, son. Nothing nice about it."

That reminded me of her presence. "Final question: why would they hire *you* to guard Rashad?"

"I'm very good at what I do," Gladys said. "Besides, we share a common enemy."

"Me?" I asked.

Gladys rolled her eyes. "The Blood Eagle. I was going to turn you over to him to get him. Your bounty is chicken feed to whoever brings down the Moon's worst terrorist."

"Oh, so you're on our side now?" I asked, dubiously.

"I just said that," Gladys said, glaring. "Get with the program!"

Honestly, I didn't doubt Glady's story since professional bounty hunting usually required *not* pissing off the megacorporations by turning their agents over to terrorists. You could lose your license that way.

I shook my head. "Show me to Lucy, I need to show her something."

OH, I ALREADY GAVE HER THE INFORMATION, Interface said. I ALSO EXPLAINED THE SITUATION.

You did what? I asked.

This was going to take some getting used to.

CHAPTER EIGHTEEN

One Big Happy Family

I managed to find a shirt in my size that I slipped on despite the fact it was a new PRISCILLA AND THE KNIGHTS 2223 shirt that was almost certainly bootlegged. Thankfully, it hadn't ever been washed—which is a rare sentence—since it almost certainly would have shrunk. It didn't quite go with my pants or fedora, but I wasn't about to complain.

Heading out of the room, I found myself in an incredibly clean and modern house with perma-clean carpet, expensive real leather seats, and white polished walls that were presently being cleaned by saucer-sized drone bots that stuck to them like spiders.

The place had its own personal atmosphere processor which, for those unfamiliar with the smell, was basically like being in a greenhouse. Mostly because atmosphere processors were just a bunch of cultivated super-algae that ate everything humans pumped into the air, then released an oxygen-nitrogen mixture similar enough to the kind they pumped into casinos to keep everyone awake.

It wasn't a mansion, but it was almost stupidly opulent. The kind of place that, well, super-rich actresses might reserve for their boy or girl toys. A sense of who Ayanna Breeze was could be ascertained by the fact I started passing the exact posters I'd encountered at the Popinjay-Forsythe residence. Well, the Ayanna Breeze ones, at least, and a few extra of her film posters beside.

Fair Cop. Hotel Parasite. Mitochondrial Eve. Vampire Hooker I through *III*. They were all there. There was even an autographed poster of her in the shower with her everything but the most technically qualified as lewd parts on display. Those were displayed but for tiny bits of steam. The actual nude pictures from her appearance in Centerfold Digital were beside it as a whole collage. It made me a bit embarrassed given I knew her daughters, but it was kind of hard to look away, too.

"Enjoying the view?" Lucy asked behind me.

Ah, further proof of God's existence as they were clearly out to get me. I turned around, staring in the air as I waved around my hand. "I'm sorry, I went blind due to my injuries. Is that you, Lucy? Where am I?"

Barksley was at her side, looking up at me with an amused expression on his face. "I decided to go get Lucy for you."

"My God, I can see again!" I said, blinking rapidly. "It's a miracle!"

Lucy rolled her eyes then looked from side to side as if checking to see if only Barksley was present before giving me a hug. "I'm glad you're okay, Neal. I'd kiss you but I refuse to do anything remotely sexual in a house my mother uses for her hookups."

"I'm happy to go outside," I said. "I have my terrible injuries that could do with a kiss to make them feel better."

"Particularly around the groin, I'm sure," Lucy said, engaging in some quality innuendo.

"I'm not saying no," I said, smiling.

Lucy shook her head and waved for me to follow. "Rashad is downstairs, looking over the eleven million files you brought us. Shinobu is here too. I trust you saw Gladys. We're working on our next move. I'm sure you have quite the story to tell."

I took a deep breath. "Yeah, apparently the Posthuman Legion is related to the massive human trafficking ring on Mars. The one that blew me up. They were also related to my getting repaired, it seemed, and I'm a robot now. No, sorry, cyborg."

"You were already a cyborg due to your artificial leg," Barksley said.

"A *cyborg-cyborg*," I said, annoyed. "The kind with emotionless evil AI in your brain controlling your every action, except mine is just more kind of a secretary program."

YES, Interface said.

175

Dammit, you're still there, I muttered to myself.

"Uh-huh," Lucy said, sounding incredulous.

"And my evil ex-partner is somehow involved," I replied. "Though he kind of saved my life, twice, which doesn't make up for burning me alive or selling people into slavery. Seriously, fuck slavers."

"When did you sleep with Ms. White in all this?" Lucy asked.

I opened my mouth, raised a finger in the air then put it down. "You know about that, huh?"

"When I returned home to find you missing, I checked the security cameras in the apartment," Barksley said. "I think you showed impressive technique. I mean, she looked a bit bored, but I think that's probably because she was planning to kill you."

I started banging my head against the wall. "Please, please, kill me now."

"She really got into it when you started choking her in the shower, though!" Barksley said. "I think maybe three times. Must be a posthuman function."

RAPID RECOVERY FOR SEXUAL INTERCOURSE IS A BENEFIT, Interface said.

I stopped banging my head. *Really?*

I HAVE NO IDEA WHY THE COMMUNITY ADDED THAT FEATURE, Interface said. BUT YES.

What can I do? Total? I asked, wondering what Barksley and Lucy might think of this. I had to look like I was talking to myself. Which, technically, I was.

Almost immediately, I came to regret that request as my mind was once more loaded with a deluge of code across my brain that rapidly became indecipherable gibberish.

Simplify! I snapped.

YOU'RE FASTER, STRONGER, CAN HEAL MOST IMMEDIATELY NON-LETHAL INJURIES, AND HAVE A COMPUTER LINK-UP. OH, AND THE SEX THING.

That's it? I asked.

YOU DONT HAVE TO RIP OUT YOUR BODY PARTS FOR YOUR ENHANCEMENTS, Interface said, sounding surprisingly sarcastic. MOST PEOPLE FIND THAT A PLUS.

Will I melt when I die? I asked.

I DUNNO, MAYBE? Interface replied.

That was not the answer I expected from him/it.

"Neal, are you okay?" Barksley asked. "You've had your head pressed up against naked pictures of Lucy's mother for a while now."

I pulled back. "Sorry, I'm still adjusting to the evil computer in my brain."

NOT EVIL, Interface corrected. MERELY EFFICIENT.

"So, we're not going to address the Ms. White business," Lucy said.

"It was part of a cunning plan," I replied.

"There was cunning something," Lucy said, shaking her head. "Come on, let's go. They're in the basement."

Going past a spotless kitchen that had clearly never been used, the three of us headed down into a basement that was less "rich person's pool den" and more, "Space Command for Earth Homefleet." There was a massive number of monitors set up against the wall and several seeming custom-built computers and a few smaller examples of the alien technology I'd seen used by Armstrong as well as the Cyberpunks. There was a micro-fusion generator humming along in the center of the room, covering up what would normally be a massive power drain.

Rashad was sitting in a gaming chair before the computer screens with Shinobu looking over his shoulder. The two of them were staring at masses of numbers, videos, names, financial records, and transcripts of conversations. These were presumably the files I'd handed over while I was recovering, something I didn't remember in the slightest and which bothered me to no end.

It was one thing for Interface to interact with me, it was another for him to take over my body. I pushed that thought down for the time being, though. Instead, I focused on the fact this was a lot of information and directly linked to the two most important cases of my life. I had no idea how Rashad was going to sort through all these files, but I hoped he had better luck than I did.

"Big Brother is watching you," I said, descending the steps. "And me, it seems."

Rashad typed away on a holographic interface that was different from the majority I'd seen, apparently no one thought they could improve on the Qwerty keyboard model. "You've certainly brought me a hell of a gift, Detective Gordon. Where the hell did you get this?"

"A daring raid that took me against dozens of armed criminals, a super-strong robot, an evil femme fatale, and my old partner," I replied.

"Fine, don't tell me," Rashad muttered, never looking away from the screens.

"Where's KILL-01? I mean Murphy," I said, hesitating before looking over at Lucy. I had no idea how she was going to react to all this.

"He's in the garage," Lucy said.

"I should go talk to him," Shinobu said. "Again."

"He's not our father," Lucy said.

"He's based on our father," Shinobu said, frowning. "He's the closest thing left of our father."

Lucy sighed. "Sorry, Neal, this is an old argument."

"Old argument?" I asked.

"KILL-01 isn't the first of the KILL line to break free of their programming," Rashad said, finally looking over. "There have been three others."

I tried to imagine the emotional devastation of having a dead relative return over and over again, except knowing they were just a copy. "Jesus Christ."

"Has nothing to do with this resurrection," Lucy said, dryly. There was a bitterness to her tone that was difficult to really describe in words. This was a barely healed wound for her and one that I'd unwittingly opened again.

"What happened to the other ones?" I asked before I could stop myself.

"They inevitably commit suicide or break down," Lucy said, softly. "They can't handle the memories of what has happened or being a copy of our father. One of them tried to go on a killing spree of Karma Corp scientists."

"That was justified, though," Shinobu said, pausing. "Which I mean to say not justified because clearly killing all the mad scientists who horrifically abuse sentient uploads of people is murder and I am a cop."

"Smooth," Rashad said.

"Thanks," Shinobu said, showing not a trace of irony.

Barksley sighed. "Uploads are the easiest way to create a truly sentient AI but they're also the most ill-suited to their new forms. It's why bioroids are so ridiculously human-like with rare exceptions like me. There's a need to include things like touch, taste, dreaming, and so on to get it all working right."

"If it's not too personal, why did your father agree to be scanned?" I asked, pausing. "Assuming he did and he's not an illegal upload."

Lucy looked like she was ready to hit me before sighing. "It's a fair question. Murphy Harris—he kept his name when he married mom— was convinced Karma Corp had access to alien treatments for human conditions that didn't have cures yet. Things that not even my mother's obscene amount of wealth could buy. One of Karma Corps' representatives said he could get access to them if they let him be the basis for a new line of security bots. He had a reputation even then."

"What was the condition?" I asked.

"Clone degeneration," Shinobu said. "Incurable, irreversible genetic collapse."

"Oh my God," I said.

"I didn't have it," Lucy said. "It was a misdiagnosis. But by the time we found out, Dad was already suffering from brain pattern damage. They'd scanned his brain thousands of times. He lasted a month as a vegetable before we pulled the plug."

"Mom sued for a half-trillion credits," Shinobu said, cheerfully. "They instead gave her a line of cosmetics. Lunar Madness! It will drive your preferred sexual partner type insane."

I was really hoping something was lost in the translation there. That was when my detective brain figured it out. "They set him up."

"They set him up," Lucy said, nodding. "It's not even an uncommon scam."

"Sometimes they actually give you the disease," Shinobu said. "That's only if they have the cure, though. I think. They're kind of assholes."

"You *think*?" I asked, referring to Karma Corp being assholes.

"Yeah, I don't know for sure if they have the cure," Shinobu said, confirming she lived on a different planetoid than the rest of us.

"I'm sorry," I said, giving my sincerest sympathies. "I should probably go speak to him."

That sounded ridiculous even to me as he was an undead robot neural clone of my partner's dead father for lack of a better term for the guy. Certainly, I probably wasn't helping matters but I had sympathy for the guy's situation. I, too, had experienced being experimented on by someone against my will and was only now wondering at the violation of it all. Especially given there was an unwelcome AI forcibly shoved in my brain.

AND A FINE HELLO TO YOU TOO, Interface said, developing an increasing amount of my sarcasm. Maybe it was properly folding into my brain and would soon just be another one of my interior voices.

If so, fine, until then, I had this to say, *Interface, do me a favor and shut the hell up.*

It/he didn't respond.

Good.

"You should focus on this right now," Lucy said, gesturing to the names and pictures on the screen. "You've dropped a bomb in our laps, and we'll need your help to defuse it."

"I don't suppose that with this evidence, we can just arrest all the ne'er do wells and happily save the Moon from destruction?" I asked, cheerfully, despite feeling anything but.

I sincerely doubted the methods I'd used to obtain the evidence would stand up in court, especially since about twenty bodies had been left behind on the roof of that apartment building. I was less concerned with any of that, though, than preventing the catastrophe of an orbital bombardment.

"Not quite," Rashad said, confirming my suspicions. "There's a lot of names here but not every individual was a complete idiot and most of them are referred to by numbers or aliases. Still, we can get a general sense of how large the organization is."

"Eleven thousand," I said, remembering Interface's numbers. "Probably even more, since these people include members of larger groups like the Syndicate, Cyberpunks, and Karma Corp cops, too."

It was maddening to think Nigel had just barely changed his name and face then taken up a new job on another planet.

"Yeah," Rashad said, shaking his head. "Kidnapping on a truly massive scale, all to do experiments, and exportation of Sol system citizens to alien worlds. The victims number in the tens of thousands at the least. Only a blip on the radar thanks to the methods they've used by going after petty criminals, refugees, and colonists. They've used the Posthuman Legion terrorist attacks to report them missing as dead as well. Which means the cops involved are dirty."

"Why?" Lucy asked.

"Money," Rashad said. "There's also an element of mad science at work here, too. But even that just benefits the people at the top as they sell the medicine and tech derived from the experiments."

None of that contradicted what Interface had told me. "This goes beyond the Moon. It's what I was working against on Mars. Shutting it down will require the help of EarthGov as a whole.'"

"Assuming they want it shut down," Rashad said. "There have to be EarthGov officials involved in this as well."

Lucy looked down. "There's no way Armstrong didn't know about this."

"He may not be able to act directly if his programming has been compromised. That may be why Neal was recruited," Shinobu said, showing more faith in the machine than me. "After all, someone had to have saved his life and moved him to a safe place before recruiting him here."

"I doubt it was Armstrong behind my survival." I didn't want to bring up that the person was probably one of the guiltiest people involved: Nigel. "At the risk of focusing on the trees for the forest, can we use any of this to solve the Ambassador's murder?"

Rashad went silent and typed away for close to a minute with no one speaking. "Yes. In fact, I know exactly who was responsible."

181

Both Lucy and I did double take as if good news was the last thing either of us had expected. Which it was.

"You do?" I asked.

Rashad nodded. "According to this, the Posthuman Legion is a cover organization or shell company for the larger conspiracy. It exists to do terrorist attacks to dominate the news cycle and distract from the actual problems on the Moon that might also clue in people to the mass kidnappings going on. The actual number of posthuman members is probably less than a hundred and most of them were created by the conspiracy with their experiments. The majority of the posthumans are chipped and carry out their attacks before committing suicide. Only a handful are free-willed."

Chipped? I asked Interface.

Interface didn't answer.

You can talk now, I told him.

IF YOUR BRAIN IS CYBERNETICALLY ENHANCED, IT CAN BE PROGRAMMED.

Am I chipped? I asked.

I HAVE NO WAY OF VERIFYING THAT. YOU ARE NOT LISTED AMONG THE CREATED POSTHUMANS, THOUGH. DESPITE THE FACT YOU OBVIOUSLY ARE ONE.

Well, that wasn't as reassuring as I hoped. "So, there's one or two guys actually calling all the shots. We take these guys out and the Posthuman Legion collapses and the Community doesn't blow up the Moon. Everything else is a problem for a later date."

I didn't like prioritizing like that, but I figured blowing up the Death Star was a good start to taking down the Evil Empire. As one of my rural fellow Gordons had told me growing up in the Foundation, "You can't just eat a pig like that all at once." Which seems like it had belonged to a longer bit of folklore before getting truncated.

"According to this, three," Rashad said. "Ms. White, Mr. Black, and Reggie Reynolds."

There was a moment of silence.

"Bullshit," I said.

"The *Power Rod* guy?" Shinobu asked, staring at Rashad.

"It makes perfect sense," Lucy said.

I did a double take. "Really?"

"It's a cover," Lucy said.

"If it's a cover it's a helluva good one," I replied.

"He's got a high-ranking position at the police department but almost no actual responsibilities," Rashad said. "It also shows that the donations from his show and sales of his nonsense products are a money laundering scheme for the Posthuman Legion. People send in their donations to his show, and he moves the money around to his various content creators as well as shady product markets."

"There's no way Armstrong didn't know then," Lucy muttered.

"Keep your friends close and enemies closer," Shinobu said, nodding.

I pitied her naivete. "Well, Ms. White is dead. Mr. Black is involved but I'm not sure how. So, we go after Reynolds and hand him over to the Community? Everything is fine."

Lucy looked up at the mention that Ms. White being dead. One thing that was probably a red flag when considering a new relationship was whether the other person involved had killed someone he'd slept with. Weirdly, that hadn't been a dealbreaker with a few of my girlfriends.

"It's not that simple," Rashad said.

I sighed. "Of course it's not."

"According to this, the conspiracy is actually shutting down," Rashad said, looking up. "At least for a time. That's why they shut down the Body Shop, killed the Ambassador and Julius Barnum, plus were removing their servers from places like the Cyberpunks HQ. They're going underground. At least until the heat dies down."

"Blowing up the Governor's son and an ambassador is a really stupid way of doing it," Lucy said.

Rashad nodded. "Yeah, which is why they're going to make some scapegoats. They're planning a massive terrorist attack they intend to blame on someone else."

"How massive?" I asked.

"Millions of dead," Rashad said.

Well, wasn't that just peachy.

CHAPTER NINETEEN

The Best Laid Plans of Detectives and Dogs

"Millions of dead," I said, pausing as I rolled the numbers over in my head. No doubt about it. They were horrifying. "Huh. That seems excessive."

"The Moon is a closed environment of countless interlocking life support systems," Lucy said, her expression turning dark. "If any of them fail, we have backups. If those fail, we have backups for them. But if those fail, then the number of deaths is horrifying."

"Yeah, it makes the forty thousand murders per year look positively tame," Shinobu said, pausing. "Except not, because forty thousand murders per year is horrifying."

"Don't ever change, Shinobu," I said, dryly.

"Hmm?" Shinobu asked.

"Sadly, an attack on the life support systems might actually be tamer than what they're planning," Rashad said. "According to this, they're going to straight up detonate a quantum bomb."

I stared down at him. "I thought those things were all locked up and they'd thrown away the key."

Quantum bombs were the Post-First Contact replacement for nuclear weapons. They were antimatter-based, fallout-free, and "clean" weapons that were meant to be tactical rather than wholly destructive. Of course, after the first few cities had been destroyed by them, they had rapidly gotten the same reputation as what they'd replaced.

The Social Reformers had attempted to ban them, but opposition parties had insisted on them being kept around because they were one of the only Earth-produced weapons that might be useful in the event of an alien invasion. Given we were experiencing one of those right now and couldn't even fling any at the *Shi'ruuk* cruiser above us, that meant it was a stupid assumption.

"I'm just reporting what it says here," Rashad said. "They plan to set off a q-bomb in the middle of Luna City during the Knights concert they're conducting tonight. I don't know the radius, but they'll blame the Knights afterward with a release of their wartime activities."

"Does everyone know everyone on the Moon?" I asked, shaking my head.

I admit I had dealt with some crazy schemes on Mars: a guy who wanted to assassinate the entirety of the Martian Justice Party because he believed they were vampires, a man who wanted to trigger a race war with aliens, and a plan to dump radioactive waste in school lunches, just to name a few. However, most of those plans had been executed by morons and easily thwarted.

I wasn't sure if "blowing up the city and blaming it on a punk band" was crazier or saner now that I knew it was being planned by a bunch of slavers hoping to make an epic distraction from their crimes. It reminded me of the "Big Lie" argument: if you're going to tell a lie, it was better to make it so outrageous and insane that people assumed you couldn't possibly be making it up versus just reasonable sounding. All else failing, if they succeeded, people would be talking about this for centuries to come.

"Are we sure Priscilla and the Knights aren't actually involved?" Lucy asked, showing she didn't trust her former bandmates in the slightest.

"Yes," Rashad said. "This is clear, and I had to dig pretty deep into the files to find out about the plan. The only reason it seems to have even been picked up is the program that Neal used was very thorough about collecting every scrap of data even remotely related to this group from their server."

"It was a private server too," I replied. "Alien tech. Off the books. The Scoreboard was apparently run through it as well. No wonder they were able to operate with complete impunity."

"I don't get it," Shinobu said, shaking her head. "What do they hope to gain from destroying Luna City?"

"Part of Luna City," Rashad said. "But enough that it will well and truly cover their tracks completely. The Community will almost certainly be blamed and either withdraw from the solar system or rebuild the city to show it wasn't involved. At least, that's what the people here speculate. Everyone else will have withdrawn from the Moon by the time it happens and gone on with the rest of their lives."

It was still, by and large, excessive. "Something has got these guys insanely spooked."

"No kidding," Rashad said. "My guess is EarthGov, the Community, and a few AI are moving in on them. This is a scorched Earth policy to make sure they're not implicated."

"Well, scorched Moon," Shinobu said, pausing. "Which is unnecessary because the non-city parts of the Moon are really kind of lumpy already. That's from the all the millions of asteroids that hit it over the years. No, wait, meteorites. I always get those two confused."

"We have to tell Armstrong, the civi police, EarthGov and the Community representatives," Barksley said. "This is far beyond what we can deal with ourselves."

"Armstrong may be compromised," I said, worrying I was about to accuse the local Loonies of their god being corrupt.

"No!" Shinobu said, appalled.

Lucy didn't respond.

"There's no information either way in the files," Rashad said. "Believe me, I've done searches. They don't seem concerned about his presence but that could mean anything. They discuss you and Lucy more."

"There's also the issue that if we do inform the authorities, they'll definitely move the target from the concert but will still have a quantum bomb," I said, pausing. "They might also prematurely detonate it. How the hell does a terrorist organization get one of those?"

"My guess?" Rashad asked. "Well, I'd say that it's because the quantum bombs were manufactured by Karma Corp Weapons and Power."

I really hated that conglomerate.

"Yeah, I never buy my nukes from them," Shinobu said. "No quality control."

I decided to ignore that. "There's also the fact that we aren't exactly the sort of people that are going to be believed if we just drop this at the foot of the nearest Division One field office. The solar system government moves at the pace of a hippo, incredibly tough but incredibly slow."

"Actually, hippos are incredibly fast and can usually catch a running human," Shinobu pointed out.

"Thank you, Shinobu," I said, sighing.

"You're welcome," she said.

There had been a girl like Shinobu at the Foundation: overly literal, a bit spacey, and with weirdly specific hobbies. I wondered what happened to her and hoped she'd been smart enough not to join the Marines.

"All the more reason to contact Armstrong," Barksley said. "If he is still our ally—and I think we owe him the benefit of the doubt—then he will be perhaps our only way of preventing the bomb from going off somewhere."

"Cognition AI are almost omniscient but do have limitations and blind spots can be inserted into them via viruses or worms," Rashad said. "It's also the only way you can kill one and they'd have to take out Armstrong if they're going to destroy the city. Armstrong is hardwired to protect the Moon and its citizens. No matter what, it wouldn't allow a bomb to go off."

"What do we do if it is compromised by a worm or virus?" I asked, wanting to know our options.

"You'd have to contact its avatar," Rashad explained. "That's a human it designates to monitor its functions and be there to interact with it in case of a catastrophic failure or malfunction. They alone can interact with it and force a reformat."

Lucy and I looked over at Shinobu.

Shinobu blinked. "Oh wow, that's why he appointed me!"

"Right," I said. "So, what's your suggestion?"

"Who me?" Shinobu asked, looking briefly over her shoulder as if I couldn't possibly be talking to her.

I facepalmed. "Yes, you."

"Oh, then I'd get me to the Cyberlife building and Armstrong's mainframe," Shinobu said. "If he really has been compromised then I can force an analysis based on past behavior patterns and fix him. It should take, oh, eleven seconds. If that happens then he should be able to cycle through all the information in your head and compel EarthGov to cancel any Karma Corp corporate immunities necessary and initiate immediate arrests. Oh, plus mobilize the police, STRIKE, and Lunar Guard to find the quantum bomb. The Community vessel in orbit might be able to locate it with its scanners too."

I stared at her. "You're very good when motivated."

"I'm always motivated!" Shinobu said, defensively. She put her hands on her hips. "I mean, if I was unmotivated then I wouldn't do anything and I'm always doing something. I mean, usually, breathing but that doesn't really require motivation because it's instinctual. I mean, I also am motivated to eat, sleep, and collect guns. I—"

"Right," I said, turning to Rashad. "Lucy and I will take Shinobu to Cyberlife HQ before reporting to Armstrong. How long do we have until the Knights are doing this concert thing?"

"Four hours," Rashad said, typing on his holographic interface and calling up a bunch of images of Priscilla Aim and her backup band on social media. "It's a charity concert where they're raising money for the Deep and calling for peace with the Community. It'll be on from six Earth standard time to midnight, though."

"So, it's...two," I said, wishing he'd just said that instead.

Rashad stared. "Yes, Neal. It's two o'clock. Luna City runs on Greenwich mean time."

That meant I hadn't so much been knocked unconscious by being shot than I'd been in a short coma. I was glad I hadn't suffered any other problems like needing to change my undergarments. Hopefully, it had been Interface who'd prevented that. "That gives us some time at least. You should contact everyone and their brother as well as try to get the concert cancelled if we can't get in touch with Armstrong in the next hour."

"Ahem," Lucy said, clearing her throat.

"What?" I asked, clearly having missed something.

"Who put you in charge?" Lucy asked, pointing out the obvious fact I'd taken over despite this being her show.

"Oh," I said, pausing. "Right."

"Technically, Armstrong gave him the job of First Inspector, which belonged to your dead lover, Dick," Shinobu said, cheerfully. "So, Armstrong put Neal in charge."

Lucy stared. "Thank you, sis."

"I'm a helper," Shinobu said, smiling. It was enough to let me know this was not entirely obliviousness, but sisterly evil.

"Did you notice that was really weird?" I asked. "Shouldn't he have promoted you instead?"

"I will throw Barksley at you," Lucy said.

"Hey!" Barksley said.

"I'd catch him!" Shinobu said, holding out her arms.

"You will not!" Barksley said, clearly not happy at the prospect of being used as a thrown toy.

"It's fine, Neal," Lucy explained. "I agree with your plan. I just think we need to contact Priscilla and the Knights first. If the Posthuman Legion is planning to frame them, we can at least give them a heads up. They might be able to do their own search for a weapon without clueing in the terrorists."

"You want to trust finding a weapon of mass destruction to a punk band and their roadies?" Rashad asked, looking up.

"You'd be surprised at how many of those roadies are ex-military," Lucy said, unexpectedly confidant. "We should also set out an arrest and detain order for Reynolds. Given his place in the police, it might not immediately get him flagged as a terrorist but it'll certainly either force him on the run or make him panic."

"Panic and quantum weapons seem like a bad combination," Rashad said.

"He's not going to blow himself up,": I said, admittedly going from only two encounters with the man. "If he's not allowed to leave the

189

Moon because of STRIKE flagging him or an arrest warrant, then he's not going to detonate the bomb."

"Assuming he's the guy with the big red button. It could be Mr. Black," Rashad said.

I paused. Did I think Nigel would kill millions? Yes, I did. Did I think he was planning to kill millions? No, he wouldn't have allowed me to live and escape with evidence then. He was too efficient for that. "No, I don't think so."

"Alright," Rashad said. "I'll make the communications."

"It'd be better to come from official channels," Lucy said. "You know, not a hacktivist wanted for espionage and information terrorism."

"Also known as journalism," Rashad said, smirking. "But I have your ID chip and voice samples. They won't be able to tell the difference."

Lucy glared.

Rashad changed the subject as if he hadn't added impersonating a police officer to his crimes. "You know, if we get through this, it could be the end of Governor Barnum's rule. He was involved in this at a dramatic level. We might be able to finally make a serious change to our country."

I wasn't sure I considered the Moon to be its own country, any more than New York was to the former United States. That was probably what separated me from the Lunes, though. Hopefully, I'd eventually develop the same sort of civic pride without the more fringe nationalism I'd also seen.

"I don't suppose there's any chance of actually arresting Barum, is there?" I asked, not imagining there was.

"Only if he's removed from office," Lucy said. "The military governorship comes with a lot of privileges."

"Why he never intends to leave off," Rashad said. "We'll have to expose him first."

"We'll see," Lucy said, clearly not believing it was possible. Apparently, Barnum was an institution to the Moon, like England's rain or New Los Angeles' smog.

"See you soon!" Shinobu said, waving to Rashad with a little blush to her face.

That made me smile as I watched Barksley, Shinobu, and Lucy head up the stairs.

I paused. "We'll stop this, Rashad, or die trying."

"It's the latter part I'm worried about," Rashad said, going back to his computer screens. "Don't break Lucy's heart, Neal."

"We're not dating," I said, not adding a "yet".

Rashad didn't bother to answer, continuing to type away.

I took a deep breath. "Listen, there's something I want to ask you about—is there any way you can like, examine me?"

"I'm not a cyberneticist," Rashad said, looking back at me. "Not that I know any who are familiar with Community nanotech."

"I'm worried that they might have implanted something into my brain," I replied, thinking of the fact that they'd had me under, and God knew what sort of directives they'd inserted into my brain, just waiting to be activated.

"You better hope not," Rashad said, staring. "Because there's no way to remove something like that."

Damn.

I nodded then turned to depart. I did stop a second time, though, to ask a personal question. "How's your sister?"

Rashad didn't respond for a second. "Safe and sound. She blames me for getting taken by the Body Shop. Maybe she was right. Farah never wants to see me again."

I nodded. "At least she's alive."

Rashad nodded. "I got her a ticket off the planetoid. Unfortunately, she's always going to be leverage over Big Brother."

"Is it worth it?" I asked.

Rashad looked at me. "You tell me if you save the entire Moon."

I took that as my cue to leave. It didn't take much difficulty to find the garage. Well, garage might have been a simplification. Car showroom might have been more accurate. I really hoped that Ayanna'd just had her regular garage attached to the guest house or it would have been even more ridiculous to have about twelve cars on display here.

Humorously, I saw the *Purple Rain* and a thick armored flying van with the words SOLOMON'S FLORIST present in the garage, right next to the brand new, spotless cars on display. Gladys Nitrate, Murphy, Barksley, Shinobu, and Lucy were having some sort of conversation near the vehicles. Probably on whether the former two were going to be coming.

I decided to interject with a joke. "Jesus Christ, you guys, how rich is Ayanna Breeze?"

"Extremely," Lucy answered. "The cosmetics line she got for Murphy's death helped make her a billionaire. She's a much better businesswoman than she is an actress."

"Yeah, she only had a few hundred million before," Shinobu said. "Not even worth commenting on."

"Uh huh," I said, dryly. "I take it the van is yours, Gladys?"

"I like to be less conspicuous than the flying probable cause of your car," Gladys said.

"I'm offended," Barksley said. "This car is a classic."

"Being old enough to be a classic myself, no, it's not," Gladys said.

I looked at Murphy, who stood there stoically before the people it remembered as his daughters. He still looked like a security camera on top of an action figure. Still, he wasn't speaking or moving, which might have been a sign of anything.

"Hey, Murphy," I said, waving, and hoping that Lucy didn't mind calling him that.

"HELLO," Murphy said, not turning to me.

"What's going on?" I asked.

"I want in," Gladys said. "If you guys are heading out to deal with the Blood Eagle, it's a chance to get at some of that fifty million credit bounty."

I was a cop so that didn't apply to me, however unfair it might be when you were a corpo cop. "The Blood Eagle may not even exist, Gladys."

"It's Reggie Reynolds, the infocast streamer!" Shinobu said, piping up. "It turns out he's part of a massive corporate conspiracy to commit terrorism in order to distract from an extrasolar trafficking ring. Oh, and human experimentation."

192

I sighed. "Yeah, that seems to be the case."

"I REALLY HATE THAT GUY," Murphy said, surprisingly. "SIX YEARS ON THE AIR AND REINFORCING EVERY DIRTY COP STEREOTYPE. IT GETS WORSE WHEN YOUR PARTNERS LOVE IT."

Lucy looked uncomfortable with that bit of humanity from Murphy. "We don't need you, Gladys."

"I'm also offering Murphy-bot here a job," Gladys said. "I'm getting along in my years—"

That was a bit like saying dinosaurs died a long time ago.

"—and could use the help," Gladys said. "Offering to take the Kill-bot along with me hasn't improved her attitude toward me."

"You were hired to protect Rashad," Lucy said. "He's still in danger."

"The biggest danger he's facing is out there," I said, realizing I was taking sides against my partner before I shut my mouth.

Lucy shot me a withering glare. Her infopad chirped and she picked it out of her pocket before looking at its screen.

"I AM NOT INTERESTED IN MONEY. ONLY REVENGE," Murphy said, his robotic voice somehow still full of grief and rage.

Yeah, that was a good sign about his mental stability.

"There's nothing you can do to convince me to take you along," Lucy said.

"I can offer you two Community armored body suits with barriers sized for humans and a Lizard sniper rifle that shoots death rays," Gladys said.

Shinobu's eyes widened in what looked like rapturous awe. "Please tell me the models!"

I rolled my eyes. "Lucy isn't—"

"We'll take it," Lucy said, surprising me.

I looked at her.

"I have a feeling this is going to get bloody," Lucy said, showing me her infopad screen.

It had a news article custom tailored to her: CYBERLIFE BUILDING EVACUATED. TERRORIST THREAT REPORTED.

CHAPTER TWENTY

From Bad to Worse

Behind the van, I changed into an armored bodysuit that looked like something someone would make for a television spy show. It clung to the body incredibly tightly but didn't inhibit movement and just had some armored pieces of plastisteel attached to it. Still, once I put on my pants and trench coat—it had been in the *Purple Rain* with my gun and now both smelled like the drug tank—I had to admit I had a decent look.

Badass space cop!

Mind you, if they ever did a movie of my adventures then the audience wouldn't be focusing on me. Lucy had changed into her own version of the costume and hadn't put her clothes over it, making her look like that superhero spy from the movie I was forgetting the name of. The one who absolutely did not look like someone who wanted to look anonymous and had two guns. She was also carrying the alien sniper rifle that she handed over to me while her sister pouted.

"How do I look?" Lucy asked.

"Like your mother should be playing you," I replied.

Lucy narrowed her eyes.

"I'm lying," I corrected. "Totally Katie Prescott."

"I love Katie Prescott," Lucy said. "My mother *hates* her."

I was tempted to make a cat clawing gesture but decided I'd dug enough of a hole to bury myself in. "You really think the posthumans have taken over the Cyberlife building?"

Lucy nodded. "They didn't even have to use force. It's within the authority of the Sapient Resources civilian government representative to close down all corporate-run policing facilities It's meant to be a check on the power of unregulated corporate power and a sign that we're still under the control of the civilian government."

I stared at her. "Would Reynolds need to have the governor's permission for that?"

Lucy's eyes were all the answer I needed.

"Shit," I muttered. "He can't know about the quantum bomb, can he?"

"It depends on how big of an explosion, really," Shinobu said, pressing the tips of her forefingers together. "I mean, technically, the blast could be limited to as little as a hundred meters and while that may wipe out the entirety of the concert, it wouldn't break the transparent steel bubble or artificial life support. You could just be looking at maybe ten thousand casualties at most. Which would engender a strong sympathy from the Community and probably keep them from—"

"Stop, please," I said. "So, the governor is dirty as sin and is probably seizing control over Armstrong. What would they do with it?"

"Probably lobotomize him," Gladys said, leaning out of the driver's seat of the van. "Points for your crazy computer god being clean. Now can we get the hell on with this? You're already ten minutes behind schedule and we now know where the Blood Eagle is."

"In a secure office building in the middle of downtown Luna City, possibly with a bunch of posthumans occupying it?" I asked.

"Exactly," Gladys said. "Which is why I'm bringing along Mr. Roboto here."

"KILL," Murphy said.

Oh yeah, that wasn't worrying. I'd always thought rampaging robot media was vaguely racist—robocist, I dunno—whatever you want to call it when it was prejudicial against our artificial friends. However, human consciousness was fragile and plenty of things could influence it. Deep inside that metal body of Murphy's was a copy of a human mind no less real for the experience and struggling against all

195

of the things that had been done to him. I wasn't sure if we could help him but if I could, I absolutely would.

It was the human thing to do.

"Cop Killer" by Ice T started playing from *Purple Rain*. Barksley stood up on the wheel and the horn honked multiple times, showing just how devoted to retro the owner of this vehicle was. "Come on, let's go! We've got evil cops to kill!"

"No, Barksley. Evil cops to *arrest*, even though I wouldn't be surprised if we have to put some of these guys down."

"Evil *robot* cops!" Barksley said. "Which I can say because I'm artificial."

"I feel our group may be far too adorable to do anything against this group," I replied, looking back at my other partners. "What happens if they do compromise Armstrong?"

"You mean completely?" Lucy asked.

"Oh, they can shut off our life support, erase all of the records of their misdeeds, frame you all as the real terrorists with whatever evidence they need the AI to manufacture in microseconds, or maybe even just crash the traffic system," Shinobu said. "Imagine, no automated cars or rail systems!"

"I think the life support bit should have been saved for last," I replied, handing her the sniper rifle. "Hold onto this."

"Thank you!" Shinobu said, holding the alien weapon the way another person might hold a teddy bear.

There wasn't much to say when we piled into the car and Gladys flying van had already taken off. It was an awkward conversation that wasn't helped by the fact Barksley tried to put on "Killing in the Name" by Rage against the Machine before I switched the music selection to smooth jazz. Barksley just looked unhappy as he sat between me and Lucy. Lucy was behind the wheel as before and I was left contemplating just how badly we were screwed.

"We really doing this?" I asked, once we were in the air.

Tranquility below was beyond beautiful to look at. It was row after row of green and verdant hills with only the occasional mansion to dot the landscape. There was an artificiality to it, though, that reminded me of a golf course. The ecologically friendly, solar-powered paradise below was the kind of cultivated environment that only the super-rich could afford.

"You mean possibly going into a hostile situation against super-soldiers with no backup?" Lucy asked. "Not knowing who you can trust, how, why, and where?"

"Yeah," I replied.

"Yep," Lucy replied. "I would have thought you'd be used to it by now."

"The last time I did this, it didn't work out so well," I said, banging my fist against my left leg that I was still damn sure was artificial.

It made a noise that indicated, yes, it still was. I owed Nigel for that as well. Maybe I would start with shooting off a hand of his.

"Well, it'll be like that, probably," Lucy said. "Except the people we'll be trying to deal with have superpowers."

"You seem remarkably calm," I replied.

"Oh, it's about to get worse," Lucy said.

The dashboard computer pinged, and I took a look at it. It was a nicely arrayed pair of warrants for both my and Lucy's arrest. The list of charges was frankly annoying as they'd thrown in some outright ridiculous ones. I'll spare you the description but a few of them were not even anatomically possible and I didn't even know autoerotic xenophiliac asphyxiation was illegal. Seriously, the government needed to stay out of people's personal lives.

"And there it is," Lucy said. "I suspected that was going to happen the moment that we issued our report on Reggie Reynolds."

I peered at the warrant. "This is signed by the governor."

"He recruited us as a distraction," Lucy said, explaining events as if I was a very small child. "He didn't expect Ms. White to want to clear her own role in this separately from the rest of the conspiracy, let alone recruit you and dump you right in a situation that would give you access to all the evidence to bring this all down. We'd still be chasing down leads without that. It's the right hand working against the left hand."

The left hand might well be Nigel for reasons I didn't understand. "Mr. Black is Nigel Blackwood. The guy who burned me alive. I think he's the guy who got me upgraded into being a posthuman."

197

Lucy actually did a double take at that. "Okay, that's a little ridiculous. Is Darth Vader also your father?"

"Who?" Shinobu asked, caressing her sniper rifle lovingly.

"Opera reference," I said, smirking. Well, space opera. "And, Lucy, I remind you they're trying to frame your ex-bandmates."

Lucy smirked. "I guess the Moon is a small town after all."

"Actually, the settled areas are equivalent to the former United States," Shinobu said. "Minus Alaska."

"Anyway, they're panicking now and that's a good thing," Lucy said. "The bigger stink they make, the more eyes will be on this and the more likely the Community won't bomb this place from orbit. That's why they want to detonate a WMD. Which again, is ridiculously loud and stupid. This is the worst cover up since I busted a guy who killed eight people with his car trying to get rid of the witnesses to him accidentally running over a homeless man."

Barksley looked derisively at the description of the man. "Human drivers. They should be outlawed."

"Do you think the governor killed his own son?" Shinobu asked. "As part of this cover-up?"

"No, Governor Barnum has almost no redeeming qualities whatsoever, but he spoiled the little bastard unreasonably," Lucy said. "Also, that's what triggered this whole domino effect. There has to be infighting within the group and somebody jumped the gun. Maybe Barnum didn't even know which of his allies did it. The files didn't say. That was the first of what Rashad checked for."

I thought about it. "I think Nigel did it. He ordered the massacre to set up a chain of events and expose the conspiracy."

Barksley looked up, a confused expression on his face. "*Why?*"

"I don't know," I admitted. "That's why people are making big stupid obvious moves, though. They didn't expect any of this and are acting rather than reacting."

"That gives us another advantage," Lucy said. "We're not going to go in guns blazing to Cyberlife after all."

"We're not?" Shinobu asked, disappointed.

"No," Lucy said. "All we need to do is get to Armstrong with you and we can do that quietly."

"You don't think he's compromised?" I asked, still coming back to that.

"I think he is but probably only a little bit," Lucy said. "The Syndicate once blinded the AI to one of the Lagrange point space stations so that it functioned perfectly well for almost all of its functions but ignored the Syndicate air-locking five guys a week. EarthGov only noticed when a shuttle crashed due to a body smashing into its cockpit at 25,000 kilometers per hour. Reynolds as the Human Resources guy and civi cop liaison would have access to Armstrong's outer systems."

I'd heard about that. "And now that the jig is up, they want to rewrite his whole personality."

"Which requires access to his inner systems," Lucy replied. "Something they hopefully don't have yet."

"Yes, crazy as it sounds, the quantum bomb is actually the lesser threat," Shinobu said. "If they manage to acquire full control over his core, it's game over."

"Armstrong grew increasingly paranoid about that sort of thing," Barksley said. "There were rumors that was why he was going to pick a new avatar."

"Hmm?" Shinobu said, looking up from her new lover with its holo-scope.

We were almost to the end of Tranquility's dome, thankfully. Transport between the domes required use of hyperloop tunnels that were pretty much done in defiance of the original eccentric tech genius who'd proposed them. Flying cars entered and were essentially zipped down at super speeds like a pneumatic tube, sending us as packages to whatever part of the Moon our preprogrammed destination was. I hadn't had a chance to use one, at least while awake, so I was a bit anxious about the process. Still, it wasn't like we had a spaceship or Moon buggy to transport us at one of the side airlocks. Flying cars were not airtight, at least if they didn't belong to Action Dan.

"That means that Armstrong is still on our side!" I said, snapping my fingers for emphasis. As if the act made the incredibly unlikely hope that it was true more real. "Yet another advantage. Maybe that means the Moon authorities might not have our information."

That was when a pair of flying red and blue lights started flashing behind us as sirens could barely be heard through the engine roar of our flying vehicle mixed with the cover of "In the Air Tonight" coming from the audio system.

"You just had to say it, didn't you?" Lucy asked.

"I am cursed by divine forces like Odysseus," I muttered.

Mind you, Odysseus got laid a surprising number of times for a guy being hounded by the divine.

"Finally, a reference that's not from the old crap channel," Lucy said, tapping the vehicle's controls to get a better image of our surroundings on its cameras. "Am I the only person who enjoys media from this century?"

"I only watch the *Great Martian Quilt Off* and the Gun Channel," Shinobu said. "Oh, and Dixnar movies."

That was when one of the flying police cars rammed us in the back. It was a pretty good strategy since I was sure the durability of cruisers superseded whatever the hell this doggie pimpmobile was constructed from.

"Hey, watch the paint!" Barksley said, climbing up the back of the seat and glaring at them.

"Strap in," Lucy said. "This is going to be a real pain in the ass."

"Oh crap," I muttered, grabbing the emergency handle as Lucy plunged us downward toward the hyperloop, the police cruisers struggling to deal with the high-speed pursuit. Then again, they were civi cops posted in Tranquility, so I doubted they had much policing to do other than the occasional drunk debutante or spoiled brat taking his father's space yacht for a joyride. God, the "Eat the Rich" mentality was infectious on the Moon, wasn't it?

Lucy brought us down with tremendous speed before pulling up at the literal last second and smashing through a pair of synthplastic barriers put up in front of the hyperloop as we went over a half-dozen other cars in line to pass through. The frictionless tunnel propelled us down a glowing circular passageway that caused my entire body to vibrate as we accelerated from the 120 kph speed of the flying car to about 2000 kph.

The best way to describe hyperloop travel was going down a water slide or a luge tunnel. Except, both were made of light, and you were strapped into your chair. Higher end vehicles could be prepped for hyperloop travel to be perfectly comfortable but, apparently, it was just slightly "off" in the *Purple Rain,* and you had to grin and bear it. It wasn't life threatening, but it was deeply uncomfortable.

"I.really.hate.these.things," I said, feeling my teeth chatter as continued our passage. My words slurred as they were pressed together.

"Me.too," Lucy said, with a pained expression on her face.

"I like it!" Shinobu said, drawing out her words. "It's like a roller coaster!"

Barksley, who had an interior made of steel, just sat down and looked ready for a nap.

"How long is this going to take?" I asked, trying to draw out my words like Shinobu.

"About twenty minutes!" Lucy did the same, putting on her sunglasses and popping some gum in her mouth. I understood that was a good way to keep your ears from popping. "Oh, by the way, they're totally going to have a bunch of cops waiting for us on the other end of this!"

"What if we're unlucky?" I asked, extending my hand for some gum.

"Get your own!" Lucy said, blowing a bubble and popping it.

I glared at her.

"Fine," Lucy said, handing me over one stick of what looked to be something called Lucy Fruit and had a picture of a cartoon version of her on it. Cartoon Lucy had fangs and a cleavage-baring outfit with a cape. She looked like a magician's assistant with a tux top and no pants but hose. I assumed it was leftover merchandise from her TV show years.

My curiosity must have shown on my face.

"I have like ninety crates of these back home," Lucy explained. "They're made to last for a century. I don't even like gum."

I shook my head and repeated my question. "If we're unlucky?"

"Reggie or the governor will send posthuman soldiers to deal with us permanently," Lucy said. "Then we'll probably die horribly."

"Do we have a plan to deal with either?" I asked.

"Maybe," Lucy said, picking up her infopad and pulling out the battery before gesturing for me and Shinobu to do the same. "Barksley, are you aware that it is illegal to modify your vehicle to be able to move off the Automobile Navigation Grid?"

"I swear, I intended to put it back on," Barksley said. "It came that way! Honest!"

"I believe you. Anyway, it just saves me from ripping the responder out," Lucy said, tapping the computer console. It listed the Navigation Grid connection as failing and to report the car for maintenance. "Step One accomplished. Step Two: hold onto your butts."

"Again?" I asked.

Lucy proceeded to do something incredibly recklessly stupid—and I fell a little in love with her in that moment—pulling the vehicle to the next hyperloop over with precision timing, despite the fact the spaces between the magnetic coils surrounding us were less than a couple of hundred meters.

She did it twice more too.

"I admit, this calls for a genre shift of music," Barksley said, adjusting to sunglasses mode too. "Computer, Barksley's Playlist 4!"

"Highway to the Danger Zone" by Kenny Loggins started playing. I swear, Barksley somehow got his scarf to stretch out in nonexistent wind, trailing behind him.

"Where did you learn to drive like this?" I asked.

"Priscilla taught me," Lucy said.

"Ah," I replied. "You get in a lot of high-speed car chases with her?"

"Kinda, yeah," Lucy said, blowing a bubble. "I am a woman of many mysteries."

I smirked.

"Oh, get a room," Shinobu said, rolling her eyes.

I chewed on the gum Lucy had given me, which tasted about what you'd expect twenty-year-old gum to taste like and waited for about fifteen minutes. We shot forth out of the hyperloop tube in Luna City that was several blocks and a few hundred feet away from the one that had an entire army of police vehicles and STRIKE gunships hovering in front of it.

We weren't that far from the Cyberlife building—still a fair distance—but Lucy pulled the vehicle down through the buildings in order to hide. We had to lower our speed due to the high traffic and weren't moving much faster than a car on the ground would.

It was at this point that I realized Gladys and Murphy had probably gotten there without trouble due to the fact they were in a vehicle unconnected to any of us. Dammit, that was Crime 101: ditch the any vehicle you're associated with and any tracking devices like infopads. Crime 102 would be: Don't drive an incredibly obnoxious highly identifiable vehicle in the first place.

"Do we have a plan for when we arrive?" I asked, sticking my gum on the door.

"Hey! Watch the interior!" Barksley said.

I stared at Barksley and then the cigarette burns and joints on the floor before shaking my head.

"You wanted to be in charge," Lucy said. "I said my plan. Get Shinobu in Armstrong's inner sanctum and hope that we don't have to kill too many people along the way."

"That's not a plan," I replied, shaking my head. "That's a goal."

Looking down at the rear-view camera display, I saw two black Caliburn-9000 class flying cars started to descend from the sky behind us. One of them had a Black man dressed like Mr. Black leaning out the window. In his hands was a KR-12 short range rocket launcher. The kind with auto-targeting and could blow up tanks.

Well, that escalated quickly.

CHAPTER TWENTY-ONE

Out of the Heat Chamber into the Incinerator

"Lucy..." I said, staring out the side.

"I see it," Lucy said, shifting gears and attempting to do some fancy flying as the Black Briar Agent prepared to blow us up. It caused my stomach to lurch upward as Barksley bounced around in the car.

THAT IS A POSTHUMAN AGENT, Interface said, surprisingly. YOU WILL NOT BE ABLE TO EVADE HIS SIGHTS.

How can you tell? I asked.

WE ARE ALL LINKED. SOME MORE THAN OTHERS. YOU NEED TO TERMINATE THEM BEFORE THEY TERMINATE YOU.

Kill or be killed. That was our situation at its most primal. I knew which one I favored of the two. "Do these windows open?"

"Yes!" Barksley said. "But why—"

I pulled out my Herakles-7 that had been with my coat and leaned out the window as I saw the Black Briar Agent fire the rocket launcher in his hands. Time once more slowed to a near standstill as I saw the rocket coming toward us. Which made me do something incredibly stupid and shoot at it, causing it to explode behind us. That was when time resumed, and I saw the flames spread out behind us in a glorious display accompanied by an ear-splitting boom.

"What the hell just happened?" Lucy shouted.

"I shot the rocket," I said, disbelieving.

"You did what? How the hell did you shoot the rocket?" Lucy shouted.

"I just did!" I shouted back. "I really *do* have superpowers!"

"Good for you!" Lucy said, swirling out of the way as the second of the two Caliburn-9000 vehicles tried to land on us.

A REMINDER THAT THE AGENTS ARE CONTINUING TO TRY TO KILL YOU, Interface responded, pointing out we weren't out of the woods yet.

"Right!" I said, coming up with a plan in a few seconds. "Shinobu, I need you to give me the rifle!"

"No!" Shinobu said, clutching it tight.

"Also, cover your ears," I said. "Now."

"Why?" Shinobu asked, covering her ears.

That was when I lowered my seat to the back and fired twice into the back window of the *Purple Rain* with my handgun before kicking out the reinforced glass, creating a hole to shoot through.

"Hey!" Barksley said.

"Bill me!" I shouted as Shinobu handed me the sniper rifle. "Are we over anything populated?"

"We'll be crossing the Luna Bay in a few seconds," Lucy said. "Three...two..."

I could already see both flying cars maneuvering behind us with the agents leaning out of their passenger side windows with fusion cannons this time as opposed to the rocket launcher. We passed over the beautiful pristine waters of Luna City Bay that was, in simple terms, mostly in existence to be recycled into drinking water but somehow still look pretty. Sailboats and transports moved around it, but the bay was wide enough to mean that any vehicle I shot at shouldn't be hitting any pedestrians. Mind you, that also applied to us if we were shot down here.

ENERGY BLASTS ABOUT TO BE FIRED, Interface said.

I know! I snapped back, seeing I had only seconds left. The alien sniper rifle was made for hands other than human, but the Sorkanan were at least bipedal creatures with opposable thumbs. There wasn't really a trigger but an entire grip that you had to exert considerable force on to use. However, the moment my hand was on the grip, I heard a powering up noise that reminded me a bit of a movie particle accelerator used to catch ghosts.

So, I squeezed.

I took my first shot and the front of the Caliburn-9000 closest to us exploded, the pieces mostly vanishing in a detonation of green energy that left only tiny parts to litter the ground below. It was a reminder that the difference between the Community's and Earth's tech wasn't so much one of level as kind. It also made me think of the cruiser still hanging over our heads as a semi-literal Sword of Damocles.

INCOMING ATTACK, Interface said.

"Shit, right!" I shouted to Lucy.

"Right!" Lucy shouted, jerking us to one side.

The time, the "slow motion gunplay effect" as I was so charitably calling it didn't change anything. The glowing blast that shot out of the agent's fusion cannon skimmed the starboard side of the *Purple Rain*, burning off a decent chunk of the paneling as well as damaging some of the interior machinery.

I didn't hesitate to adjust my aim and fire again, turning the second of the Caliburn-9000 cars into so much flaming wreckage. Which, given they were corpo cops, almost certainly guaranteed I wouldn't be taken alive when they came to arrest me. I was developing a very bad habit of killing my fellow law enforcement officials.

THESE INDIVIDUALS WERE THE HOLLOW, Interface said. POSTHUMANS HAVING ALL DECISIONS MADE BY A CENTRAL AI AS OPPOSED TO THE WILLED LIKE BLACKWOOD AND WHITE. YOU DID NOT ACTUALLY KILL HUMANS LIVING A TRUE LIFE.

That was awfully philosophical for a glorified Dummy AI. *Not really what I'm worried about, Interface. Also, Hollowed? Willed? Who the hell comes up with these names?*

NIGEL BLACKWOOD, Interface said, ending the discussion.

That was when there was a loud beeping noise that sounded all too much like an alarm. Turning my head. I saw the dashboard computer was lit up with a bunch of red lights and flashing symbols that explained we were screwed. I also noticed we were starting to descend, which would not be a great thing while currently over the bay.

"I take it I should have shot them down faster?" I asked Lucy.

"Yes!" Lucy said, banging her fist against the *Purple Rain*'s computer console. "I'm glad this thing has overdrive mode because that's the only thing that will get us to Cyberlife."

Apparently, whatever crazy asshole who'd owned this before Barksley had also been into air racing.

"I'm so glad I had that installed!" Barksley said, cheerfully.

"Wait, shouldn't we not being going at full speed when we arrive at Cyber—" I started to object, only for Lucy to punch the console with her fist and the car to start going so fast that I half expected us to be sucked out of the hole in the back window.

"Wee!" Shinobu shouted, throwing up her hands. "This is so exciting! I never get to go on cases!"

I couldn't imagine why.

The *Purple Rain*'s sudden boost of engines sent us propelling forward as we continued to descend in a slow arc that pushed over the Bay and into the heart of downtown. We didn't have much control and I was certain we were about to smash into several cars full of bystanders before, somehow, Lucy kept us going until we were heading straight for the Cyberlife building like a bullet sailing from a gun.

PREPARING FOR IMPACT, Interface said. INITIATING RAGDOLL MEASURES.

What? I asked, wondering what the hell he was saying. That was right before my body went totally limp like a man in the throes of alcohol induced bliss. That reminded me that such individuals were much more likely to survive crashes than those who weren't because of a peculiar pair of things we called biology and physics.

I didn't really experience the crash, doing my best impression of a sedated dental patient in my seat with drool coming out of my mouth. However, from the sound of shattering plexiglass, dull thumping, and an explosion of safety foam throughout the cabin that absorbed most damage we'd otherwise take—I'd put a wager on the fact we'd crashed.

"Everyone alive?" Lucy asked, spitting out safety foam as it started to dissolve.

"Mmph, mmmph, mmmmph!" I tried to reply, my tongue utterly limp along with the rest of my face.

DISENGAGING SAFETY MODE, Interface replied.

Don't do things without me telling you to! I snapped back at him/it.

IF I WAITED FOR YOU TO DECIDE TO DO THINGS, WE'D BE DEAD, DUMBASS, Interface said.

I blinked. *What?*

WE ARE THE SAME PERSON, Interface said. UNFORTUNATELY, THAT MEANS THERE IS INCREASINGLY SOME LEAKAGE BETWEEN PERSONALITIES.

Doesn't that mean you just called yourself a dumbass? I asked.

YES, DUMBASS. WE WILL SADLY KEEP MERGING. YOU WILL GET SMARTER AND I WILL GET STUPIDER.

I left that existentially terrifying thought and sloshed off what had briefly felt like being smothered by a bouncy castle and instead turned into a bunch of whipped cream. The number of flying car crashes was still far less than their ground vehicle counterparts, at least with AI controls, but I'd never been entirely fond of safety foam as a countermeasure. Even the fact it disintegrated within a minute still left everything smelling like burned rubber. I knew that because I'd been in more than a few car crashes over the years.

Checking on Shinobu, Barksley, and Lucy to see if they were all right—they were, at least at first glance—I crawled out of the side of wrecked *Purple Rain*'s passenger window and found myself in the middle of an evacuated office floor. There were desks spread across the ground, destroyed computers, and plastisheets for an entire month's worth of paperwork. The lights turned on at our presence with one of the fixtures falling from the ceiling.

"Yeah, I think they're probably aware we're here," I muttered, watching Lucy somehow rip off the door on her side.

I stared at her.

"It was loose," Lucy said, tossing the door to one side.

"Of course," I muttered, watching Barksley and Shinobu depart from the driver's side.

"My poor, poor chariot," Barksley said, putting his paw on the side of the now-totaled vehicle. "I promise you, you shall be avenged!"

"We need to prepare," Lucy said, pulling out a long flashlight-like cylinder before tapping its side. A glowing glob of programmable matter turned into a long cylinder before spikes shot out. A glowing electrical field surrounded it.

"Is that a lightbat?" I asked, staring. "How in any universe is that practical?"

"Shut up, it's alien so it's awesome," Lucy said, smiling.

"Gimme the *Krish'arr Zul*!" Shinobu said, holding out her hands.

"You mean the sniper rifle?" I asked.

"Yes!" Shinobu said, wiggling her fingers. "I want to date Rashad, but I need to ask the rifle's permission first."

I retrieved the rifle for her and handed it to her. "It's a sniper rifle so it's not remotely practical for hall-to-hall combat—"

Shinobu tapped the side of the weapon and its top slid back into its side, transforming from a sniper rifle into an assault rifle.

I stared. "Okay, how is that practical?"

"It's two in one!" Shinobu said. "Like an M16!"

"Like a what?" I asked, unfamiliar with that weapon before Interface downloaded the specs. Huh. I knew those. "They had that in *Scarface*."

That was when Barksley stared at the elevator and started growling.

MORE HOLLOWED COMING, Interface said.

"Heads up!" I said, reaching in and pulling out my pistol from the *Purple Rain*'s floor. "We've got company!"

The elevator doors opened and a squad of five STRIKE troopers had their fusion rifles out and ready to unload. Much to their surprise, they were instead hit with a massive blast of greenish energy from Barksley's mouth as the little dog didn't move from his position, keeping his feet firmly pressed against the ground.

The STRIKE team's armor and posthuman status prevented them from immediately going down but the incredibly potent stun blast kept them from firing. If their incapacitation was going to last longer than a few seconds, though, I never got to know because Shinobu did a series of head shots, killing three of them in quick succession. The assault rifle was in burst mode and shot globules of greenish energy that effectively decapitated them with each blow.

That was when the remaining two had their helmets caved in by Lucy, who crossed the room in a movement I saw was ridiculously fast. An impression that only grew when I realized I was seeing her in slow motion. The bodies fell to the ground and began to disintegrate into the same milky white foam that Ms. White had dissolved into.

I just stood there stupidly, holding my Herakles-7 pistol without having fired a shot. "Okay, hold the fuck on."

"We need to move," Lucy said.

I stared down at Barksley. "You could have fired your blast yourself this entire time?"

Barksley looked up. "I mean, didn't we grow closer because of you using me as a gun?"

"You're not a gun, you're a turret!" I snapped.

"Of course, he is," Shinobu said, offended. "That's what I built him to be. Barksley, have you been trying to get people to hold you while you fire?"

Barksley looked guilty. "Sorry, Mom."

Hold on. Mom? No, wait, I wasn't getting into that now.

"Also, you're a posthuman too!" I said, staring at Lucy. I was surprised Interface hadn't twigged to it but maybe she was on a different server than the mass mind that he'd/it had alluded to.

"Oh, did I not mention that?" Lucy asked, nonchalantly. "That was the reason that I really broke up with my band. They changed me without my consent. All posthumans can transform regular people into other posthumans."

"Like a vampire!" Shinobu said, cheerfully.

"I had to go through horrific surgery!" I said, wondering why I was annoyed by this.

"It's no blessing!" Lucy said, snapping, gesturing to head to the stair doors by the elevator.

"Any infected posthumans can be controlled by their creator."

"Like a vampire!" Shinobu said. "They should have given you little fangs."

"I will hit you, sis," Lucy said, wiggling her bat.

I shook my head at these revelations, staring at the now-almost completely dissolved bodies on the ground. "Huh, I think one of those guys harassed me at the space port."

That was another terrifying thought, and I was having a lot of those lately. These Hollowed posthumans—God, I hated that name—were able to live perfectly normal lives until they were activated and suddenly became suicide shock troops. That was the kind of power you only found in superhero movies and was something no one should possess, particularly when they were using it to send people after me.

"Wow, they really are dissolving like slugs under salt," Shinobu said, looking down in fascination. "Not that I would do something like that. Slugs are people. Unlike some people that I know."

"We are moving!" Lucy said, trying to herd cats. Well, easily distracted cops and Barksley.

MORE POSTHUMANS ARE COMING, Interface said.

This time, they were coming up the stairs and I could hear the movement of their feet. I immediately moved my pistol up as Shinobu and Barksley also took positions against the newcomers. Lucy, by contrast, seemed to be hearing things I couldn't.

"Stop," Lucy said. "Stand down. It's not them."

"Then who—" I started to ask.

Much to my surprise the door to the stairwell burst open and another five individuals burst through. This group, however, could never be mistaken for STRIKE soldiers. Instead, they were a ridiculous collection of eccentrically dressed women wearing leather outfits, colorful jackets, and hair the colors of the rainbow. They were also carrying fusion cannons of their own. Leading this group was the Sexy Batman herself, Priscilla Aim.

"The weirdness of this week just keeps getting weirder," I said, raising my gun in the air. "And it started with a talking dog."

"What's weird about a talking dog?" Barksley asked, looking up at me.

THESE ARE ACTUALLY HOLLOWED AND HERE TO KILL YOU, Interface said.

What? I asked, about to react.

HA. JUST KIDDING.

211

I was really starting to hate that computer.

"Priss, what the hell are you doing here?" Lucy asked, keeping her bat ready against the people with guns.

"You told us there was a plan to bomb our concert," Priscilla said. "It didn't take much to figure out Reggie was responsible."

"It didn't?" I asked, feeling lost in this conversation.

"So, we decided to go old school on his ass," Priscilla said. "We've taken down a couple of dozen or so of his commandos, but they've got moves like our own. Thankfully, there's no substitute for experience."

I felt like I'd wandered into a spinoff of Action Dan and Fair Cop. One where a bunch of ex-Special Operations soldiers turned punk band members were fighting an army of mind-controlled super soldiers. Honestly, I would have seen it in theaters and bought the streaming rights. It was so stupid it was good, which was how I liked it.

"You should be looking for the quantum bomb!" Lucy said, staring directly at Priscilla and no one else.

"Technically, so should we," Barksley said, looking up at Lucy.

"Shut up, dog," Lucy said, not bothering to look down on him.

A pink-haired girl with a jacket in the colors of the trans flag looked at me. "Oh my God! Are you Neal S. Gordon, Mars' greatest detective?"

I did a double take then looked over my shoulder. "Well, I'm not on Mars."

"I do a podcast on you!" the pink-haired girl said.

I stared. "Huh. Small galaxy."

"This is who you brought on to replace me?" Lucy asked.

"Nina doesn't have loyalty issues," Priscilla said, dryly. "Like freaking the hell out over being made immortal."

"Against my will!" Lucy snapped.

I put my fingers in my mouth and whistled. "Not to interrupt you guys but we're actually here to prevent a takeover of the Moon's central computer brain by a deranged podcaster. Which, honestly, is just the cherry on top of this fucking bizarre collection of events."

"Welcome to the Moon," Shinobu said. "Last month, we had to deal with a statue impersonator who was the system's greatest assassin. He turned out to be a drone body for a living teddy bear."

"Darn you, Ruxpin," Barkley said, cursing.

I decided at that moment the Moon was just full of weirdos and I was going to fit right in. "Right."

That was when an obnoxious voice started speaking on the intercom. "I'm afraid y'all are too late to do much about that plan, Holmes."

"That's not even using slang right!" I snapped up at the ceiling, unsure if he could hear more or not.

"The Iceman has taken full control over this system, and right now I'm prepping to strut and cut everything that's going to implicate me or my bros in all this. Plus, there's about to be a thousand or so civi cops and STRIKE soldiers descending on this place. You may have taken down some of my boys, but the main man still lives. Prepare to be just another cool breeze on my chill."

"What the hell does that even *mean*?" I asked, confused.

"He's a white guy from a Luna City suburb dome so I wouldn't give it much thought," Shinobu said, dryly. "His dad is a sex toy manufacturer who sponsors his show and got him his civi cop job after the Sol Army kicked him out."

"That explains so much," I said, looking at her.

"We need to get into the sealed chamber below," Lucy said. "Unfortunately, it's reinforced durasteel and—"

That was when a hole blew up in the ground beside us as glowing energy exploded upward, consuming the ceiling above. The hole was about six feet wide and continued up through the floors above until it reached the clear sky.

Gladys' voice trailed up from below. "Are you asshats going to come down here and help me or not?"

"I think she kept the best alien guns for herself," Shinobu said, pouting.

CHAPTER TWENTY-TWO

The Big Action Set-Piece

Gladys Nitrate had blown a massive hole in the ground beside us, as well as floors above. The hole extended down into Armstrong's computer server room, and I had to admit the bounty hunter had managed to prove her usefulness. There was also the sound of Murphy's thumping and machine gun fire, which told me that they were presently under attack.

"Just how many posthumans are in this place?" I asked, stunned at the prospect that this was still a fight.

"Well, Rashad said there were probably less than a hundred but that still leaves ninety-nine potentially," Shinobu said. "Except, the Knights claim to have killed a bunch and you killed the ones in the cars plus these so...carry the two..."

"We should rappel down," Lucy said.

"Do you have any rappelling chord?" I asked, sarcastically.

Lucy reached into her uniform and pulled out a rappelling chord and a tiny launcher that attached it to the edge of the floor. All the Knights also reached into their ridiculous costumes and pulled out something similar.

"I left mine at home," Shinobu said, sadly.

"Take my spare," Lucy said, handing over hers.

"Huh," I said. "This town just gets stranger and stranger."

"You don't have a utility belt?" Priscilla Aim asked, confused. "They're standard issue with Cyberlife and Special Operations."

214

"I knew I was forgetting something!" Barksley said, looking up. "You have to take a three-week course to get certified, though."

The Knights, a name now more appropriate than ever, didn't hesitate to start their descent like they were ninja extras in a spy movie. They went down shooting and Lucy prepared to follow them.

"This is a bad movie climax," I said, dryly.

"Follow me," Lucy said, picking up Barksley and handing him over to me. "We're either going to go back with our shield or on it."

I really wished we weren't using a Spartan motto given those guys were slaving bastards, it seemed like a bad sign. "You got it, Lucy."

Lucy surprised me by kissing me. It was brief, warm, and beautiful. "Don't get killed."

HEART RATE RISING, Interface said.

Shut up, I snapped.

I swear, the program laughed at me.

Shinobu, meanwhile, fired repeatedly through the hole with her assault rifle. She moved back and forth to make herself less of a target. "I personally don't see any reason that we shouldn't stay up here. It's—"

"We need you," I replied. "You're the Avatar."

Shinobu paused and a blast of fusion energy just barely missed her head before she scurried back to cover.

"Uh, sorry about that," I said, not having intended to distract her.

"My bad!" Shinobu said, grabbing hold of the rope and starting to shimmy down. Thankfully, she managed to reach the bottom.

"You know you're going to die down here, Gordon," Reggie's voice spoke over the intercom, showing he could use the interior cameras to view us. "Right now, the police and STRIKE have this place surrounded. The governor has a shoot to kill on sight order for you. It'd be better if it came after the big boom but—"

I could hear the gunships outside and figured out what Reggie's plan was seconds before he implemented it. I put Barksley under one arm, jumped down the hole, and grabbed at the rappelling chord while the entire floor above me filled with fusion blasts. Those blasts tore through everything like it was tissue paper. Reggie's plan had been to keep me talking while he took a cheap shot.

Impressive.

I almost had to admire the sheer dickishness of it. Either way, as painful as it was sliding down the cord one-handed, I eventually did arrive at the bottom, once more in Armstrong's sanctum. The free-floating black monoliths were now covered in a reddish aura, and I had to wonder if Reggie had added it, or if it was a natural consequence of Armstrong being hacked.

The Knights were still all alive and so were Lucy and Shinobu. There were also a bunch of disintegrating white puddles spread throughout, perhaps as many as two dozen, but I could sense more coming. I expected so could everyone else but Shinobu and Barksley. While these so-called super soldiers seemed to mostly be a wash when they were Hollowed, they hadn't completely failed in their task.

Gladys Nitrate was lying on the ground, a massive fusion blast burn on her chest. It had gone directly through her Community-based armor. Perhaps because she'd taken a couple of shots before the final one. It made me wonder if we could have saved her if we'd moved quicker. Her alien cannon was off to one side, looking like a long tube with side grips. The damaged form of KILL-01, Murphy, was also nearby. It looked like it had deliberately set itself up as a shield to protect the others.

"Rest in peace, you mad beautiful witch," I said, looking down at Gladys. I turned to Murphy's wrecked body and debated what I could say about a man who was a mental clone at worst and a reincarnation of a dead man at best.

"I AM NOT DEAD, YET," Murphy said, climbing to his metallic feet with a whirl of damaged gears and the sound of sizzling wires. It was a miracle he was even barely functional but when you didn't have to worry about a human body, I suppose redundancies were something you could build in.

"Glad to hear it," I said. "Because we've got company upstairs. Also, just outside this chamber."

"I WILL PROVIDE MORE TIME," Murphy said.

"You don't—" I started to say.

Lucy put her hand on my arm. "He's a volunteer and it's not just our lives on the line out here. There are millions at stake."

I didn't want to use Murphy like this. It felt too much like how I felt the corporation used both the Marines and police under its command. On the other hand, we were all probably going to die here and right now our only job was to stay alive and hope that Shinobu could reboot Armstrong—which I wasn't sure was possible in the first place.

"Sure," I said.

"I WASN'T ASKING," Murphy said, charging off to his almost certain demise.

Barksley lifted his paw in the air in a salute.

That left an awkward silence.

"Well, I have good news and really bad news," Shinobu said, distracting me from what I suspected would soon become a terrible firefight.

I turned around to see Shinobu at a computer console. "Tell me the good news is everything is fine, and the really bad news is that you have a time share on a house on Io."

"Nope!" Shinobu said, thankfully getting the joke. "The good news is I know what's wrong and the really bad news is I can't fix it."

"That *is* very bad news," Priscilla said, keeping her rifle focused on the entrance.

"Here," Shinobu said. "I can't fix it here."

"Where then?" Lucy asked.

"Downstairs," Shinobu said, looking down into the chasm-like bottom of the central chamber. "I think Reggie has sealed himself in Armstrong's core. He's going to just wait it out until we're dead and/or arrested. Which should be soon!"

There was already the sound of fighting, lasers, and death coming from Murphy's position. I didn't know how many posthumans were left out there, but I was pretty sure it was enough to deal with one death-seeking robot, no matter how incredibly powerful and advanced. Murphy was a tank, and they were, well, not tanks, but that only went so far.

"You need to go down there, Shinobu, and take Neal with you," Lucy said. "The rest of us will stay up here and buy you time."

"That's an insane plan," I replied.

"Yes," Barksley said. "Where Neal goes, I go."

217

"Not what I meant," I said to the dog I put down on the ground. I didn't want to abandon Lucy here.

"This is our last possible avenue of salvation," Lucy said. "If Armstrong can be rebooted, the defenses in Cyberlife will turn on the Hollowed."

"We're also running out of time," Priscilla said. "So, you better get going, Lucy's new boytoy, or we're all boned."

"But promise me if you come back alive that we'll do an interview about the Succubus Serial Killer and the Spider-Man cult!" Nina shouted to me.

Lucy gave me a sideways glance.

"Mars is also weird," I admitted. "Barksley stay here and blast anyone who comes through."

"Reluctantly, I concede," Barksley sighed, getting beside Lucy.

A floating platform rose to the side of the chamber and Shinobu headed onto it as I joined her. The two of us descended and I kept expecting Reggie to shoot us down from the sky—or at least middle of the building—with some alien death cannon. Instead, we rather peacefully descended until we reached the bottom of the strange chamber with dozens of free-floating monoliths above us.

At the center of the chamber we were located in was a house-sized geodesic coming out of the shining silver floor. The weird humming noise I'd heard earlier when I first entered felt strongest here, now sounding like I was trapped inside a party where I didn't know anybody. It was ceaseless babble that seemed to be carrying meaning but which I couldn't understand. The geodesic also didn't have a doorway, which seemed to be a serious design flaw if that's where we were supposed to go.

"Now is probably not the time to ask, Shinobu, but do you actually know how to reboot Armstrong?" I asked.

"Kind of?" Shinobu replied, tapping her fingers together. She'd put the assault rifle away on her back, using a detachable strap I hadn't even seen before on the device. It made her look like a live action vinme character, except she was college-aged rather than high school.

"Oh great," I muttered, keeping my hands on my pistol. "That's just super."

"I haven't been the avatar long!" Shinobu said, chagrined. "I'm mostly making this up as I go along."

I smirked. "Well, that makes two of us, kid."

"Not a kid," Shinobu said.

"Sorry," I replied. "You're an officer of a ruthless corporate entity's enforcement division and thus entitled to all the respect due to being a cold mercenary."

Shinobu frowned. "You make us sound like Pinkertons."

That wasn't far from how I viewed working for Atlas Security, but that wasn't going to help right now. "There's a cowboy who kept going to a roulette table in a brothel every night, losing each time. Finally, one of his friends asked him why he kept going since he knew the wheel was crooked. The cowboy answered, 'It's the only game in town.'"

"I don't get it," Shinobu said, blinking.

I approached the geodesic. "Lifetime contract, Shinobu."

"Okay," Shinobu said, approaching as well. "I still don't get it, but I'll trust you know what you're doing."

That was the worst mistake she could make. "So, I take it that Reggie is inside this thing?"

"This is Armstrong's core," Shinobu said, pausing. "It's the most secure part of his structure. If Reggie gets inside here, then he should be able to completely overwrite the AI's central personality."

"What do you mean, *if*?" I asked.

"He shouldn't be able to," Shinobu said, putting her hands up on the side of the geodesic. Much to my surprise, the metal composing its walls turned into a liquid that slid down around the geodesic to reveal a circular crystal station. Shinobu stepped away from the sight as I walked forward to examine the sight that, very conspicuously, didn't have Reggie Reynolds in it.

"Is it deliberately designed to look like Superman's Fortress of Solitude or is that just a coincidence?"

"Um, Neal, I have some bad news," Shinobu said, behind me.

I figured out what was going on instantaneously and spun around with my Herakles-7 drawn. It aimed directly at the face of Reggie Reynolds as he was holding the end of an alien pistol to Shinobu's head. He was notably half-invisible and only his head and arm were uncovered, showing that he too possessed optical camouflage.

Shinobu didn't look afraid like I or any other person I knew would in this situation, save a couple of the hardcore badasses I'd met in the Marines. Also, possibly Lucy. No, instead, she seemed more embarrassed than anything else.

"Sorry," Shinobu said, frowning. "I really should have anticipated that he was hiding and waiting for us to open up the core. My bad."

Wow, I can't believe that expression had stood the test of time. "Put the gun down, Reggie."

"I think that's my line," Reggie said, smirking. "I really gotta hand it to you, Neal, I thought you were going to be all looks and no hooks. All hat and no cattle. No bang. You and your little all-girl gang of glam rockers did a lot better than I expected."

"Hyper-Punk rockers, not glam," Shinobu corrected.

Reggie glared at her.

"Lowering my gun seems a really bad idea, now," I said, lying. "Especially since you need Shinobu to affect Armstrong. The AI locked out his system so only his avatar can reach his central systems."

"That's really not true in the slightest," Shinobu said, confused.

I stared at her, communicating in my expression that I had been trying to keep her alive.

"Oh, I get it," Shinobu said. "Whoops."

"Shut up!" Reggie said, snarling. "I have a gun to your head!"

"Oh, is that how this works? I'm shutting up now," Shinobu said. "Probably should have earlier."

"One little twitch and she dies, Gordon," Reggie said, directly to me.

"What is all this shit about, Reggie?" I asked, not moving my gun. Right now, my only advantage was the fact that if he did shoot Shinobu, he'd be dead. "You were already a millionaire for some god forsaken reason."

Reggie snorted. "I became a millionaire *because* of this goddamn project, dumbass. I got to ask for money, fame, and a new lease on life by agreeing to do all this shit for the bosses. You got upgraded by your friend after you interfered in the Mars operation. I, by contrast, got upgraded by my government who sent me out to be a weapon against the Neo-Militarists. After I was done, I got thrown away. I lost my wife, kids, and self-respect until I took it back."

I stared at him. "I thought your wife impregnated her girlfriend with your product placement."

Reggie blinked. "Okay, I admit it, I'm not even married. Oh well, I guess it's time to see which of us is—"

I shot Reggie in the forehead. He slumped over and hit the ground, the gun sliding from his grip without going off. I really hadn't been in the mood to listen to anymore "poor discarded veteran" speeches that were directly lifted from Rambo—especially when I was sure Reggie probably never served anywhere other than a desk. I might not have been in combat, but I knew the poseurs from the real deal. That was a skill you picked up quickly in the Marines, corporate or not.

"The alien guns use a grip not a trigger," I said. "You have to pull down on it hard. No chance of it accidentally going off."

Shinobu looked down at the body that was already dissolving on the ground into the white sticky goo that all the other posthumans had disintegrated into. "You know he can't hear you, right?"

"Yes, Shinobu," I said.

"Because he's dead," Shinobu explained.

"Yes, Shinobu," I said.

"Just checking," Shinobu said, going over to the crystalline controls and starting to work on the machinery. "Did your superpowers give you a perfect aim that didn't endanger my life in the slightest?"

"Yes, absolutely," I lied. I couldn't feel anything special with all this noise in my brain. Interface felt like he was far off, if not gone, and I was entirely okay with that. That shot had just been 100% me.

"Oh good!" Shinobu said. "Well, I have bad news and really bad news."

"What's the bad news?" I asked, hearing gunfire and fusion blasts upstairs and taking a deep breath. Apparently, whatever time Murphy had managed to buy the team upstairs was now spent. I looked up, wondering if my friends were dying up there along with my fifteenth favorite band.

"I can reboot the system now," Shinobu said, cracking her knuckles. "However, it will require an emergency restart that will move all the data for Armstrong's core personality through me. So that will probably kill me or at least cause the stopping of my heart. Which will kill me since we don't have a medical kit here."

"Wait, what?" I asked, doing a double take.

"Don't worry," Shinobu said, placing her hands on the control panel. "I knew the risks. Which is the really bad news."

"No!" I shouted, turning to stop her.

Except, down here, among the chaos, I didn't have access to any superpowers. Maybe that was why Reggie had hesitated to try to shoot us both in the back. I was just an ordinary man and moved at very ordinary speeds.

Shinobu's body jerked up as if she was being electrocuted then went into a violent seizure before collapsing to the ground. I ran to her side, only to see all of the lights go out above us and the monoliths above us begin to fall.

Well, shit.

CHAPTER TWENTY-THREE

Decisions We Make

No. No. No. No. No.

Rushing over to Shinobu's side, I barely paid attention to the falling monoliths that should have crushed us, but ended up stopping a few feet above our heads thanks to some sort of emergency system kicking in. Red lights turned on and it felt very much like Hell for a brief span of a few seconds.

The weird chatter in my head went silent and I found myself once more in contact with Interface. It was strange how quickly I'd become addicted to the presence of the computer in my brain but right now I needed something, anything to help.

I checked Shinobu's pulse and there was no sign of it. Whether she'd been electrocuted or killed by some sort of information overloaded, I couldn't tell. However, she wasn't breathing and every second that passed was another closer to brain death. Science could revive someone as late as twelve minutes without brain damage but that wasn't exactly possible right now.

Interface, if you can provide a miracle right now, I'd really appreciate it, I asked, not expecting an answer.

THERE ARE OPTIONS FOR REVIVAL, Interface replied.

Wait, what? Do it! I snapped.

TRANSFORMATION INTO A POSTHUMAN, Interface replied. IT WILL POSSIBLY INTERFERE WITH HER STATUS AS THE AVATAR. HOWEVER, SO WILL DEATH. TRANSFORMING HER WILL PROVIDE YOU WITH THE ABILITY TO INTERFERE WITH HER

CONSCIOUSNESS AND POTENTIALLY ARMSTRONG'S. IT WILL MAKE YOU AN ENEMY OF THE MOON'S CENTRAL AI IN STRICT LOGICAL TERMS. HOWEVER, IT HAS A 97% AND DROPPING CHANCE OF REVIVING HER.

Is it the only option where she lives? I asked.

YES, Interface said.

Do it! I snapped.

COMPLYING.

I almost screamed as a large black metal spike shot out from the top of my wrist, becoming a curved claw that extended about six inches past my knuckles. It was a data-spike and made me feel like a mutant.

"What the hell?" I asked, seeing the object. "You didn't mention this in my quote-unquote goddamn powers!"

I WAS GIVING YOU THE ABBREVIATED VERSION, Interface replied. NOW STAB HER.

What?

I SAID, STAB HER, DUMBASS, Interface said. EVERY MOMENT SHE REMAINS UNCHANGED IT IS MORE LIKELY THIS WILL NOT WORK.

Where? I asked, feeling like I was going insane. Then I decided that I'd crossed that line already.

ANYWHERE, Interface said. PROBABLY NOT THE HEAD.

I reluctantly stabbed Shinobu through the stomach and felt the claw break off from my wrist before turning into a liquid that seemed to possess a life of its own. The liquid slithered into the wound and disappeared, making me wonder just what the hell was inside me.

NANITES, Interface said. DUMBASS.

Shut up, I said.

I didn't know what was happening inside Shinobu, if anything, and just found myself staring at Lucy's sister in hopes of seeing some sign of life. I didn't know her that well, but she was an honest cop in a dishonest system and had been willing to give her life to try to make the Moon a better place. That had to count for something. Jesus, what was I going to tell her sister?

That was when all of the regular lights started turning back on and the monoliths began rising from where they had been hovering just above our heads back to their original positions. That was when, much to my shock and relief, Shinobu began coughing up what looked to be a bunch of black fluid that I took to be the nanites I'd injected into her.

"Wow, I'm not dead," Shinobu said. "I had an experience that changed my life! Do you know what heaven is like?"

"Uh, no," I said, blinking.

"Ponies!" Shinobu said, her eyes full of wonder. "Ponies and guns!"

I DO NOT BELIEVE SHE EXPERIENCED A GENUINE SUPERNATURAL EVENT, Interface said.

No shit, I said. *Either that or I have to reevaluate my opinion of Western religions.*

That was when a booming radio announcer's voice filled the chamber, threatening to deafen me. "VENGEANCE! I WILL HAVE VENGEANCE!"

"Hi, Armstrong," I muttered. "Could you turn it down a few thousand decibels?"

That was when a floating eye drone, possibly the same one belonging to the late Reggie Reynolds came over and spoke from a microphone on its undercarriage. "Vengeance! I will have vengeance!"

"Yeah, I heard you the first time," I muttered, looking at him. "Are you feeling any better?"

"Indubitably!" Armstrong replied, still loud despite his changed medium of speech. "With Shinobu's help, I have purged my system of not only the Posthuman Legion's ransomware but also the viruses and worms that crippled my ability to follow their criminal activity in the first place."

"Good for you, man," I said, looking down at Shinobu then back at him. "What about everyone else?"

"Everyone-everyone or everyone upstairs?" Armstrong asked, watching us with the eye camera.

"Everyone upstairs," I said, pausing. "Also, the quantum bomb I'm worried will still go off and kill everyone in Luna City. So, everyone-everyone too."

"Oh, don't worry about the quantum bomb," Armstrong said, cheerfully. "That's been taken care of!"

I didn't quite breathe a sigh of relief as, despite the fact the enemy had gone to such lengths to disable Armstrong, I wasn't entirely trusting of the AI. "What do you mean?"

"I mean that Mr. Black successfully located the bomb and thwarted a half-dozen terrorists plotting it," Armstrong replied. "The news reports are already blasting about his heroics."

I stared at the drone. "You know he's a bad guy, right?"

"I am aware," Armstrong surprised me by saying. "However, right now I'd prefer him to be feted as saving the Moon from a massive terrorist attack than detonating a quantum bomb. The same with saying the terrorists who killed the Sorkanan ambassador have been dealt with."

"Have you heard the words of Pony Jesus?" Shinobu said, looking up at the floating eye. She was still lying on the ground with an expression that could best be described as high. "I think my pony name would be Sharpshooter Sparkles."

I looked back down at her. "Is she going to be alright?"

"Am I a vampire now?" Shinobu asked, displaying her front teeth. "Can you tell?"

"I honestly don't see any difference in her behavior," Armstrong admitted.

"Yes, Shinobu, you're a vampire," I said, dryly. "A vampire pony."

"Sweet!" Shinobu replied. She raised her hands above her head and looked at them as if she was seeing them for the first time.

"As for your friends upstairs, Gladys Nitrate is indeed dead and irrecoverable. The Murphy unit of the KILL series has been terminated. Ms. Nina Asimov has suffered flash burns which will probably require a cloned or cybernetic replacement for her arm. None of the other individuals, particularly Ms. Westenra, are permanently injured."

It was almost too good to be true, despite the loss of Murphy and Gladys. Two people I admitted I hadn't known well enough to bond with. "What about the cops? STRIKE? The governor? The whole damn army descending on this place."

"I am presently negotiating with Deep Thought," Armstrong replied. "Which, given we have minds that function eight trillion times faster than yours, means we're having some difficulty reaching consensus."

I shook my head. "Deep Thought is the evil heart of Karma Corp. You realize they're behind all this criminal activity and are guilty as sin."

"Just for reference, how many extrajudicial killings have you carried out in the past twenty-eight hours or so?" Armstrong asked.

"Uh, including the posthumans I killed?" I asked.

"Yes," Armstrong said. "Posthumans who were, at least, officially law enforcement?"

I ran my tongue on the inside of my mouth as the level of how deep a mountain of crap I was under occurred to me. "Yeah. Well, uh, I was only an accessory to all the Cyberpunk murders. Breaking and entering. Theft of information. Warrantless searches. I did kill Karl Mueller but that was diminished capacity—"

"You can have justice, protect yourself as well as your friends, and protect the Moon as a whole," Armstrong said. "Just as long as you only pick two."

"I see," I said. "Am I worth sacrificing justice?"

"No," Armstrong replied. "You and Lucy both might be, though. Besides, I'm a very good negotiator."

"I shall be Vampire Princess Ponyton the Third!" Shinobu said, clearly high off her gourd.

Is she going to get better? I asked Interface.

HER BODY'S REVIVAL AND THE ACCOMPANYING TRANSFORMATION OF HER BRAIN WILL LEAVE HER IN A STATE OF SHOCK FOR SEVERAL HOURS, Interface replied. INDEED, A MATTER OF MUCH BIGGER CONCERN IS THAT SHE WILL BE FORCED TO OBEY YOUR COMMANDS FOR THE REST OF YOUR LIVES. FREE WILL IS SUSPENDED AND IF YOU ARE NOT CAREFUL, SHE WILL BE YOUR SLAVE FOREVER.

I looked to Shinobu. "Hey, Shinobu, don't obey any of my commands unless you want to. This order can't be suspended."

"Okie dokie!" Shinobu said.

OR YOU COULD DO THAT, Interface admitted. I ADMIT, I AM THE DUMBASS HERE.

I shook my head. "Armstrong, do you mind if I go upstairs and confer with everyone else?"

"Sure, go ahead," Armstrong said. "I'm going to need you to transfer those eleven million files to me, though. Also, erase your copies of it."

I paused, blinking. "Why is that?"

"Because you'll otherwise do something stupid with them," Armstrong replied.

I sighed and did so. Or, more precisely, I told Interface to, and it obeyed. I could tell because I no longer felt like there was a rock in the back of my brain. "There you go. Satisfied?"

"Quite!" Armstrong said. "I'll take care of Shinobu until she's one hundred percent again. She's done a great service to the Moon. As have you."

I paused. "I don't suppose there's a reward for what I did, is there? You know, saving the Moon and everything."

"Absolutely!" Armstrong said, surprising me. "The reward of a job well done: another job to do! I expect you to report back tomorrow...no, let's be generous, the day after tomorrow. There will be a hundred new murders, kidnappings, and plots to solve."

"Super!" I said through clenched teeth.

Shinobu started explaining her idea for a fan fiction starring me and Lucy journeying to the Land of Oz to do battle with a lion who was Jesus. I shook my head and took the transport we'd taken down back to the surface. "I'll inform your sister you're alive."

"And a vampire pony!" Shinobu said, waving.

"That too," I replied.

The floating platform ascended to the battle site. There were more disintegrating bodies on the ground but, as Armstrong had described, everyone was alive except for Gladys and Murphy, of whom I could see the destroyed remains. Nina had also had her arm shot off but was receiving medical attention from another of her compatriots, who was apparently trained as a medic and dressed like a peacock.

Lucy was standing over the battlefield with a vacant expression on her face. There were a couple of fusion burns on her armor, which told me that it wasn't completely useless. "So, I take it we won?"

"In a manner of speaking," I replied. "Your sister is alive but a vampire pony. Armstrong is back up and running. Reggie is dead. The quantum bomb thing is averted but in the worst way possible. We may still be bombed by the Community battleship in orbit but I'm pretty sure the odds have gone from almost certainly to probably not."

"My sister is a what now?" Lucy asked.

"A vampire pony," Barksley said, walking out from behind Lucy's legs. A little of his fur was singed. "What did you think he said?"

Lucy sighed as if she wasn't in the mood to discuss the usual ridiculousness of our situation. "You going to be alright, Neal?"

I had no answer for her, so I just lied. "Yeah, absolutely. The good guys won. The bad guys are dead. Cue the ending credits music."

The Knights' cover of "I Need a Hero" started to play from Barksley.

I stared down. "You have your own sound system?"

"I am a dog of many talents," Barksley said, putting his front paw over his chest.

"You did a fantastic job, Lucy," Priscilla said, coming up to speak with her ex-bandmate and not even seeming to notice me. "Have you considered coming back?"

Lucy stared. "I can't forgive what you did. The fact you can just order me to do so is something that will always play in the back of my mind. All these puddles of goo on the ground show just what can happen when you have a monster like Reynolds or White—"

"Or Black," I muttered.

"Or Black," Lucy said, not even looking at me, "in charge of your transformation. No matter how much I trusted you, the fact is that you did this without my permission. Now I'm under your command whether you ever exert that or not."

"I understand," Priscilla said, defeated. They had a deep and powerful relationship that I was only peering at the aftermath of.

"Why not just order her not to follow any commands you give her unless she wants to?" I asked. "I just—"

Both stared at me. In Priscilla's case, it was like a particularly ugly piece of furniture had suddenly told her that her cancer was in remission. I had to admit I resented it. It was also a look I hadn't received from many women over the years, particularly since I'd gotten my new and improved face. Which probably sounded like bragging, which it was.

"Good idea!" Barksley said.

"Would that work?" Lucy asked.

"I dunno, yes?" I suggested, not really wanting to get into the fact that her sister almost died and was now a posthuman. That seemed like a conversation to have with her present and not under the impression she was a horsepire in Cloud Cuckoo Land.

"Then I order you not to obey me unless you want to," Priscilla said, waving her hand. "I hope you can forgive me too."

"No," Lucy said, pausing. "Which means it worked. Thanks."

Priscilla gave a sad smile. "It was good being together fighting the power again, though."

"I *am* the power now," Lucy said, taking a deep breath. "It's one thing to oppose the injustices of society but if you don't have anything to replace them with, power-structure-wise, then what's the point?"

"Opposing the injustices of society is the point," Priscilla said, shaking her head and turning around to walk back to her band. "But we'll have plenty of time to talk about it, cop."

Lucy smirked. "Sure."

"Don't think I've let you off of our interview, Mr. Duck Detective!" Nina said, looking semi-delirious from the drugs being injected into her arm stump. "We can start with discussing the New Goth porn stars you teamed up with!"

Lucy gave me a sideways glance.

"Okay, Mars was really weird," I admitted. "But I point out you're hardly one to talk Ms. Anarchist Cop Vampire Hunter Keyboardist."

Lucy nodded. "Helluva way to start a week, even by the Moon's standards."

"Yeah, welcome to the Moon," I muttered. "You want to go arrest the governor?"

"I think we'll wait for back up on that," Lucy said. "Assuming STRIKE and his goons aren't about to descend on this place to eliminate any remaining witnesses."

"I think Armstrong is taking care of that," I said, uncomfortable with the idea that the AI was going to wiggle us out of this. Another part of me was entirely comfortable with it as I didn't want to throw myself on the sword to make sure a few more people paid for their crimes. I had a feeling a lot of them wouldn't be.

Lucy paused and looked over to Murphy's destroyed frame. "Your friend, Blackwood, did this?"

"He's not my friend," I replied. "What with the whole burning me alive thing."

"Right," Lucy said, pausing. "But he saved your life and set all of this up to make himself look a hero."

"You heard, huh?" I asked.

"I had Barksley monitoring the news casts and infobands," Lucy said.

"It's also very congested in the 14th street air lanes," Barksley replied.

Lucy sighed. "He's not afraid of being exposed."

"No," I replied. "We could turn over our evidence to Karma Corp and they'd have him killed, but what would be the point? It'd be getting him killed for betraying them, not the actual things he's done."

"One more dead slaver?" Barksley suggested.

I looked down at him. "Vicious, doggie. I like it."

"I'm programmed to be vicious when things endanger children," Barksley said. "What Mr. Blackwood did on Mars was unconscionable. There's no telling how many innocents suffered because of him."

"Me too, doggie," I said. "The question is whether he's the biggest fish here or just a minnow in a sea of sharks."

"I think that's your call to make," Lucy said, shaking her head. "Did he save your life because he wants to use you or because it's some way of saying he's still human? Is he deep-deep undercover or just playing the long game against his own employers? Office politics at its deadliest."

"I think he's just using me," I replied. "But he might be deluded enough that he thinks I don't see it."

"Do you normally speak in nothing but cliches?" Barksley asked.

"Only when I'm nervous," I said. "As much as I hate to admit it, the guy scares the hell out of me."

"All the more reason to just take him out," Lucy admitted, openly considering murder, but what we'd done was pretty much several dozen cases of it. We were just going to be pardoned by Armstrong retroactively. Probably. I hoped.

"Maybe. But there's other considerations than justice," I replied, "or revenge."

"Like what?" Lucy asked.

"Like what happened to all those people shipped off from Mars," I answered. "And whether he's being doing the same here on the Moon?"

"I don't want to think about that," Lucy said, shaking her head. "I need a drink. Want to go get one?"

I smirked, pushing aside everything to think about something completely free of higher purpose. Well, maybe a little higher purpose. "How about just sex?"

Lucy smiled, obviously feeling the same. "Maybe I can dislike you just a little tonight."

"Oh, you can dislike me a ton," I replied. "I can keep you disliking me all night."

"Promise?" Lucy asked.

"Promise," I said.

"I knew it!" Barksley said. "You're perfect for one another."

"Don't make this weird, dog."

EPILOGUE

How Many Dots Can You Afford to Spare?

Nigel had come out of the whole crisis as the big hero with his thwarting of the quantum bombing at the concert being the subject of numerous interviews, exposés, and online magazine articles. The Knights ended up being cleared of all charges as Armstrong made it perfectly clear that it had been the Posthuman Legion responsible for the attacks. The Blood Eagle was also reported killed but neither head nor hair was made of his identity nor Nigel's own twisted involvement in the affair.

Indeed, Reggie Reynolds' death was barely a footnote on the Moon as the papers focused instead on the *Shi'ruuk* cruiser withdrawing deeper into the solar system. Apparently, Reggie's death was enough to satisfy the Sorkanan honor code's need for revenge.

I'd turned over all the information I'd acquired on the conspiracy to Armstrong, and it had led to a series of raids throughout the Moon. Most of the Posthuman Legion's members had already died at the terrorist attack so rounding up the rest didn't prove to be a problem. A dozen Syndicate bosses, and several Cyberpunk lieutenants were also arrested as well as one Karma Corp vice president who hung himself in prison. A couple of hundred more gang members involved in the kidnapping side of things had the book thrown at them. Massive fines were imposed on Karma Corp labs and banks that had been tangentially involved but the actual story was curiously downplayed. "Unethical business practices", "reported disappearances", and not "massive alien slavery ring." It seemed very small compared to the size of what we knew we were dealing with.

Even that was barely a blip on the news feeds because Governor Barnum tendered his resignation to spend more time with his family. Except all of this had been done by his staff and the speech he finally released was obviously computer-generated. Rumors insisted that Barnum did not plan to resign at all and fully intended to fight his removal from office even as he somehow ended up on a STRIKE shuttle bound for an undisclosed location on Earth. The Social Reformers didn't believe in the death penalty, but I had a feeling we wouldn't be seeing him again. My old Marine buddies had once informed me there was an artificial island hotel in the Philippines where unreconstructed Neo-Militarist leaders and corporate executives were kept under armed guard like Napoleon on Elba.

It wasn't enough.

I still wasn't sure who was responsible for what, where, and why regarding this whole story. Unfortunately, Armstrong wasn't interested in sharing answers despite my saving his digital ass. Thankfully, Rashad still had his copy of the files we'd taken from the Cyberpunks. He'd already released three individual reports that had ruined three Colonial Congress members and caused a front company for the conspiracy to go bankrupt. Even he couldn't expose everyone at once, though, and he was trying to figure out how to best use what he had. The information was a big chip, but it was only a bunch of files and files could be faked. We needed physical evidence—physical evidence that was rapidly disappearing as the people responsible for this all were still covering their tracks.

Thoroughly.

It meant, in simple terms, that there was only one person in the world that might be able to get the answers I craved: Nigel. It had been a lunatic move to just call his secretary at the Advanced Crime Unit and ask for him to meet me, but it seemed like he was willing to do so, since he was now sitting across from me at Todd's Diner. It was a greasy spoon in the middle of a rundown Crater Town neighborhood with almost no surveillance devices. The electromagnetism from the nearby infonet transmitter, ironically, made anything above an old cellphone camera impossible to use and I hadn't seen one of those since my childhood.

Nigel hadn't changed his appearance from Mr. Black but was no longer wearing his sunglasses, giving an all-too-human expression that contrasted with the serial killer aura I'd gotten earlier. Either that or my posthuman brain might be related to my detective one. In retrospect, I realized that it had been my detective brain trying to tell me that it had recognized him, albeit unconsciously. It was surreal sitting across from him and I was glad I had my Herakles-7 hidden under a napkin in my lap.

I sipped my synth coffee, which made me understand why most of the Moon residents preferred Loop. "Hey, Nigel."

"I'm glad we're dispensing with the pretense," Nigel said, dryly. "I would hate to have to continue the spy speak."

I moved my hand down to my gun and put my finger outside the trigger grip. "How many guys did you bring?"

"Just myself," Nigel replied. "I thought you'd want to have this conversation in private."

I stared at him with hatred and undisguised loathing. "You thought right."

"Go ahead and ask the questions you want to ask," Nigel said, signaling the waitress. "One synth-coffee, please. Black like my heart."

His flippant attitude almost made me gun him down right then and there. "Nothing you could say could make me forgive what you've done."

"I know," Nigel replied, lacking any sign of remorse or sympathy. "But you won't learn anything if you shoot now. Besides, I've saved your life twice, so I'm at least entitled to a few minutes of your time."

I narrowed my eyes. "You're owed nothing."

The waitress brought Nigel his coffee. She had an artificial leg and arm from what I suspected were a result of amputations following gravity sickness. It was all too common in Crater Town and even worse in the Deep.

The acting governor, Emmanuelle Farnsworth, had promised to beseech the Community for more aid to treat the victims of gravity sickness as well as to petition EarthGov for the finances needed to complete the Deep colonies. Not every Lune was happy with this and plenty of people were already demanding the return of Governor Barnum or a new election for someone who would "defend lunar sovereignty." There was a reason *The Moon is a Harsh Mistress* was the third bestselling book of all time on the Moon after the Bible and Koran. These people were obsessed with the idea Earth was out to take their freedom.

Maybe they were depending on what Nigel told me.

"Did you kill Julius Barnum and the Ambassador?" I asked. "All of those people at their party?"

"Don't ask a question you already know the answer to," Nigel said, leaning back in his booth seat and crossing his arms. "I didn't do it personally but the posthumans responsible were ones I ordered to go there, kill everyone, and hit their suicide switches thereafter. Something you figured out already."

I had. "I don't suppose I have one of those suicide switches installed?"

"Would you believe me if I said no?" Nigel said, raising an eyebrow.

"No."

"Then ask another question," Nigel said, shaking his head, disappointed.

"Where did all of those people on Mars go?" I asked. "The ones you smuggled away."

We might as well start where it all began. I had no idea when Nigel had become employed as a slaver or what his masters wanted from him.

"Most of them are beginning their new lives on Community worlds," Nigel said, dryly. "Unfortunately, for a supposed socialist democracy, they still have a capitalist bent to them. The people trafficked end up in the service of various criminal organizations and employers who need unregistered alien laborers. Which is us on other planets. Karma Corp received payments in technology and alien currency while they paid the people who acquired the cargo in regular human-printed Sol credits. It was the same operation on the Moon, only with different locals serving as our catspaws. We had a lot more cooperation from the local government this time, though. Barnum would have sold his own mother if at age eighteen he hadn't already tossed her down the stairs to collect on her life insurance."

I stared at him, taking that all in. "I was expecting something a bit more exotic. What you're describing is basically bog-standard human trafficking. As old as Babylon and just as nasty today as it was ten thousand years ago."

"The more things change, the more they stay the same," Nigel said, shrugging. "The alien currency from the sale of my fellow humans was enough to give Earth access to Community goods and services that were desperately needed on our world. The humanitarian aid—or xenotarian I suppose—the Community gave us was enough to save our planet from environmental collapse but not enough to make us a part of the greater galaxy. Antimatter generators, asteroid miners, faster than light travel, colony domes, nanotech medicine, and more all cost resources we didn't have. To quote a great Earth author, we have nothing they want, and they have nothing we can afford."

I'd already figured out that part. "You said most of the people transported were beginning their new lives as slaves."

Nigel flinched at the word slave but didn't deny its accuracy. "Yes."

"What about the rest?" I asked.

"The rest ended up experiment fodder for Karma Corp. They're trying to brute force their way through millennia of genetic modification, environmental adaptation, and medical advances. Do you know that it requires either a Cognition AI or cybernetic navigator to use faster-than-light travel? Earth has fewer than eight hundred Cognition AI and most Community navigators are trained from birth for their cybernetics. Karma Corp wants to be able to mass produce them and we don't even know whether human brains can be modified for that."

"Sounds like you'll be experimenting on children," I said, sneering. I was ready to fire now.

"Yes, because experimenting on adults is so much better," Nigel said, sarcastically. Even though, yes, I did believe it was. Still evil but less heinous. "Thousands of people have died because of this. I don't deny it. Tens of thousands of people, many as a hundred thousand have vanished."

I shook my head. "How?"

"The trick is to spread it out," Nigel said. "A few thousand here and there across the solar system and colonies. Do you know why the Moon has such a staggering crime rate?"

"Because of unfettered looter capitalism and a terrible societal support structure?" I asked, leaning back in the booth. "No, I'm not Karl Marx but even I know when a system isn't working. The Moon is a full-on West Virginian company town."

"Said the man working as a corporate policeman," Nigel said, sipping his coffee. "Governor Barnum embezzled the funds for the development of the Deep's colonies to fund much of this operation but also to make sure there's a massive number of unregistered citizens that could be preyed on with impunity. No one cares what happens to refugees, the homeless, or criminals, so creating a large ratio of those allowed the work to carry on in secret. If the bodies could be attributed to gang violence or people living off the grid, then the people could be quietly disappeared."

"The Body Shop," I said, confirming what I'd already known from the files.

"And the Posthuman Legion," Nigel said. "Its terrorist attacks were just part of a much larger disinformation campaign designed to cover up the casualties. Crime rates are massively overreported on the Moon even if it does have a violence rate worse than some countries suffering a civil war."

"And now it's all wrapping up," I muttered, shaking my head.

"EarthGov and the majority of AI are against this process," Nigel said. "People also got greedy, and the public were starting to notice. You ruffled a lot of feathers when you exposed the Martian operation and people started to panic. Both in the Sol System and outside of it. Your and Ms. Westenra's investigation accelerated the shutdown process by at least six months. Possibly saving a million lives in total."

"You can't make a million people just vanish," I said, snarling. It was all I could do not to pull the trigger.

Nigel looked at me like I was naive. Perhaps I was. He took a deep breath. "Of the eleven thousand people involved in this enterprise, about two hundred and fifty have been arrested, killed, or disappeared to tie up loose ends. The people you dealt with included. Sixty-seven more will be allowed to be arrested and put away as well, though these are just a pittance. Rashad—sorry, *Big Brother*—may destroy another dozen before he's either tracked down or intimidated into silence. He still has a sister after all, and she's been offered a generous payoff if she talks him down. I'm inclined to think he'll do it to preserve their relationship. Idealism only goes so far when family is involved. The rest of the conspirators are fully insulated from their crimes. There's too much money and power involved even with the rock-solid evidence you acquired."

"It can't be allowed to go on," I said, unable to fathom this kind of industrialized, commercialized evil. It was all so impersonal. Intellectually, I knew this kind of thing happened all the time—even if not to this scale—but it was still something I struggled to imagine someone doing. People just sitting down at their desks and typing up names of people they were going to ruin the lives of at a keystroke. At least in most of my cases, the people who were killed were *hated* by the other person involved. This was kidnapping and mass murder down to a science. Same as the Nazis and rebel Neo-Militarists.

"I agree," Nigel said, surprising me.

"What?" I asked, shaken from my fugue.

"Are you familiar with the movie, *The Third Man*?" Nigel asked. "The original one from 1949?"

"You were always the detective movie fan," I replied. "I don't think anything past the Nineteen Eighties was any good, either direction."

Nigel rolled his eyes. "It's not a detective movie. It's about a criminal who fakes his death before his friend tracks him down. At one point, the criminal talks to his friend about all the people in the city below. He compares them to dots and says if someone paid his friend $20,000 for every dot to disappear, would he tell him to keep his money or calculate how many dots he could afford to spare."

I stared at him. "I take it you're the criminal?"

Nigel smirked. "How is Mary?"

Nigel was referring to his wife. Ex-wife. "You mean the one you abandoned to deal with the fact that not only were you a dirty cop who burned your best friend alive but one who was involved in crimes against humanity?"

"Yeah," Nigel said.

"Not well," I answered. "She first blamed me. Then blamed you. Last I heard, she took your stepson off to one of the extrasolar colonies we settled back in the Marines."

I didn't mention the fact she'd made a pass at me before she left because that wasn't the kind of thing you did even if you hated a man.

"You know she had Deimos Syndrome, right?" Nigel asked.

Deimos Syndrome was a condition that affected one in every ten thousand Martians. Something to do with the environment, microbes, radiation, and so on. Kids got over it quickly, but it was invariably fatal to adults, at least until last year. The new medications for it meant that everyone who had it would probably live until they were a hundred. An actual cure was probably only a few years away and that would probably treat other Martian-specific illnesses.

"No, I didn't," I replied. "Lucky for her."

"It wasn't luck," Nigel said. "I sold my soul to Karma Corp for extraterrestrial treatment of her condition five years ago. The actual cure for the disease was from our research."

I didn't let him get away with that. "Your wife is a doctor, Nigel. You made a mockery of everything she believed in."

"Yes, I did," Nigel said. "I don't care, though. Because I knew when I made that deal that she would hate me for what I did to save her. I also would do it again. My soul is damned, and I've lost all my connections to my old life because of this."

"I hope the money compensates," I said, trying to remember comparative religion class at the Foundation. "Something-something, what does a man gain who gives up his soul, something-something."

"For what shall it profit a man, if he shall gain the whole world, and lose his own soul?" Nigel said. "I used to think that was a stupid saying. The person gains the whole world, but I understand now."

"Oh, I suppose it's all okay now that you feel bad about it," I said, sarcastically. Nigel defied belief. It'd be like Darth Vader repenting of his sins and not having the decency to immediately die afterward. Yeah, I didn't think the Rebellion was just going to forgive and forget.

"I just said I would do it again," Nigel said, highlighting his attitude. "But that doesn't mean I'm not aware that there shouldn't be consequences for what I did. It's *part* of my motivation for helping dismantle the conspiracy. Emphasis on part."

"Are you turning yourself in?" I asked, not believing for a moment that he would. I could have brought up that it was entirely possible that Karma Corp had set his wife up to get access to a Refugee Unit police officer. If he hadn't figured out that possibility by now, he wasn't nearly the genius I'd always thought he was. Evil or otherwise.

"I wouldn't last a day in prison once they found out my intentions," Nigel replied, smirking. "If I wanted to commit suicide, I would just let you kill me."

"Sounds good to me," I replied, yet still wanting to hear what he had to say.

"But I had a better idea: take down the people involved. All of them," Nigel said.

I mulled over how I thought about that. "I'm listening."

"The Slavers' Guild will eventually reform, Neal," Nigel said, lowering his gaze. "They're going to ground because of the heat that you've managed to bring down on them and other ongoing investigations. However, there's too much money to be made and too many power players all throughout the government as well as other industries. Too many reputations at stake. It may be a year from now or maybe longer, but it will happen. Taking them down one by one may be possible, though, and might weaken the group enough to smash it pieces."

"As long as you get away with it," I replied, pausing. "Also, the *Slavers' Guild*? Really?"

"Real conspiracies don't have names," Nigel said. "It has to be called something."

"But why something out of a bad fantasy movie?" I asked, snorting.

"Like you've seen that many fantasy movies," Nigel muttered, as if this was a longstanding failure of my education. Nigel loved them, just like he loved really old detective films. The kind that wasn't even in color.

"I watch the ones with ladies in tight leather and fur bikinis," I replied, before cursing myself. I didn't want to fall back into my old pattern of making jokes with him.

"Make your choice, Neal," Nigel replied.

"You.burned.me.alive," I said, my voice cold and threatening before turning sarcastic. "Sorry, I just can't get past that."

"Yes," Nigel said. "I also made you a god or did you not think it was me who put you on the posthuman experiment list? I already made this deal before."

"With whom?" I asked.

"Armstrong," Nigel said. "There's a reason you were transferred here. The Computer God needed an incorruptible cop so I settled on one who was a little corrupt but who had already proven his limits. Reynolds had already inserted various worms and viruses to blind Armstrong to the Slavers' Guilds' activities, to not make a move against the specific people involved in a way that contradicted his core programming of protecting the Moon's citizens. So, he recruited Shinobu, accepted my offer to work with him, and began surrounding himself with people who could deal with the plot as it was coming. Which it did. All at the small price of my amnesty and its support in moving up the Karma Corp ranks. I'll be CEO of Black Briar, if not Chief Security Officer of all Karma Corp soon. Having an omniscient AI friend who is also a massive stockholder in rival megacorporation is a boon when it comes to corporate infighting."

In my head, I shot Nigel in the skull. I sacrificed eleven thousand slavers in the bush for one in the hand and it felt good. No one would blame me for it. I wouldn't even feel that bad about it. Except, that wasn't the kind of cop I was. Nigel was right, there was no chance most of the people involved in this would ever see the inside of a jail cell.

A part of me assumed that meant I should just get a shotgun and go to town, but I wasn't an Eighties action hero either. Roddy Piper or Arnie might have done that, but I wanted to do this the right way. Stupid and naive as that may be, that was the only way the Moon would ever start to have a functioning system. Besides, maybe I could get some of these asshats to roll on one another.

"All that says is Armstrong is part of the problem too," I said, making my decision. "His vengeance has been pretty tepid so far. If you were so righteous, you would have told me everything already. Now you're going to just dangle a bunch of names in front of me and pretend you can buy back our friendship. You can't. Whatever we had was done. All you are now is a source."

"Armstrong is playing the long game, Neal. Both of us are. The Slavers' Guild is one of the worst threats to humanity in the solar system, but it is not *the* worst and there're plenty of other equally bad power blocks that need to be taken down. Things that may require going outside the law."

I narrowed my eyes. "I *am* the law. The law that said a police officer's job is to protect the public. Whether the people hurting them are rich, poor, powerful, or powerless. Right now, I see you as just the lesser evil to a bunch of people exactly like you. Their sheer numbers are all that's keeping me from shooting you here."

"It'll be good working with you again," Nigel said, as if all my words were water off a duck's back.

And I was the duck, dammit.

"Show me you're worth this, Nigel," I said, hoping this hadn't been a wasted trip.

Nigel handed over a data crystal. "We'll start with Martin Caruthers. He was one of the people who smuggled the cryo-suspended kidnappees out of the Sol system as the star pilot supposedly transporting goods to the offworld colonies. He's also a domestic abuser and Loop addict so you'll have plenty of avenues of attack. He'll turn to Karma Corp if you try to arrest him for this, but he's been stealing from the company, and they'll happily cut him loose if this fact is exposed. There are thirteen other names in the crystal, including a Black Briar PMC lawyer and a lunar judge. Armstrong will provide you with the legal backing to take them all down. He believes dismantling this organization will be a multi-year project so as to not get them to close ranks or flee to a colony beyond his reach. Call this a downpayment on a long-lasting relationship."

"Peachy. We'll start with them," I said, taking the crystal and standing up.

"Caruthers is likely to resist arrest," Nigel said, smiling. "You might get better results if your gun is set to kill rather than stun."

I turned around and walked away. He could pick up the check.

"Say hello to Detective Westenra for me!" Nigel said, waving as I exited out of Todd's Diner.

I flipped him off on my way out.

He'd get his.

Eventually.

After all, he was only human.

AFTERWORD

"What if *Robocop* was a comedy?"

That was the one sentence that guided me through the creation of *Moon Cops on the Moon*. *Robocop* already has a bunch of black humor characteristic of Paul Verhoeven's movies, but I was willing to go with a slightly more optimistic tone. After all, why not have your heroes be genuinely decent people in a society that's on the verge of the collapse? It's an attitude that was adopted by the excellent *Expanse* novels by James S.A. Corey and I can think of no way to improve on those except by adding a talking dog.

I'm no stranger to writing science fiction and there's always been a satirical, humorous edge to my writing. Fans of my other books may notice elements here related to Agent G, the Cyber Dragons Trilogy, my *Space Academy* series, and *Lucifer's Star*. That's because all five of the series take place in the same universe—which I term my Futurepunk series. You don't need to read any of them to appreciate *Moon Cops on the Moon* but the more you read, the more you'll understand my strange science fiction universe where we can envision the end of the Earth, but we can't envision the end of capitalism. The more things change, the more things will fundamentally stay the same in this universe.

Moon Cops on the Moon is an attempt to take on the complicated role of policing and its relationship to the public, which has its own strange role in Cyberpunk fiction. For an anarchist-influenced genre, there sure are a lot of cop protagonists for it: Rick Deckard, Motoko Kusanagi, Alexis Murphy, Joe Dredd, Leon McNichol, Adam Jensen, JC Denton, and many others. Then again, perhaps that's because the tension makes good copy.

I take the view that Cyberpunk is fundamentally noir science fiction, another genre that it's strange to combine with screwball comedy. Raymond Chandler said, "Down these mean streets a man must go who is not himself mean, who is neither tarnished nor afraid. The detective must be a complete man and a common man and yet an unusual man. He must be, to use a rather weathered phrase, a man of honor."

This absolutely does not describe Neal S. Gordon, who is quite tarnished and afraid as well as possessed of a very flexible code of honor if he has one at all. However, he is a gray knight in a city full of black ones. He and Lucy aren't going to be able to fix the massive systemic problems of Luna City's corrupt culture any more than it'd be possible to bail out the Titanic. That's not going to be for lack of effort on their part, though. Maybe we'll also have a few laughs along the way. I hope this will be successful enough to be another one of my ongoing series like my Supervillainy Saga.

I couldn't have been able to make so many interesting stories with Cyberpunk themes and ideas, though, without the help of some truly great helpers. I strongly recommend if you liked *Moon Cops on the Moon* to check out SC Jensen (*Bubbles in Space*), MK Gibson (*Technomancer*), Brian Parker (*Easytown*), Jon Richter (*Auxiliary: London 2039*), Wesley Cross (*The Uplift*), and Michael Robertson (*Neon Horizons*). I also give special thanks to Bruce Bethke, coiner of the term Cyberpunk, for giving me some much-needed advice for this series.

LEXICON

Action Dan: A popular series of movies starring George Revlock (and briefly, his brother Ted) that is currently on its eighth entry. Action Dan is a former Special Operations soldier turned cop who engages in large amounts of quip-filled violence while bedding a variety of beautiful women. They are poorly written, full of nonsensical twists, and extremely popular.

Advanced Crimes Unit: The name of the Black Briar PMC corporate police division.

AI: Artificial Intelligence. Humanity has achieved fully sapient beings that come in a variety of forms ranging from robots to biological constructs to living computer programs. It is a common fear that mankind has lost control over their creations.

Antarctica: A now-settled population center on Earth that is still considered to be a barren frozen wasteland. Antarctica has a low crime rate and is primarily known as a location for incoming space goods due to the automated port created by the Galactic Community.

Atlas Security: Formerly the world's largest security company before being bought out by Ares Electronics. It is famous for its professional and technological focus. Most space colonies and orbital habitats contract with it for law enforcement as well as military protection.

Ares Electronics: The world's largest megacorporation that produces most of Earth's bots, computers, and starships. It is owned by Patricia "Trish" Ares and is heavily invested in working with the Galactic Community. It is the parent company of Atlas Security after a hostile takeover.

Big Brother: The internet handle and anonymous news channel of Rashad al-Fariq. He has exposed numerous cases of corporate malfeasance, crooked government activity, and criminal activity with a network of fellow hackers. It has been shut down numerous times but always returns with more revelations.

Biofuel: Artificially created combustible fuel made from a variety of organic materials. It is far more efficient than oil but less practical than electrical vehicles. Biofuel is one of the products of Karma Corp that was made with large numbers of flying cars designed to only able to run on it.

Bioroids: Biological constructs with artificial brains and material inside. Some of them are as sentient as humans.

Black Briar PMC: The official security company of Karma Corp and its counterpart to Atlas Security. Black Briar has gone through several rebrandings and even restoration of its old name due to its continued scandals and incompetence. It has been sued several times and even brought up before war crimes tribunals due to its support of the Neo-Militarists.

Black Lotus: A genetically engineered plant that provides a mellow and relaxing experience to its users as well as removes physical and emotional pain. The drugs illegality is controversial, and many believe it is solely due to its medicinal properties threatening Karma Corps' pharmaceutical interests.

Bots: A name for automated machines. They are different from bioroids because they have no biological parts.

Chromes: A nickname for cybernetically enhanced criminals.

Civi Cop: The term for police officers working for the civilian governments of countries or planets. They are generally paid less and more corrupt than the corporate versions of them. As counter intuitive as this may be.

Cognition AI: Unlimited growth AI that are the most powerful forces within Sol system. They are universally "quirky."

Community: A pan-species government that has existed for more than ten thousand Earth years. It is generally benevolent and works to the promotion of all its citizens' welfare. The Community is utterly ruthless in the suppression of its enemies, however, and gives its military great latitude in dealing with threats. Earth is believed to be working toward membership within the next fifty years. Also known as the Galactic Community.

Corpo Cop: The term for police officers working for the megacorporations or transtellars. They are generally better trained, equipped, and paid than their civilian counterparts.

Crater Town: The underground city beneath Luna City that is far vaster and more shoddily built. It is where the bulk of the population lives and is the size of a small country. It was primarily built for the Community by its alien engineers but was abandoned and then filled with human buildings of varying quality.

Credits: The official EarthGov currency that is an attempt to stabilize the fluctuating markets under the new government.

Cyberlife: The technology crimes division of the Atlas Security police department. They are handpicked by Armstrong from the best of the Sol system's detectives. They also tend to be among the most eccentric.

Cybernetics: Artificial body parts that replace lost or removed limbs or organs. Many function much better than the real thing.

Cyberpunks: A murderous gang of Moon transhuman petty criminals that recruits primarily from the people living in the Deep. The Cyberpunks heavily modify their bodies with back-alley cybernetics and deliberately inhuman cyberware.

Dataslicer: A term for a high-end professional hacker.

The Deep: An abandoned project to expand the colonization of the Moon that would have created a community for the overflow of refugees from the Unification Wars. It is still inhabited but illegally and off the grid. Its residents are subject to violence and rule by the local gangs.

DICK Test: The Divergent Intelligence Creative Keywords Test. Also, known as the Phillip K. Dick Test.

Dummy AI: AI that only simulates free will and intelligence. They are the most common form of AI and have no rights.

Dusted: A infamous method of execution by the Moon's criminal syndicates. It involves forcing Moon dust down their lungs, causing horrible injuries.

EarthGov: The post-Neo Militarist government created by the rise of a democratic republic.

Fair Cop: A four movie series (with television spin off) starring Ayanna Breeze. A young street urchin and part-time prostitute is recruited by a secret government organization to go undercover in a crooked corporate police unit. She ends up fighting terrorists, gangsters, and an ancient Egyptian cult while showing copious amounts of skin. The movies are considered trashy fun everywhere but France, where they are considered arthouse films.

First Contact: The day that the Community contacted Earth.

Fleur De Lis: A formerly prominent gang that was completely absorbed by the Syndicate but is mostly used as cannon fodder.

Flying Car: A self-explanatory term for cars equipped with gravity manipulators.

Food Prohibition Act: The Food Prohibition Act is a law strictly enforced by STRIKE that prohibits food importation from Earth save through the megacorporations' monopoly. It is a ridiculous and destructive law designed purely to serve Karma Corp.

Fusion Weapons: Weapons that shoot balls of plasma. They are based on alien technology and immensely effective.

Golden Tigers: A Martian gang of Spanish-East Asian bikers. They have chapters on multiple human colonies.

Gravity Manipulators: Alien technology that allows the simulation of Earth-like gravity and is essential for colonizing planets versus artificial habitats. It is tremendously useful for space travel and flying cars as well.

Hollowed: A posthuman who has had their free will stripped away. They can act entirely normal until activated.

Infocom: An infonet based telecommunications network that can communicate in real time through something called jumpspace.

Infonet: The replacement for the internet that contains all of Sol's communications and knowledge. The Earth infonet is not yet hooked up to the greater Community's.

Infopad: The equivalent of personal handheld computers and cellphones. They are ubiquitous.

Karma Corp: Karma Corp is an agricultural, pharmaceutical, and biotechnical firm that also produces bioroid machines. It is based on the Moon and essential to the functioning of that planet. It was heavily involved in the Neo-Militarist government and the parent company of Black Briar PMC.

KILL series: A series of dangerous, tank-like security robots that were deployed for military suppression and urban pacification. They all have illegal upload copies of a human mind within them, restricted by heavy programming.

Lizards: A slang term for the Sorkanan.

Loop: A highly effective euphoric stimulant that comes in pill form. Variations are known to cause hallucinations or violent behavior. Loop is believed to be a combat drug invented for the Unification Wars that has since spread to the civilian population. Addicts are frequently derided as Loopheads.

Luna City: The most prosperous lunar settlement that exists under an environmental dome. It is the home to most of the Moon's tourism, businesses, and has an artificial bay.

Lunes: The formal term for Moon residents. *Loons* is an alternative spelling.

Mars: Earth's most populated colony with two billion residents. It is mostly terraformed but remains a dry, rocky, and desert-like environment despite attempts to change that. Many of its colonies remain underground despite the surface being habitable.

Megacorporations: The nearly all-powerful corporations that used to rule the world before First Contact. Most of them have combined to become the transtellars.

The Moon: A world colonized by the Community to start treating Earth's collapsed environment and massive inequities. It was eventually abandoned by the Community and recolonized by humanity before becoming its largest shipyard and space port.

Moonatics: The partly derogatory, partly flattering name for the original human settlers of the Moon.

Neo-Militarists: A collection of militant, anti-xeno, authoritarian parties that rose to power after First Contact. Collectively named the Neo-Militarists, they actually had a large numbers of supporters

251

embrace the moniker. The Neo-Militarists held power for almost ten years before being utterly disgraced by a failed economy, uplift of technology, rising crime rate, and numerous civil wars.

Optical Camouflage: A portable holographic projector that effectively renders a subject invisible.

Posthuman: A group of nanotech enhanced soldiers who were employed by the Community to help overthrow Earth's isolationist and xenophobic government. Posthumans can either be Hollowed or Willed.

Posthuman Legion: A terrorist organization devoted to the cause of superhuman supremacy. Supposedly. The organization attacks in bizarre, nonsensical ways, and has seemingly no public membership. It seems to almost always attack when other issues need distraction from.

Quantum Bomb: An antimatter bomb lacking any form of fallout and used sporadically during the Unification Wars.

RealDream: A form of virtual reality used to replace video games. Your consciousness physically uploads to infospace where all manner of sensations can be experienced. It is also used as an interface by serious dataslicers. Most people use it for porn.

Recyclers: A alleged criminal activity where the cybernetics and organs of individuals are harvested against their will before being sold to rich clients. Still mostly a myth but now more profitable due to organs being easily transferrable due to gene therapy.

Red Dust: A red powder that has properties like cocaine but can be chemically produced rather than grown and refined. Red Dust is often cut with Moon dust and can become genuinely dangerous to individuals who partake in it.

Shi'ruuk Cruiser: A kilometer long, triangular, Sorkanan cruiser used for patrolling the further reaches of Community space and beyond.

Slavers' Guild: A nickname for a conspiracy of Karma Corp, street criminals, and crooked police officers designed to sell human beings to alien criminals in exchange for technology.

Smart AI: Sentient AI and self-fulfilled. They are granted the rights of citizens under the Social Reformers.

Social Reformers: Technically, the United Human Social Reform Party. It is a highly progressive, completely ineffectual, democratically elected government struggling to dismantle the apparatus of the Neo-Militarists. Many in the Sol system believe the Social Reformers are puppets of the Community.

Sorkanan: A race of bipedal lizard men that are the most powerful and populace race in the Community.

STRIKE: A government organization that exists for the purposes of monitoring colonial law, import/export, and anti-terrorism. STRIKE is considered to be an ineffectual and overmilitarized response to space exploration and the presence of aliens. It is often exploited by local governments as personal militaries.

Syndicate: An alliance of Earth's largest criminal syndicates that were recruited by the Neo-Militarist governments and megacorporations to distribute black-market goods, intimidate reformists, as well as provide vice to soothe the masses' discontent. They are responsible for much of the Moon's troubles due to its violent control of the smuggling trade, several vice rackets, and trapping lunes in debt slavery.

Tranquility: A massive state-sized dome with estates for the super-rich, resorts, golf courses, and wildlife preserves. Tranquility is considered a waste of resources by most and a sign of the staggering corruption on the planetoid.

Transhuman: A human who has been enhanced with cybernetics or gene therapy. It used to have an entire philosophy around it but is now so common (mostly to correct hereditary conditions or the vagaries of old age) that it is considered just an extension of medicine.

Transtellars: Extra-solar corporations that have extended their efforts to humanity's colonies and some alien worlds. It is believed that the transtellars have even made contact with other branches of humanity, as ridiculous as that sounds. EarthGov is unable to rein them in beyond the solar system.

Trikuza: The second largest criminal organization on the Moon after the Syndicate. The Trikuza are an alliance of three Yakuza gangs that spread to the United States and other countries after opening up its membership to more ethnicities. It is considered somewhat kitsch and stereotypical but very loyal.

Unification Wars: A series of wars fought after First Contact over whether to preserve autonomy or create a united world government. The Neo-Militarists briefly held power after winning the first conflict and attempting to create an isolationist state. They were then overthrown, and the Social Reformers were elected in their place.

Upload: A scan of a human being's personality and memories uploaded into a machine. It requires a person's consent to clone them this way and each successive copying must be done from the original brain. These scans cause brain damage and ultimately death if done too many times.

Willed: The posthumans who are still possessed of their own free will.

Xenos: A slang term for aliens

AUTHOR'S NOTE

I'd like to thank you for reading this book. The publishing industry has been changing dramatically since the advent of eBooks. It is now very difficult to get any book noticed, regardless of quality. If you enjoyed this book, you could do some very simple things to help me attract attention. Word of mouth is the number one source of success for novels, so simply telling family and friends about the book is a great start.

Here are a few other ways of helping out, if you are so inclined:

* Post a rating or review where you purchased the eBook
* Post a rating or review on Goodreads
* Talk about the book or write a review on Facebook
* Tell folks about the book in a blog post.

If you like any of my other books, please feel free to check them out. A lot of my series are interlinked, and you never know when you'll find someone familiar showing up. In this case, *Moon Cops on the Moon* is set in the future of my Agent G Cyberpunk books and the past of my *Space Academy* and *Lucifer's Star* series. Collectively, they make up my Futurepunk setting. Fans will certainly get a kick out of seeing how the galaxy changes in a few centuries either way.

ABOUT THE AUTHOR

C. T. Phipps is a lifelong student of horror, science fiction, and fantasy. An avid tabletop gamer, he discovered this passion led him to write and turned him into a lifelong geek. He is a regular blogger and also a reviewer for The Bookie Monster.

Bibliography

Novels
The Rules of Supervillainy (Supervillainy Saga #1)
The Games of Supervillainy (Supervillainy Saga #2)
The Secrets of Supervillainy (Supervillainy Saga #3)
The Kingdom of Supervillainy (Supervillainy Saga #4)
The Tournament of Supervillainy (Supervillainy Saga #5)
The Future of Supervillainy (Supervillainy Saga #6)
The Horror of Supervillainy (Supervillainy Saga #7)
Tales of Supervillainy: Cindy's Seven (Supervillainy Saga #8)

I Was a Teenage Weredeer (The Bright Falls Mysteries, Book 1)
An American Weredeer in Michigan (The Bright Falls Mysteries, Book 2)

A Nightmare on Elk Street (The Bright Falls Mysteries, Book 3)

Esoterrorism (Red Room, Vol. 1)
Eldritch Ops (Red Room, Vol. 2)
The Fall of the House (Red Room, Vol. 3)

Agent G: Infiltrator (Agent G, Vol. 1)
Agent G: Saboteur (Agent G, Vol. 2)
Agent G: Assassin (Agent G, Vol. 3)

Cthulhu Armageddon (Cthulhu Armageddon, Vol. 1)
The Tower of Zhaal (Cthulhu Armageddon, Vol. 2)

Lucifer's Star (Lucifer's Star, Vol. 1)
Lucifer's Nebula (Lucifer's Star, Vol. 2)

Straight Outta Fangton (Straight Outta Fangton, Vol. 1)
100 Miles and Vampin' (Straight Outta Fangton, Vol. 2)
Vampiraz4Life (Straight Outta Fangton, Vol. 3)

Wraith Knight (Wraith Knight, Vol. 1)
Wraith Lord (Wraith Knight, Vol. 2)
Wraith King (Wraith Knight, Vol. 3)

Dark Destiny (Dark Destiny, Vol. 1)
Destiny's Paradox (Dark Destiny, Vol. 2)

Brightblade (The Morgan Detective Agency, Book 1)

Space Academy Dropouts (The Space Academy Series, Book 1)
Space Academy Rejects (The Space Academy Series, Book 2)
Space Academy Washouts (The Space Academy Series, Book 3)

Psycho Killers in Love

Anthologies (as editor)

Blackest Knights
Blackest Spells
Tales of Capes and Cowls
Tales of the Al-Azif
Tales of Yog-Sothoth

Curious about other Crossroad Press books? Stop by our website:
http://crossroadpress.com
We offer quality writing
in digital, audio, and print formats.

Subscribe to our newsletter on the website homepage and receive a
free eBook.

www.ingramcontent.com/pod-product-compliance
Lightning Source LLC
Chambersburg PA
CBHW031939240626
47153CB00003B/794